THE
KINDNESS
OF
STRANGERS

THE KINDNESS OF STRANGERS

BERNARD TAYLOR

St. Martin's Press
New York

Design by Paolo Pepe

Library of Congress Cataloging in Publication Data

Taylor, Bernard, 1934–
    The kindness of strangers.

    I. Title.
PR6070.A884K5   1985   823'.914   85–10065
ISBN 0-312-45399-X

First Edition

10 9 8 7 6 5 4 3 2 1

This is for Debal

THE
KINDNESS
OF
STRANGERS

1

He sat at a small table in his room, looking out onto the walled garden below.

He felt restless and despondent. He could never wait to get away from the restaurant for a couple of hours after the lunch session each day, but when he was free he didn't know what to do with the time.

After a while he got up and went out onto the landing. The house was quiet, apart from the distant hum of the vacuum cleaner somewhere below where Sarah, the old cleaning woman, was earning the pittance his grandparents paid her. He stood listening; there was no other sound; his grandparents were still out. Turning, he made his way to the stairs and slowly climbed up to the top floor of the house.

Reaching it, he went into a room on the left. It had once been a workroom; a row of shelves still bore boxes of nails— now rusting—and worn-out tools. Near one wall lay a mattress with pillows and blankets. He had brought them up here long ago, and sometimes in the hot summer nights when his grandparents had gone to bed he would creep up here to sleep. Now, moving past the mattress, he crossed to a flight of wooden steps and climbed them to the top where he opened a pair of shutters and a window and stepped out onto the roof.

The May afternoon was unusually warm and humid, but up here a slight breeze could be felt. Sitting on the flat part of the roof he looked out over the parapet. There was nothing much to see. Beyond the garden wall the quiet cul-de-sac seemed more forgotten than ever. It didn't bother him, though; on the contrary, he was glad; he liked the quiet. He liked the roof, too, and sometimes in the really warm summer weather he would take off his clothes and lie naked, letting the sun play on his pale body. Shielded by the parapet he was quite safe from critical, prying eyes; no one could see him from the garden or the street below, while neither his grandparents nor Sarah ever set foot above the house's second floor.

The house—the only home he had ever known—was Victorian. It was very tall—tall even for its four stories. It was set in Carshalton Gardens, in Kew, on the outskirts of London. Gray and ugly, it reared above its shabby surroundings, the three semidetached houses opposite, the remains of a demolished row of terrace houses to one side, and a small, squat bungalow on the other. Once, long before, the house had stood in fairly spacious grounds and, marking the line of some old parish boundary, had been something of a landmark. Over the years, though, the demarcation line had been forgotten and most of the land sold off. Now, in the present constricted confines of its walled garden, the house was nothing more than an ugly curiosity.

And, he reflected, it was not practical for a small family with just one aging cleaner. His grandparents would have been much more comfortable in some smaller, modern house or bungalow. They required comparatively little space and could afford whatever they wanted; there was no shortage of money. But they had been in the house so long now they wouldn't think about moving. He was glad. He loved the house; he always had, and he looked forward to the day when it would be his alone. And when that happened he would transform it—for *her*.

For the time being, though, he had to put up with his grandparents' presence. Still, in the summer there would be a respite; in July they would be leaving for their holidays. When that time came he could relax.

As he sat there idly gazing off, his eye was drawn to a

movement near the front garden wall. A cat. The tabby cat from one of the houses on the other side of the street. It had come into the garden and now, after stretching its limbs, was settling on a small patch of grass beside the herbaceous border. He sat staring at the animal through narrowed eyes. He had hated cats for as long as he could remember—ever since that time when, hardly more than a baby, he had been sleeping in his cot and his grandparents' sleek Siamese had jumped up and lain across his face. He had come close to suffocation then, only his grandmother's appearance on the scene saving his life.

Now he remained quite still, watching the cat for a few seconds, and then, getting up and turning to his left, he began carefully to make his way alongside the parapet.

At the front of the house he came to a stop beside a rusty old bucket and stood there, and he stooped, dipped his hand into it and brought out a stone the size of a small hen's egg. He had placed the bucket there as a child, so many years ago, since which time he had filled it with missiles—stones brought up from the garden—many, many times over. Now, judiciously grasping the stone, he steadied himself against the parapet, drew back his arm, took careful aim and let fly.

He missed. With a dull thud the stone struck the grass just a few inches in front of the animal, bounced up and skimmed past its ear. In a flash the cat, taking fright, was on its feet, leaping up onto the front wall and jumping down on the far side. It was gone.

The young man cursed. He must be out of practice, he said to himself. Any other time he'd have scored a direct hit.

He sat down again and, putting back his head, closed his eyes against the sun. He couldn't settle, though, and after a while he sighed, got up again, climbed back through the window and made his way down to his room.

There, sitting at his table, he opened the drawer and took out a paper bag containing a slice of apple pie that he had brought back from the restaurant. He ate it slowly and when he had finished he brushed the crumbs from his lap. Opening the drawer again, he took out a large scrapbook. After placing it on the table before him he took from the same drawer a magazine that he had bought on the way back to the house that afternoon. Placing it beside the scrapbook, he opened it to a particular page and sat gazing at a photograph. It was of a young girl in Victorian dress, holding a lantern.

Some moments later, after listening carefully for any warning sounds, he opened the scrapbook to a blank page, carefully cut the picture from the magazine and pasted it in. That done, he sat back and looked at the picture in its new setting.

He began then, slowly, to turn the pages. Besides the pictures taken from magazines and newspapers there were glossy photographs of the same girl, bearing her signature, photographs that she herself had sent to him. There were drawings and paintings of her, too, quite a number of them, executed by himself in pencil, crayon, and watercolor. To his mind they were all quite inadequate, none of them doing her the justice she deserved. No, but even so, he reminded himself, they had been done with love. And anyway, if he kept working at it, one day he would do a portrait of her that he could be proud of. Perhaps he should take some classes, get some expert instruction. Yes—that would be a good idea. Then when he drew or painted her likeness he could do her some justice. . . .

He turned his thoughts back to the album. Every picture in it was of her—Shenna. He had been collecting them for almost three years now, ever since he had seen her in *Child's Play*. It was the first of her films he had seen, and the memory of it would stay with him forever. One day, he told himself, he would have her photographs all round the house, and his paintings of her, as well—wherever he chose . . . one day when the house belonged just to him—and her; for someday she would be be there too, sharing his life. She might be far away on the other side of the Atlantic right now, but that was a barrier that would be surmounted. . . .

Suddenly into the quiet came his grandmother's voice as she called his name up the stairs, and quickly he closed the album and the magazine and slipped them back into the drawer. After a few moments footsteps could be heard from the landing, and then the voice came again, now just outside the door: "Why don't you answer me?"

"Yes?" he called back, and then turned as the door opened and she came into the room. She had just come in from the street and was still wearing her coat. Eyeing him coldly, she said, "I was calling you."

"I'm sorry," he said, "I didn't hear you."

"Didn't hear me." There was contempt in her voice and in the thin curl of her mouth—the mouth that for as long as he could remember had only ever been set in grim disapproval—often the lips turned in so far that they disappeared altogether—or mouthing prayers to a god who seemed to have completely ignored her, for surely no one to whom God had listened could be that unhappy. Now, she sniffed the air, her nostrils dilating.

"Have you been eating up here?" she asked.

"No." He shook his head.

"No," she repeated disbelievingly, and then added, "You eat up here, you'll attract the cockroaches." She stood glaring at him with small, gleaming, loveless eyes—a short woman, slight and wiry, her gray hair drawn back on the small round head and twisted into a bun.

As he looked back at her he became aware of the depths of his hatred; hatred for her and for his grandfather. And they hated him, too, he had no doubt of that; at this moment his grandmother's glance was full of such malevolence that he almost quailed before it. But why should they hate him? And then he told himself it was because he was a constant reminder of their daughter's sin; more than that, he was the fruit of it. And in addition, of course, he was also—through his mother—the fruit of their own union.

With the thought in mind he tried to picture their ugly, joyless coupling, the old woman and the old man (he could never see them as young)—her short, hard, wiry body beneath his tall, heavy, shapeless form. The image made his throat contract and he quickly dispelled the picture from his mind.

When he thought of his mother, though, it was different. When he pictured *her* making love she was always eighteen years old, with her naked limbs thrashing and her forehead beaded with sweat while some faceless man pounded away at her body. It was an image shaped by what little he knew of her, and the fact that he had no idea of who his father was.

He had been only a child when his mother had been killed—decapitated by a truck while driving in France. At the time of her death he had been staying with her parents, and he had continued to live with them ever since, a constant source of unhappiness to them both. No matter the education they had acquired for him and the plans they had formed, he had fallen short of all their expectations. Not for him a career as a musician or a scientist or a teacher or, like his grandfather, that of a highly paid civil servant. To their disappointment he had aspired to become nothing more than a deliveryman for a local hospital and, following his boredom with that job, a waiter at an Italian restaurant—the job that he held right now.

Now his grandmother turned away from him and he watched as she stepped toward his neatly made bed. After looking down at it for a second she glanced back at him, narrow-eyed, holding his gaze for a moment or two, then stooped slightly and pulled back the covers. He watched as she peered closer at the sheets. She had been doing the same thing since he'd been ten years old. At that time he'd had no idea what she had been about, but later, with his sexual awakening, he'd realized that she was looking for signs of the evil nature within him—as it had been in his mother and was surely in every young man and woman. And in those earlier days when she had found the evidence she sought, he had been beaten for it. Now, as she turned away from the bed, he inwardly smiled. He had learned his lessons well. She might have caught him out in the past, but she never would now.

She moved back to the door, stood gazing disapprovingly at him for a moment, and went from the room. He sat there listening to the receding sound of her feet on the landing, and then pulled open the drawer again, first taking out the album, which he opened on the table before him, and then a small, shallow, wooden box, which he set down beside it. Lifting the lid of the box, he looked at the contents. There was a gold wristwatch there, a pair of gold earrings shaped like daisies, and a gold brooch; things that had belonged to his mother. He picked up the brooch and looked at it. Victorian and very large, it was ornately fashioned and set with rubies and small pearls. He was keeping it for her: Shenna.

After a while he laid the brooch back in the box and returned it to the drawer. After that he took out a hardback notebook—his diary.

He had begun to keep a diary many years ago, while still a child, the inception of it springing from his need for some receptacle for his most secret thoughts, his hopes, and his fears—a receptacle that was at once accepting and uncritical, which no person he had met had ever been, least of all his grandparents. Of course he had had to keep his diaries hidden away from where prying eyes might find them, and most of the time he had managed to do that—though not always. He could still recall how, not long after his fourteenth birthday when he was home on holiday from boarding school, his grandmother had found his current diary and had been shocked and horrified at its contents. He had watched then as the book was destroyed, after which his grandfather had punished him. Following the beating, he was made to swear on the Bible that he would offend in such a way no more. His vow had lasted unbroken for only a matter of days. It was the first serious vow that he had discarded. After that the breaking of vows became easier, and then easy. As time went on the act had brought pleasure.

He had kept his diaries faithfully over the years, not writing an entry regularly each day, but as the mood took him. During the dull days he wrote little, but on other days, when on the crest of some wave of happiness or optimism or submerged in the depths of despair, frustration or anger, he spent long hours pouring out the expressions of his feelings.

Now, opening the book, he wrote the date at the top left-hand corner of a new page, sat in silence for some moments, and then wrote:

> *I feel lately I'm living in a silence—a silence that comes from* her *—and it's so complete that inside myself I'm crying out. Not that it matters to her. She doesn't care; she can't, or she wouldn't allow me to be so unhappy.*

He sighed, put down his felt-tip pen, and looked down onto the garden. In his left temple a small nerve pulsed beneath the skin. His feeling of melancholy had grown and now became touched with guilt. After a moment he took up the pen once more and wrote:

> *I shouldn't have written as I did just now. It isn't true that she doesn't care. I couldn't bear to believe such a thing even for a moment. There will come a time, someday, when it will all be sorted out. And when that happens I shall read back over these pages and laugh. No, together we shall laugh at it all—but most of all at my foolishness and my lack of faith. And in many years to come the world, too, will read these pages (long after my death—our deaths)*

and of course, knowing the outcome, the whole picture, the world will smile at me in tolerant amusement and wonder how I could have doubted as I have.

And while I reassure myself over it all I'm left sitting in this room, alone, surrounded by reminders of her. I'm so close to her in so many ways—and yet so far away.
If only she would write!

If only she would write. Some kind of response—he had to have some kind of response. And then a question came into his mind: *Was she getting his letters?* Perhaps there was someone at the studio, some snotty little clerk who was taking his letters and destroying them. It was possible. Someone jealous, of course—it would have to be. And Shenna would have no idea it was going on; she would probably just believe that she had been forgotten. She would never know how much he was thinking of her, how much he was wanting to hear from her.

On the other hand, though, perhaps she was getting his letters and was just ignoring them. But if so, *why?* Had he done something to offend her? If so, she should tell him— not punish him like this with her silence.

After a moment he went on writing.

Apart from my life with her (and I do share it with her, even though she's not here) everything goes on without variation. Six days a week I get the bus into town to the restaurant, and whenever I take Miss Collins her lunch tray I check to see whether there is any mail for me. There never is. And how dull my life is. In every way. Each day I see the same faces, and I talk and smile, while all the time I'm despising everyone. They don't know what goes on inside me. How could they? They think I'm like they are. One day, though, they'll realize I'm not; they'll know the truth.

Closing the cover of the diary, he pushed it away from him. Depression was settling over him like a blanket. After sitting there in silence for several minutes he opened the drawer and brought out writing paper and envelopes. He would write to her again.

The address he wrote at the top of the page was not his own. He never used that when writing to her. He had never dared. His grandparents had always been very curious about any mail arriving for him, and if letters from *her* had come to the house they would soon have found out. It was because of this situation that he hadn't written to her at all at the start, no matter how much he had wanted to. But then, suddenly, and like a gift from God, there had come the answer to the problem.

The answer had come about through his work at the Soho restaurant, where one of his regular jobs was to deliver lunch to a woman who occupied a small office on the top floor of an old building across the street. Four times a week he would ring her doorbell, and she would press the buzzer to release the lock and allow him in. He would carry the tray up the dusty stairs, past the other offices, the doors of which bore signs saying things like CAMDEN EXPORTS, JOSH HENKER PHOTOGRAPHICS, SIDNEY CALLENDER LTD., HARVEY DILKE ENTERPRISES.

The routine had been going on for some time, and then one day just over a year ago he had gone as usual to deliver the lunch tray and, while pushing open the door, had turned and seen the postman approaching. "Here, a little present for you," the postman had said, and placed several items of mail on the tray beside the covered plate. When the postman had gone he'd entered the building and made his way up to the top floor where Miss Collins, middle-aged, unattractive, and running some kind of lonely-hearts introductory service, waited for her lunch. "The postman gave me the mail," he said as he put the tray down on her cluttered desk, and she picked up the letters and cards and, muttering about people not doing their jobs properly, went through them. A few of the items she laid aside, saying, "These are mine," while the rest she shuffled into a pile. "I've never heard of some of these people, though I suppose they must have been here at some time. Moved away, I expect." She handed him the little stack of mail. "Put it with the other stuff in the hall on your way down, would you, please? I imagine somebody'll pick it up sooner or later."

It was all very casual. He took up the empty tray from the day before, left the room, and went back down the stairs. Then, near the front door, he dropped the letters onto the hall table where there was already quite a stack of mail— some of it, judging by the postmarks, having been there several weeks. He glanced at some of the envelopes. So many names.

The next morning he wrote Shenna a letter asking her for a signed photograph, addressing the letter to her care of Columbia Pictures in Hollywood, where *Child's Play* had been made. At the top of the page he wrote not his own address, but the address of the office building across from the restaurant. When it came to signing his name he sat for some moments trying to think of one—he couldn't use his own—and then his glance fell on the cover of his diary, in the lower right-hand corner of which was neatly printed in tiny gold lettering: A COSGRAY PRODUCT. After a second's further consideration he wrote with a flourish at the foot of the letter: *John Cosgray*.

After he had sent the letter off he just waited. And then at long last there had come the day when he went to deliver Miss Collins's lunch tray and found on the hall table the envelope with the American stamps in the corner. Seeing the date of the postmark, he realized it had probably come by sea—which would account for its delay. He felt a shiver of excitement go through him as he looked at the name written there: *John Cosgray*.

Carefully opening it, he found inside a letter and a photograph. And *such* a photograph. It was a glossy head-and-shoulders portrait that showed Shenna smiling and leaning against a fence or a gate. Across the bottom of the picture she had written, *My best wishes, Shenna Preston.* The letter with it was brief and typewritten, but even so it was still more than he had dared expect. He read:

Dear John,

Thank you so much for your letter. I'm glad to hear how much you enjoyed *Child's Play* and *Circuit.* I hope also you like the enclosed photograph, which I'm sending with my very best wishes.

Sincerely,
Shenna Preston

He read it through several times. After the initial thrill he was somewhat disappointed in the fact that she had given no address for herself; at the top of the page was printed simply in elegant, blue italics: *Shenna Preston.* But it didn't matter, he told himself, he would get her address later; in the meantime it was thrilling enough that she had written and sent the photograph.

The photograph was the first of three she sent in response to various letters from him over the months—each one arriving at the office building across from the restaurant. After those first three replies, though, there had been nothing, no matter how often he had written or how he had expressed his deep affection for her.

Now, sitting writing to her in his room, in the close, overcast May afternoon, he wished for the thousandth time that he could get her private address—her home address. This was no way to carry on a correspondence—writing to her care of some huge, faceless organization. He sighed. There was nothing he could do about it right now.

When he had finished the letter he read over what he had written. He had begged her to write back to him. Begged.

He had never done such a thing before. He didn't care, though. He wasn't too proud to beg where she was concerned, for he knew in the end it would all be proved worthwhile. And she would answer the letter; she wouldn't ignore his plea—not this time. But—what if she did? No. *No*. He didn't dare think about that. He *had* to get a response. Quickly he made some mental calculations: say a week for his letter to get to her—and then two or three weeks for her answer to come back—that was allowing for it to come by sea. A month. Except—what if she was away? So, add two weeks for that eventuality. That made six weeks in all. Six weeks. Surely he must get an answer in that time.

Opening the table drawer, he took out a small calendar and saw that six weeks took him up to the second of July. The date rang a bell, and he suddenly remembered that that was the day his grandparents were leaving on their holiday: a two-month cruise of the Mediterranean. And then he discovered, by means of his past diaries, that the date had further meaning for him, too. The second of July was the date, three years ago, when he had gone to a cinema showing *Child's Play* and had seen Shenna for the first time. The second of July—where he was concerned it was clearly a significant day. He smiled. He knew now with certainty that by that day, just six weeks away, everything would have come out right.

He folded the letter and put it in an envelope. Then, after sealing the flap, he wrote Shenna's name on the front, and below that: *Columbia Pictures, Hollywood, California, USA.* In the lower left corner he printed in large letters: URGENT. PLEASE FORWARD. When he had put a stamp on the envelope he propped it up before him on the table.

Suddenly, from the corner of his eye, he became aware of movement, and turning his head he saw a large, dark brown spider moving across the tabletop. He recoiled, eyeing the creature with disgust as it moved over the writing paper and the cover of his diary. And then, in horror, he saw it move up onto the open album—right onto the photograph of Shenna, the first one she had sent him. Feeling rage and loathing swell within him, he slowly raised his hand and slammed it down.

He felt the hideous body give beneath his palm and he shuddered and screwed up his eyes. After a moment he lifted his hand and opened his eyes. The crushed spider lay on Shenna's face, some disgusting matter oozing out across her mouth. He cried out in a kind of moan and, snatching up the album, frantically shook it till the spider's body fell onto the floor. Then he ground it in, his feet moving as if in a frenzy, pounding at the carpet long after there was any recognizable trace of the creature left to see.

2

The girl moved slowly, stealthily in the gloom, holding her breath, teeth gritted in concentration. Then, after a moment, she stooped, reached down, pulled off her shoes, and laid them silently on the floor. That done, she peered about her and listened. She waited a few moments more and then crept out from behind the rack of clothes and started slowly and soundlessly toward the door of the store. She had gone only a few yards when suddenly a dark shape leaped out at her. *"You're too late—again!—goddamn it!"* she said under her breath, while in almost the same moment she opened her mouth and screamed. A second later the weary voice of the director, Dave Linden, was heard.

"Cut."

The actor who was playing the pursuer gave a little chuckle, waved the knife, and said, "Not literally, I hope," and the girl raised her eyes to the roof and silently said, *Just knock it off with the dumb jokes, why don't you, and try to get it right for a change.*

A moment later, after the working lights had come up, the director moved forward onto the set. "Okay, Shenna," he said, nodding to the girl, "that was fine, just fine." Then, turning to the man, he shook his head. "Larry, you're still taking far too much time. For Christ's sake, she could be out of the store and halfway down the street. You've got to be quicker—a lot quicker."

Shenna moved away to her nearby chair and sat down. It was almost six-thirty, and she was tired. All she wanted to do was finish the scene and get away. If Larry Freeman didn't get it right, though, they were going to be here all night. She listened as he stood justifying his actions and talking about his motivation. *Aw, come on*, she wanted to say, *we've done eight crummy takes already. Just do what's asked of you and let's get out of here.* To talk about motivation in relation to garbage like this was like trying to teach table manners to a gorilla.

While the scene was set up again she was checked by makeup and hairdressing, and then at last everyone was ready and the scene was shot once more. And this time it worked. Obviously Dave's words to Larry—whatever they had been—had hit home, for when Dave called "Cut" a few moments later he added a smile of satisfaction. "Fine," he said. "Now one more and that's it."

Twenty minutes later another take was in the can, a wrap was called, and Shenna was walking to her dressing room. At last. Now she was free till Monday.

When she had changed out of her costume she set off toward the parking lot. The evening was balmy and pleasant, and a light Santa Ana wind lifted her blond hair and ruffled the white silk of her blouse. In the distance the Hollywood Hills were surprisingly clear.

In her new Mercedes Roadster she drove off the studio lot, made her way along Washington Boulevard, and onto the San Diego Freeway toward Westwood. The house where she lived with her mother was at the foot of a hill in Beverly Glen. They had bought it just two years before. It was spacious and well proportioned, with a pool and a large garden.

The first thing Shenna noticed as she let herself into the hall was the music coming from the den. At first she couldn't place it, but after a moment it came to her. Of course—it was from *The Dowry*. Her mother must be playing it on the VCR.

Opening the den door, she looked across to the two women who sat before the TV screen. "Hi, there," she said. Aunt Cissie—who had come from the East Coast to stay for a while and was returning home in the morning—smiled warmly as she returned the greeting, while Doris, Shenna's mother, showed more reserve, smiling briefly and then turning away, picking up the remote control for the TV and stopping the tape's progress. Doris was forty-four-years old, slim, fair-haired, and attractive. Cissie, three years older, was heavier in build and going gray. "We're watching *The Dowry*," Doris said.

Shenna smiled as she studied her mother's face, trying to read the signs. "So I notice," she said. "You're gluttons for punishment."

Giving a little laugh, Cissie asked how the filming was going and Shenna shrugged. "Okay. I'll be glad when it's finished."

Doris patted the sofa cushion at her side. "Are you coming to join us?"

"No, thanks." Smiling ruefully, Shenna shook her head. "I've seen it."

Doris ignored this. "You must be hungry," she said, starting up from the sofa. "I'll get your dinner. We had ours a while back."

"No, I'll get it." Shenna gestured for her to stay where she was. "You watch the movie. I want to take a shower first, anyway."

As she turned to the door, Cissie's voice followed her: "What's all this I hear—about you giving up acting to go and join the London hippies?"

Shenna was silent for a second, then, forcing a grin, she said, "Well, it looks as if Mom's already given you the full story." She glanced across at Doris, but her mother was once again studying the remote control in her hand. A moment later the picture flashed back onto the screen and Shenna, hesitating in the doorway, watched as a girl in Victorian dress—played by herself—went through the hall of some old New England house, unfastening her cloak. She watched as the girl climbed the stairs and went into a bedroom, where she dropped the cloak on the bed and, turning to the mirror, pushed her thick blond hair back from her face. Here the camera moved in for a close-up, showing strong, well-shaped features, and eyes with a blueness that owed nothing to any tinted contact lenses. It was a face that possessed character and individuality, and a prettiness that had nothing of the empty, button-nosed, Hollywood look that stamped the faces of so many young actresses.

Turning away from the TV screen, Shenna closed the door behind her and went into the kitchen, where the smell of the beef casserole came from the oven. She poured herself a Coke and carried it out into the hall. As she trudged up the stairs, she could hear the sounds from the television, the music swelling to a climax. At any moment the screams would begin. *The Dowry* was the last picture she had made—and she hated it. It had been beautifully scored, beautifully designed and costumed, but it was garbage.

Reaching the top of the stairs, she came to a stop and stood there as the sound of the music grew, hung for some moments on the crest of a swell, then abruptly dropped and ceased. She winced as the first of the screams rang out; then, turning, she went into her studio and closed the door on the sounds.

This room, in which she had spent so much of her spare time lately, was on the north side of the house. It was large and light, the walls hung with her own oil paintings; others leaned against the walls and stood stacked in a nearby closet. Sipping from her glass, she stood before an easel on which hung an unfinished oil painting. The still-life grouping had been set up on a small table a couple of yards beyond the easel, composed of apples and onions on a pale blue cloth next to a tall, green glass jar holding some dried grasses. She would be able to get back to the painting tomorrow—and she had the rest of the weekend before her.

She left the room after a while and took a shower, then, still in her bathrobe, she went down to the kitchen and prepared a tray with a little green salad and some of the casserole. Bringing the tray back upstairs, she sat at the window. As she ate she thought of her work at the film studio that day. She had been working on the movie for two months now and there were about seven weeks to go before it would be finished. Those seven weeks couldn't pass quickly enough. If *The Dowry* had been a bad film, this one, *Chain Letter*, was worse. It was like so many others in the current run of money-makers—"mad slasher" or "splatter" movies as they were often called: put a bunch of pretty girls together and then kill them off one by one, and try to make each death more imaginative and gruesome than the last. Still, she consoled herself, it wouldn't be too long now before the shooting, with all its depicted horrors, would be over.

The prospect of those last days was far more bearable. They were to be spent in London—which was part of the reason she'd agreed to do the picture in the first place. Going to England, to London—that was the important thing; for the sake of that she'd put up with half a dozen movies like *Chain Letter*.

When she thought about it—the future—she was filled with excitement, the way it had been when she was a child and had looked forward to those rare summer vacations on Cape Cod. And now, as in those earlier times, she wished she could make the hours move faster. She must be patient, though; the time would come eventually, and when it did it would be a new beginning.

On a nearby table stood a silver-framed photograph of a man of about twenty-eight, with handsome, regular features and a wide, bright smile. Although she had never seen the man and although the photograph was black and white, she knew his coloring well, she could see clearly that his hair was a deep, rich brown and that his eyes, with their black, black lashes, were gray. As she continued to gaze at the photograph, she thought of her mother's words some weeks before: "Your coloring's not the same, but even so—you get to look more like him all the time." Her mother so rarely spoke of him, and to Shenna the words had come as a surprise. They had pleased her too, so much.

Shenna slept late the next morning, not surfacing till just after nine, when Doris woke her with the information that she was about to drive Cissie to the airport and that Shenna should get up if she wanted to say good-bye.

Putting on her dressing gown, Shenna came downstairs, where she kissed her aunt and then waved from the front door as Doris drove them away in the station wagon.

Doris had left hot coffee on the stove, and Shenna poured herself a cup and was sitting drinking it in the kitchen when the telephone rang. It was Amy Michaels, one of her friends. The two girls had tentatively agreed to get together that morning, and Amy was calling to check that it was still on. After a minute she agreed to drive on over to the house.

Amy arrived some thirty-five minutes later, by which time Shenna had showered and dressed and made fresh coffee. Carrying their cups upstairs to Shenna's studio, they sat down on an old sofa. Amy had a round, pretty face with a wide mouth and short, pert nose. As blond as Shenna, she was a little taller and, at twenty-one, two years older. They had been friends for a number of years now, ever since, as children, they had played sisters in a movie. At present, though, Amy was at UCLA majoring in English, her acting career having taken a back seat to her studies. A college education was not her own idea, but that of her parents, who wanted her to be equipped for something other than acting in the event that her chosen career should founder.

"Though God knows what I'd do," Amy said, shaking her head. "Acting's all I've ever been interested in. I can't see myself working in some newspaper office or teaching school or anything like that. It's different for you—you've got your painting." She grinned. "Or so you tell me. I think acting's the only thing I'm any good at."

"Oh, come on—actors always say that—you know they do." Shenna gazed at her for a moment then asked, "But what do you mean—*or so I tell you?*"

Amy shrugged. "Well—I don't know—I guess I just find it difficult to accept that you don't see your acting as being the most important thing. . . ."

"Oh, don't—please." Shenna frowned. "You sound like my mother."

Amy gave a rueful smile. "Is she being difficult?"

"A little."

"Well, you're all she's got. She's going to miss you."

"I know that."

"I'm going to miss you too, Shen. I wish you weren't going."

"Oh, don't worry—I'll be back."

"Yes, but when? Maybe you'll become a famous painter and settle in Europe somewhere." A pause, then Amy went on, "You know, I don't find it easy to believe that—that you could give up your acting."

"Why not?"

Amy sighed. "Oh, I don't know." She was silent for a second or two, then gave a little nod. "Yes, I guess I *do* know. I guess it's because I've never done as well as you—in the business, I mean. And I find it hard to accept that someone who *is* doing well in it should think of giving it up." She shrugged. "I mean, it's all I've ever wanted. Give me a chance to do as well as you and *nothing* would keep me away. Nothing would persuade me to do anything else."

"But you've never really *tried* anything else. Who knows, you might discover that you have a real talent for writing or something."

"No." Amy contemptuously brushed Shenna's words aside. "But," she added, "there's another reason I don't understand you giving up your acting."

"Listen, I don't know that I'm *giving it up.*"

"Well, you are for the time being."

"Okay. Anyway, what's your other reason?"

"Well—you're so damned good at it, that's why. It's as simple as that."

By the time Doris returned from the airport and shopping Amy had gone.

Entering the hall, Doris called up the stairs that she was back, and then went into the kitchen to put away the groceries. After that she prepared more coffee. Some minutes later when Shenna came downstairs she found her mother in the study, sitting at her desk and sorting through the mail.

"Did Aunt Cissie get off okay?" Shenna asked.

"Oh, yes," Doris said absently. Then, shaking her head, she looked up and said, "Yesterday's mail as well as today's. I have to take care of it before Susan comes in on Monday." Susan was the stenographer who came in to do the letters. Shenna picked up a magazine and perched herself on the edge of the desk. A moment later Doris said without looking up, "I read the script Jack sent last week." Jack Tanner was Shenna's agent. "You should look at it," she added.

"What's the point?" Shenna said. "A few weeks from now I'm not going to be here, am I?"

Doris gazed at her for a moment with her lips pursed, then replaced the letters on the desk and stood up. "I'll get back to it in a minute." She started out.

"Mom, please," Shenna said, "let's not get like this."

Doris turned to her in the doorway. "Like what?"

"Going on as if you don't have any idea what I'm talking about. Is it going to continue like this until I leave?"

Doris looked at her in silence for a moment, then turned away again. "I'll get the coffee," she said.

She left the room and after a few moments Shenna leaned across the desk and idly picked up the mail. Much of it was addressed to herself, forwarded by her agent from the television or film company to which it had been sent. Doris opened all Shenna's mail that didn't appear to be private— the fan mail among it. The routine had started many years before when Shenna was much younger and had continued ever since. The only mail that Shenna herself opened was her personal correspondence, which came addressed to her specifically at the house. She rarely bothered to read any of the fan mail. There was never any point. One piece was pretty much like another; it was generally predictable and never interesting.

She began, now, to go through the fan letters, first reading one that had come from Westchester, New York. In it the writer told her that he'd seen *Child's Play* three times and then ended by asking for an autographed picture. The next letter, from Kansas City, Kansas, also requested a photograph and went on to ask if she was working on any more movies. The third letter, from Maine, also asked for a photograph, "preferably one from *Circuit*."

The fourth letter was a much longer one and Shenna was still reading it when Doris entered with the coffee. "Have you read this?" Shenna asked as Doris set the tray on the desk.

There was a pause before Doris answered. "What's that?"

"This letter from England. From London."

Doris shook her head. "Oh, that one. I've just glanced at it. He's one of the regular creeps." She sat in the wing chair by the window and sipped her coffee. "What does he have to say this time?"

"You sure you can stand it?"

"I'll try."

Shenna cleared her throat and began to read.

Dear Shenna,

What must I do to get some kind of response from you? I've written to you so often, but all I get for my efforts is silence. Please don't imagine that I'm like those other people who write to you. I'm not just one of your fans, so please, don't treat me like one.

If you think back you will recall that I've spent considerable time writing to you—letters giving you encouragement and, at times, advice and friendly criticism—and all well meant, I hope you realized. And what, lately, have you given me in return? Nothing—though trust and affection are two-way things. Right at the beginning, as I'm sure you remember, you did *respond, writing to me and sending me signed photographs of yourself—photographs which, along with your letter, I still prize greatly; and because of your very positive reaction I was encouraged to believe that our friendship would develop. Unfortunately, though, it has become very one-sided. Of course, it may well be that I'm misunderstanding the silence and that there's a perfectly good reason for it. If this is the case then please,* let me know*—then I shan't worry so much. As it is, I don't know what to think, and I go around imagining the worst.*

As I sit here I feel you are in my room with me. I have so many pictures of you—photographs, and drawings of you that I've done myself. I keep them all very secret (like my love for you, which is very private, very special, and not a thing any ordinary man would understand). Did I ever tell you that I'm a creative person as well? Well, I am, in my own way. I love to draw, and I intend taking some classes one day when I get some time. We artistic people, we should stick together, don't you think?

Anyway, all that apart, I just want to ask you to write back to me. Please write back to me. I need reassurance—to know that I'm not deluding myself. I'm sure you'll tell me I'm not, but so often in the silence of my room the doubts come creeping in and I feel very much alone.

Shenna came to a halt and Doris asked, "Is that it?"

"No, there's more." Shenna paused. "Has this guy written often in the past?" She turned to the last page of the letter. "John Cosgray," she added.

Doris gave a nod. "Yes, quite often."

"He says I wrote to him. Did we say anthing in particular, can you recall?"

Doris shrugged. "No, it couldn't have been anything special. It's all pretty much the same formula. Susan could do it on her own most of the time. As you know, I just thank them for writing, and then when you've signed the letter we send it off with a picture. You know the routine as well as I do. It never varies."

"He seems to think I encouraged him."

"That's nonsense. He's never been given any encouragement. On the contrary—I remember that when he started writing too often and making too many demands I just ignored his letters. That's what I've done in the past when others have gotten a little too persistent, and it usually works. They get the message sooner or later and eventually stop writing."

"Not this one."

"Apparently not." Doris shook her head. "What else does he have to say?"

Shenna turned back to the letter and went on reading aloud.

Anyway, on to brighter things. Are you working on anything at the moment? If you're doing another film, I hope you've chosen wisely. I say this as I don't believe you have always made the right choices in your career so far. I'm thinking about your role in The Dowry. *The film seemed to me to have such a strong undercurrent of sexuality about it and when I recently saw it I was horrified and embarrassed for you at some of the reactions engendered by the sight of you up there on the screen. I'm sure you can't be aware, but there are many in our so-called civilized society who see such films purely for the purpose of getting sexually aroused, and when you are the object of that attention it distresses me beyond words. Bearing this in mind, I've been reading several books looking for a good property for you— something that would make the right film vehicle for you. I wondered about* Tess of the D'Urbervilles. *I think the part of Tess would be an excellent part for you. I know it was done a few years ago with Nastassia Kinski, but I think you would be so much better in the part—with some of the more sexual overtones subdued a little, of course. I'll write to a few producers and suggest you for the role. There are several Dickens heroines, too, that would suit you very well, and I've also thought that you would make a marvelous Ophelia or Viola. I've got lots of ideas in mind—but leave them with me for now.*

Well, Shenna, it's time to take my leave of you once more. I shall write again soon, though, rest assured. In the meantime, please, please write me a few lines and let me know how you are. I think of you constantly and am anxious for news of you. Don't let me down. You can depend on it—I shall not let you down. Whatever happens I shall be here.

With love, always,

John Cosgray

P.S. Apart from the miles between us I feel more distanced than ever always having to write to you at the studios. To make it simpler, when you write back don't forget to include your home address. Oh, yes, and your phone number, too. It'll be expensive to phone from here but it will be worth it. You can't imagine how important it is to me, the knowledge that I am not alone, that I have someone—a friend. You.

If you write to me I shall be so happy. If you don't, then I don't know what is to become of me. I have invested my life in you, and without you I shall have nothing worth living for. I beg you again, write to me. Please, please write.

Shenna put the letter down on the desk. "God alive," she said. "What gets into these people? Some guy writes in for a picture and you send him a picture and a polite little note, a note that nobody in his right mind could misunderstand, and suddenly it's as though you mean everything to him. And here he is writing as if we've got some kind of relationship going. What do you do about something like this?"

Doris got up from her chair and picked up the letter. "Don't worry, I'll take care of it," she said, "as I've taken care of the others in the past. I'll write to him, and I'll try to let him down lightly so that he's not too upset. He's got to be discouraged, though, otherwise it'll only get worse. But don't worry. I'll sort it out." She dropped the letter back on the desk, turned to the window, and looked out over the garden. There was a little silence, then she said, "Cissie thinks I should take a vacation in the fall, after you've gone. Go and stay with her for two or three weeks."

"I think that's a good idea. The fall's the prettiest time of year on the East Coast. Will you go?"

"Oh, I doubt it."

"Why not, for heaven's sake? You're always saying how much you miss the place, how much you loved it there."

Doris and her sister had been born on a small farm in Orange County, in upstate New York, very close to where Cissie now lived. Over the years, Doris had frequently spoken of growing up in the country and of how much she would like to go back there one day. Now she nodded and said, "I do love it, and I *will* go to see Cissie for a visit. But not yet." She smiled, ending the discussion, and gestured to Shenna's cup. "Your coffee's getting cold."

Shenna nodded, drank from her cup, and then looked at her watch. Doris frowned. "What's the matter? You have an appointment somewhere? Why can't you sit and relax for a while?"

Shenna shrugged. "I just want to get on with my painting." There was so little time now before she was due to leave and she was anxious to do as much as possible on her own before starting the course. As she put down her empty cup she glanced up to see Doris flicking through the script that Jack Tanner had sent.

"It's a very good part—your part," Doris said.

Shenna smiled. "*My* part?"

"You know what I mean. But really, it's very well written. You should read it." She paused. "Aren't you even interested anymore?"

With a sigh, Shenna said, "I told you, Mom, there's no point. If they offered me a remake of *Gone With the Wind* I couldn't take it. Please—things are different now, you know that."

Doris turned away. "Nothing's gonna make you change your mind now, is it? You're so set on this—business."

"Yes, I *am* set on it—this *business*, as you call it. Why should I change my mind at this stage? Why?"

Doris shrugged. "Oh, I don't know. I guess I just keep hoping that you'll stop thinking about it all, that you'll—settle."

"Mom," Shenna said, "I'm nineteen years old. I'm not ready to settle *anywhere* just yet. And I'm not just *thinking* about going away. All my arrangements are made. You know that. I've been offered a place and I've made my plans. It's all set. I can't just go and forget it—not now."

"You seem to be doing that to your career."

"What career?"

"*What career?*" Doris shook her head in angry exasperation. "Shenna, sometimes I don't know what goes on in your mind. I swear I don't. Are you saying you don't get offers? You get offers. You might choose not to take them up, but you get them."

"Yes, I know that."

"Yes, and you do a lot better than most other young actresses your age. Look at some of them. Look at your friend Amy. She'd be glad just to get a *chance* at some of the jobs that come to you. *And* some of the jobs that you turn down."

"All right, I know I get offers, but look at them. Can you wonder I turn most of them down? I've done nothing that's been worthwhile over the past couple of years. Sure, the money's been okay, but as far as satisfaction goes, no—there's been precious little of that, and that's something I want."

"Your movies have been very successful, most of them."

"Yes, like *The Dowry*. Mom, it's crap, and you know it is. And what about this one I'm doing now? It's even *worse*."

"Well, I have no say in your choice these days, so don't blame me. You insist you're capable of deciding what work you want to do. . . ."

"I know I chose to do it—but that doesn't mean I have to admire it."

"Then why did you do it?"

"For the *money*. If I can't get satisfaction I've got to get *something*. And that's what I think of whenever I look at that crummy script—the money—and what I want the money for."

"To go to England."

"Yes." Shenna paused, then added quietly, earnestly, "Mom, please try to understand. I want to study painting— and at a good school. It was never possible before when I was busy with one picture after another. For God's sake, I'm not asking anything of anybody. I've got enough money for my fees and to live on."

Doris turned away. "What are you saying?—that in the past I stopped you from doing what you wanted to do? Shenna, I only ever thought of you—always. That's why we left New York in the first place—uprooted ourselves to come here. It was for you."

"I know that. I'm aware of that."

"Are you? I worked damned hard to get you started. And it wasn't easy. But you had talent and I knew you could do it. And now here you are, looking on it all as if it were some kind of—of penance—and determined to give it all up." She shook her head. "God, will you listen to me! This is really pathetic, isn't it? I sound like Mama Rose."

There was silence in the room for a moment, then Doris went on: "Success came pretty easy for you, Shenna. Maybe *too* easy; *you* didn't have to do the struggling. You think I enjoyed giving piano lessons all those years?—and half the time to smart-ass brats who never wanted to be within fifty feet of a piano? Well, let me tell you I *didn't* enjoy it. I didn't then and I don't now. But we had to manage somehow." Doris had continued to give piano lessons even after Shenna had begun earning a top salary. Though now the number of her pupils was much smaller, still they came, and, conserving her independence, she conscientiously taught them.

"Most other mothers had husbands and most other girls your age had fathers," Doris continued. "*We didn't*. We had to get along as best we could. And thank God we had my music. With that we *did* get along."

"Listen," Shenna said. "Wait a minute—"

Doris overrode her. "No, *you* wait a minute. *You* listen. When you've had things really hard in the past it's stupid to get complacent—and that's something you should remember. But you—you'd toss it all aside—everything we've worked for, for some dream—some dream that has no practicability whatsoever."

"Who said anything about my giving it up forever?"

"Oh, you think your career's going to wait around for you? That you'll be able to come back to it in two or three years and pick up where you left off?" Doris shook her head. "I don't understand you. I really don't." She paused. "Tell me something—what does Amy think about your going away?"

Shenna didn't know how to answer. Doris waited a moment and then gave a nod. With a note of triumph in her voice she said, "You don't need to say anything—she thinks you're crazy, right? Of course she does. You know something? I just wish you had her dedication. Amy Michaels and all those other girls—they'd give their eyeteeth to be in your situation."

"Mom, I'm not talking about Amy and all those other girls. I'm not concerned with them. I'm only concerned with *me.* Besides, acting has always been Amy's choice. It was never mine."

"Oh, I see—you're saying I pushed you into it, is that it?"

"I'm not saying any such thing. I'm just saying it was never a conscious choice I made. I—*we*—just got into it. And I know that it's been good to us, but . . ." She shrugged. "Well—now it's different. Now I can make a choice. And I want to choose while I'm young. While I *can* choose. And right now it's my choice to—to try to paint. At least to see whether I've got any ability."

"And you have to leave home in order to find that out?" Doris shook her head. "If you want to paint, then what's wrong with Los Angeles? Why can't you study at UCLA, for God's sake? It's right on your doorstep. And Amy's there. You wouldn't have to leave all your friends. *And* you could study in your spare time, while you keep acting. You could go to evening classes. You don't have to go to England in order to paint a few pictures."

"England's hardly the end of the earth."

"Maybe not." Doris was silent for a moment, looking at her daughter coldly, then she said, "What are the other reasons you want to go there? Is it because of—your father?"

Shenna shrugged. "What would be the sense in that?"

"What would be the sense, indeed? He's dead, Shenna. There's no point in trying to raise ghosts."

"I know that."

"Good. As long as you accept the fact."

Yes, *I* accept it, Shenna wanted to say. When are *you* going to?

As Shenna looked at her mother's set face Doris turned away to the window. When she turned back a moment later Shenna was surprised at the look of bitter anger on her face.

"Well, *good luck!*" Doris laughed humorlessly and gave a withering shake of her head. "Believe me, Shenna, you've got a few surprises coming to you. You think you can manage for yourself? We'll see. You'll come running back. You've had everything done for you up to now. You'll soon see what a difference *that* made in your life."

"Mother, for God's sake! I'm nineteen now and—"

"Sure, nineteen and has all the answers." Doris moved to the desk and sat down. "Anyway, I've got work to do." She picked up the script. "I'll return this to Jack and tell him he's wasting his time."

"No." Shenna reached out and took the script from her hand. "*I'll* send it back. If I'm going to start managing my own affairs, I might as well start now."

"Fine." Doris shrugged, tight-lipped. Pushing the John Cosgray letter across the desk, she added crisply, "And while you're at it, you might as well take care of this one, too." She paused, glaring at Shenna across the desk. "If you *can*."

In silence Shenna held her mother's gaze for a moment, then, picking up the letter, she crisply tore it across and dropped the pieces into the wastebasket. "Sure I can," she said.

3

The days passed so slowly, and each time he took Miss Collins her lunch tray he looked to see whether there was anything for him on the hall table. There never was, and each night in his room he crossed off another uneventful day on the calendar. When he had crossed off the thirtieth of June he put his head in his hands. Only two more days. In just two days it would be the second of July. He *must* hear from her by then. He *must*.

The next day, when he entered the hall of the office building and looked through the assortment of mail, he saw once again that there was nothing for him.

He stood there for some moments, aware of the thudding of his heart. What was he going to do? Then, as he tried to fight the disappointment that threatened to overwhelm him, he reminded himself that there was still time. There was still tomorrow, and tomorrow was the special day. Yes, of course, it would be tomorrow—the actual day of the second. *Of course.* He should have realized it before. Everything in the past pointed to it. The second—it was *the* day in his calendar. All he had to do was wait another day.

The following morning he was up and dressed earlier than usual, anxious to get away. He ate his breakfast hurriedly and with little appetite, hardly aware of the bustle going on around him as his grandparents made final preparations for their departure. They would be leaving that afternoon; their suitcases had stood packed in the hall since yesterday.

As he made his way to the front door, his grandfather followed him into the hall and asked if he would be coming back to the house after lunch as usual. He turned to the old man. "Yes, of course. I'll see you both then to say good-bye." He would like never to see them again, but he had to be patient; soon everything would be different. It had to be. With Shenna beside him he would have the courage to live his own life.

At the restaurant he watched the hours and the minutes crawl by. Then at last Mario handed him Miss Collins's tray, and he took it and carried it across the street. In the hall of the office building he put the tray down on the table, picked up the mail, and went through it.

Nothing.

There was nothing for him.

He couldn't believe it. It couldn't be. He must have made a mistake.

He went through it again. Nothing. But she *had* to have written. She *had* to. He went through it again, and then once more. Still nothing. Nothing. Nothing. After a while he dropped the mail back onto the table and turned and moved to the door. Behind him the lunch tray lay forgotten and growing cold.

He returned to the restaurant without giving any thought to where he was going or what he was doing, and once there went straight to the lavatory, where he sat and hugged himself in his misery. He had no thoughts of work, no thoughts of anything but the knowledge that all his hopes had gone for nothing.

After a time the door rattled as someone tried the handle, and then there came a knocking, followed by the voice of one of the waiters, Valentino, asking if he was all right. He didn't answer. Valentino's voice came again, after which there was the sound of footsteps receding, and then footsteps approaching, and then Mario's voice was there, anger and impatience in its tone. What did it matter if they got angry? They had never liked him, anyway. He knew they laughed about him behind his back. He had never fit in with them, never shared in their conversations, their dirty jokes, their after-work activities. He didn't care. *Nothing matters now*, he said to himself, and found himself silently repeating the words while inside him it seemed that he was nothing but one great, continuing groan of anguish.

"Are you all right in there?" Mario called. And then more loudly: "Are you?"

"Yes."

"At *last*. Are you ill?"

"No, I'm not ill."

"Then come out. *Now*." A pause. "Come out or we break the lock."

He got up and opened the door. They were all there, all standing looking at him as he emerged: Mario, Carlos, Simona, Valentino, Trevor, and Alan. He ignored them and, with an air of calm, pushed past them and began to change into his street clothes. When he was ready he walked out. He would never go back.

After leaving the restaurant he walked around in a daze, only aware in intermittent flashes of where he was and what he was doing. At one point he found himself waiting at the side of a busy road for a heavy-goods lorry to pass, and, looking at the huge wheels, thought how swift would be such a death—if he had the courage. He didn't, though; yet all the time in his mind was the thought of how much he wanted to end it all. He had to find some kind of oblivion where the hurting would stop.

Later he found himself in Hyde Park, on a bench. As he sat there two young boys came charging by on roller skates, moving perilously close, and the old woman reading her newspaper on the seat beside him clicked her tongue and spoke of hooligans of today who had no respect for anyone. He nodded, hardly hearing what she said. Closing his eyes, he leaned forward, hands on his knees. He would never recover, he knew.

He remained on the bench for a long time. And as he sat there his feelings slowly changed, shifting from the dreadful hurting ache to a feeling of anger. And the anger grew. Shenna—she had never had the slightest consideration for his feelings. She had made a complete fool of him. She had simply played with him for her own amusement. She had led him on to gain his love and now that she was bored with the game she had just tossed him aside.

The thoughts went over and over in his mind till it seemed that they filled his head and at any moment his skull must burst. And as the sensation grew, his anger screwed up his eyes and knotted his hands into fists while the nerve in his temple throbbed with pain. Once she had been everything in the world to him, the only reason for living through each dreary, monotonous day. He had loved her so much. Now he hated her.

Reaching into his inside pocket, he took out his wallet, opened it, and extracted a small photograph. Shenna. He gazed at it for long seconds with his eyes wide and gleaming, then with rapid, violent movements tore it to pieces. Then, looking down at the pieces scattered at his feet he stood up and ground them into the asphalt. With the destruction of the photograph he knew it was the end, the end of it all, and with the realization he sank back onto the bench, lifted his head and yelled out to the sky.

"No-o-o-o-o-o-o-o-o!"

Then he hung his head and wept.

He didn't know how long it was before he turned and saw through tear-wet, incurious eyes that the old woman had left the seat beside him and gone away. He had not been aware of her going. He had been aware of nothing but his desolation.

After a time, vaguely, on the periphery of his grief, he realized that she had left her newspaper behind on the seat.

Without interest he turned and glanced at it—and as he did so the wind briefly lifted the top page—and he suddenly froze. . . .

It couldn't be possible.

For a moment he sat quite still, and then slowly, almost timidly, he reached out, picked up the paper, and opened it to the page he had glimpsed.

Yes. *Yes.*

The small photograph down on the lower right-hand side was of Shenna.

Disbelievingly, he stared at it. She was shown full-face, smiling at the camera. The text beneath was headed, ACTRESS TO STUDY IN BRITAIN. Underneath it was written:

> Actress Shenna Preston, it is reported from Hollywood, is temporarily to give up her career in favour of a course in art at the Greenwich School of Art in southeast London. Miss Preston, nineteen, has starred in several major Hollywood film successes, including *Circuit*, for which she was nominated for an Oscar, *Child's Play*, and *The Dowry*. Jack Tanner, her Hollywood agent, says that naturally he is disappointed over her decision, but that she will be doing something she has wanted to do for a long time.
>
> At present the actress is working on a new suspense drama called *Chain Letter*, which will bring her to England for shooting of the final scenes. When this work is completed she will embark on her studies at Greenwich, taking the Foundation Course in Fine Arts, lasting a year. After this, it is understood, she may go on to a degree course.

It couldn't be true.

She was coming here—to London.

While the tears dried on his face he sat looking at the photograph and reading the piece over and over. He looked at the date of the paper. It was that day's, the second of July's. His prayers had been answered after all.

With the paper clenched in his hands, he closed his eyes in anguish. *He should have known.* How could he have thought the way he had? How could he have imagined such things of her? Lifting his head, his lips moved in a silent plea. "Forgive me, Shenna. Forgive me for doubting you. Forgive me . . ." Everything now was explained. Of course she hadn't written—she hadn't had time. She had been preparing to come to England. What did it matter if he had had no letter from her? She was coming here in person—to him.

Carefully, he tore the page from the newspaper, folded it, and put it in his pocket. Then, with a smile on his lips and his step light, he made his way home.

Arriving at the house, he met Sarah, the cleaning woman, coming from the front gate, her work finished for the week. As she came toward him she smiled and said, "Well, see you next Monday," and he remembered that his grandmother had arranged for her to continue coming in while they were away. He wished it otherwise; he would have liked the house to himself.

Entering the hall, he found his grandparents ready to leave and waiting for the taxi they had ordered. "You're late," his grandfather said, as if suddenly realizing it. "If you'd been much longer you would have missed us."

He made no reply but turned and went upstairs. As he reached the landing a few moments later, he heard the ringing of the telephone down below. He went on into his room and closed the door on the sound. Sitting down at his table he took the page of the newspaper from his pocket, unfolded it, and very carefully cut out the picture. Then from the drawer he took out the scrapbook and opened it. As he sat there he heard the door open behind him and he quickly covered the album with his arm. Turning, he saw his grandmother in the doorway. "That was the restaurant," she said. "They say you just walked out. Is that true?"

". . . Yes."

"Why?"

When he didn't answer she came forward, and as she did so her glance fell on the open album beneath his arm. "What's that?" she said, her eyes narrowing.

"Nothing—it's nothing." He closed the album and moved to put it in the drawer, but she leaned down and snatched it from his hand. She began to turn the pages. After a few seconds she raised her eyes and said, her voice laden with contempt, "You disgust me." Then, as he watched, she ripped a page from the book and thrust it in front of his face, holding it as if it were contaminated. The photograph was of Shenna sitting beside a pool.

"You disgust me," she said again, then put the album down on the table and tore the photograph across and across and let the pieces fall—fragments of Shenna's perfect body falling like dead leaves onto the carpet. As he watched, he was back again in the park with the pieces of the photograph around his feet. He shook his head as if in pain, then saw her reach out to take up the scrapbook again.

"*Don't touch it.*" His voice was steely cold as his hand flashed out and closed around her thin wrist. Holding it rigid in his grasp, he peered into her hard, hostile little eyes. "Don't touch it," he said again, grinding out the words in a low voice. There was silence for a brief moment and then she laughed, a dry, brittle sound, without humor and now touched with uncertainty. Then, raising her free hand, she struck him in the face.

Rage exploded within him as he felt the sting of the blow

and he leaped to his feet. As he did so she recoiled, and he saw fear naked in her face. Seeing it, he suddenly became aware of his own power, and almost as if his movements were measured, he lifted his hand and hit her hard across the mouth. She screamed and he hit her again and saw a smear of blood appear on her upper lip. Again she screamed, and then from the hall below came the sound of his grandfather's voice calling up the stairs, demanding to know what was going on. He took no notice, but hit the old woman again and continued to hit her, over and over, while the sound of his grandfather's footsteps came nearer.

4

The remaining few days passed in a chaotic whirl of final preparations, but at last everything was ready. Then, on the afternoon of Friday, July 30, with Amy and other friends bidden farewell, Shenna set off for the airport to catch her flight to London. Doris went with her—a little cold, a little reserved—and it wasn't till they were actually on the point of saying good-bye that she unbent and, putting her arms around Shenna, held her close and kissed her.

A while later, as Shenna stepped aboard the plane, she felt as if she were stepping forward into a life of her own. She felt free.

The flight arrived at Heathrow airport just after noon the following day. Emerging from Customs, Shenna hurried past the waiting press photographers and was met by a young man from the film production company, who took charge of her luggage, placed himself between her and the reporters, and led the way to a waiting limousine. Soon afterward she had left the airport and was on the motorway heading for the city.

It was exciting to be back in England, to be here on her own. On the three occasions she had worked here in the past her mother had been with her, and each time, invariably, Doris had insisted that they return to California as soon as shooting had been completed. This time it would be different.

The film company had booked her into a hotel in Mayfair, and as soon as she had checked in she showered and changed and had a light lunch brought up to her room. After she had eaten she went out and made her way to the National Gallery, where she stayed looking at the collection until closing time. The rest of the evening she spent relaxing in front of the television, after which she had a good night's sleep.

She spent the next day, Sunday, visiting the Tower of London and the Tate Gallery. The following morning, just after ten, she telephoned the art school's registrar, Miss Greer, and arranged to meet her between eleven-thirty and twelve to discuss the matter of where to live. Then, armed with directions and the map that Miss Greer had sent to her in Westwood, she set off for Charing Cross, where she took a train for the few minutes' journey to Blackheath.

Blackheath had been spoken of by Miss Greer as a "village," and when Shenna emerged from the station at her destination she found it to be just that; it *was* a village—compact and fairly attractive, and retaining something of a village atmosphere in spite of the progress of time—progress that had all but obliterated any sense of character and individuality from much of the area surrounding it.

After taking in her immediate surroundings she consulted her map, and then crossed the street and set off to the right, heading for the school. A few minutes later she came to it—a large, red-brick Victorian building on a pleasant, tree-lined street off one of the main thoroughfares leading from the village. After standing looking at the building for a few seconds, she went up the steps and into the foyer.

The only person in sight was a porter, who lifted his balding head from his newspaper and asked whether he could be of help. Shenna told him she wanted to see the housing officer, and he directed her along a corridor to a door at the end, where she entered and was met by Miss Greer, a pleasant, attractive woman in her mid-forties with a Park Lane accent one could have cut with a knife. Introductions over, Shenna sat down while the woman took from her desk a short list of apartments and rooms owned by private landlords—properties available for rent that the various owners deemed suitable for students. "Though," she said dryly as she handed Shenna the list, "I'm afraid that suitable for art students in the eyes of many private landlords often means accommodation that no one else will look at. I don't know why it is, but so often people assume that *art* students will be prepared to live in just about anything. I suppose it all comes from the old ideas of bohemians starving in their garrets." She smiled. "I wouldn't imagine many of them foresee the possibility of a film star for a tenant."

"Good," Shenna said, smiling in return, "because I'm here as a student—and that's the way I want it to stay."

When she got back to the foyer she stopped on impulse by the porter's desk and, after telling him that she would be starting school there with the new term, asked whether there was any chance that she could look around some of the studios. The winning smile she gave him didn't seem to work, though, for he shook his head and said, "I'm sorry, miss. I wish I could let you in, but I can't."

"Ah, too bad . . ."

"I'm sorry. Most of them are locked, anyway."

She shrugged. "Oh, well, it was just an idea. Thanks all the same." She turned away and as she did so he said, "You're American, are you, miss?"

"Yes, I am."

"I thought so. Have I seen you somewhere before?"

She shrugged, aware of being touched by a flash of annoyance; so much for her thoughts of being plain Shenna Preston, student. "It's possible," she said coolly.

"It's just that your face seems a bit familiar. *Have* I seen you before?"

She smiled then; what was the point of getting uptight? She was going to have to get used to it. "As I said," she told him, still smiling, "it's possible." Then she turned and went out onto the street.

There were nine properties on the list that Miss Greer had given her, and all within walking distance, though one glance at their details was enough for Shenna to immediately rule out five of them (she wasn't about to share a kitchen or a bathroom with anybody), and she set off to view the remaining four with her hopes less than high.

And she soon found that Miss Greer's pessimism was well founded. Of the remaining four, three turned out to be set in streets that were dirty and depressing while the fourth was on a frantically busy corner where she knew she would never get used to the sound of the traffic thundering by. It was after seeing this last that she returned to the village, bought a copy of a local paper, and sat in a small café looking over the ads. To her relief, there seemed to be no shortage of apartments available; she'd wait until filming on *Chain Letter* was finished and then look at some of them.

He was walking through the village when he came to a sudden stop. He had caught sight of her through the window of the café; she was sitting at a table, reading a newspaper. After a moment, his heart thudding, he moved on; he didn't want her to turn and see him looking.

That evening he sat in his room, opened his diary and wrote:

> *She's here. I've seen her. It was true what the papers said. Now I must find a place closer to the school. Closer to her. I must be near her, as near as possible.*

Over the next week Shenna went on location in and around London, filming the last scenes for *Chain Letter*. At last, on Friday, the final wrap was called. Now there'd just be a couple of sessions of post-sync dubbing and her involvement with the project would be finished.

The following Monday, after a weekend of sightseeing,

she got the train to Blackheath, where she bought copies of local newspapers and resumed her search for somewhere to live. Two days later she had found a studio apartment in a Victorian house in Elm Court Road, a narrow though pleasant little street situated less than a mile from the school and near the area of Lee Green. The house had recently been converted into four apartments and Shenna had been shown two that had just become available.

Reasonably well furnished, both apartments (she *must* get used to saying "flats," she told herself) were on the ground floor, on either side of the lobby. She chose the larger of the two—flat one—which was situated on the left of the hall. It was comprised of a fairly large bed-sitting room, with a small incorporated kitchen and, off to one side of a hall the size of a postage stamp, a bathroom and toilet. All she had to do was provide linen, cutlery and pots and pans, and get the telephone installed. Compared to the spacious dimensions of the house she had left in Westwood, the flat was tiny, but it didn't matter—there was enough room for her and, more importantly, enough space for her to set up an easel and paint. She took the apartment on a six months' lease, the minimum time possible—that way, she figured, if she wasn't happy there she would soon have the opportunity to move to some other place. When she had paid a deposit and the first month's rent she got her key and was all set.

That evening she called her mother and told her of her find, describing the apartment and its surroundings. In answer, Doris said how pleased she was, but her tone was disappointingly unenthusiastic.

The next day Shenna left the hotel to move in, and at once set about getting a telephone. This didn't prove as easy as she had anticipated, but eventually she succeeded and a date was set for its installation. After that she went shopping, buying, among other things, an easel and painting and drawing materials.

During her first days, while she settled in, she met her neighbors from the floor above, the elderly Miss Martin, and a middle-aged widower, Kenneth Drake. They both seemed pleasant enough. The flat opposite her own on the ground floor remained empty.

The telephone was due to be installed on the morning of her second Monday there, and while she waited for the phone men to arrive she slipped out to nearby Lee and got a copy of *The Times*, which she brought back to read over a cup of coffee. On the arts page was an advertisement for an exhibition of new paintings that had just opened at a Kensington gallery, and she decided to go there that afternoon.

After the telephone men had come and gone, leaving behind a bright new cream-colored telephone, she worked for an hour at the still life she had begun, had a light lunch, and then left to get a train to Charing Cross. From there she took the tube to South Kensington and then walked the short distance to the Simpson Gallery.

The paintings on view were the work of three up-and-coming young artists, students from London schools. She found the work fascinating—in particular that of one of the artists, who had displayed paintings of still lifes, landscapes, and portraits. She was standing before one of his larger canvases—a study of a child against a patterned curtain—when she heard a voice at her elbow and, turning, saw beside her a middle-aged, gray-haired man dressed in a light tan suit. She had seen him earlier, sitting talking to the gallery's receptionist.

"It's beautiful, isn't it?"

She nodded. "Yes. I keep coming back to it."

The man told her that his name was Alfred Carson, and that he was one of the gallery's directors. When Shenna introduced herself he smiled and said, "Yes, I recognized you." Then, after a pause, he added, "Didn't I read that you're over here to study painting?"

"Yes. At Greenwich."

He was curious about her work and ambition to be a painter, and they talked for several minutes. Then, just as Shenna was about to make her excuses and break away, Carson said, looking over her shoulder, "Ah, here's an old friend," and she turned and saw another man coming toward them. He was introduced to her as Ian Bradley. Dressed casually but expensively, he was tall and broad-shouldered, with keen blue eyes, thick, dark hair, and a smile that looked very bright against his suntanned skin.

As the three of them chatted, the time went quickly, until Shenna, looking about her, suddenly realized that the other viewers had gone and that the receptionist, too, was preparing to leave. It was five-thirty; she herself must be going, she said; she had to get back to Charing Cross for her train to Blackheath. Carson waved a dismissing hand. "Relax," he urged. "It's the rush hour and it'll be hell on earth right now. You might as well take it easy for a while." Then, when Shenna acquiesced, he locked the door behind the receptionist and, while Shenna and Ian sat down, set about pouring glasses of chilled white wine for the three of them.

It was almost six-thirty when Shenna once again got up to go. This time Ian said he had to be leaving too and offered to drive her to the station. Shenna thanked him. As they reached the door, Alfred said, "Just a minute . . ." and came after them. "Tell me," he said to Shenna, "have you got any examples of your work here in London?"

She shook her head. "No, but I've got a stack of photographs of my paintings—ones I took to send to the school when I applied for a place."

"Could I see them?"

"Yes, sure."

"Soon? Very soon, I mean."

"Yes, of course. Why?"

He paused. "I'll talk to you about that later. But let me have the photographs as soon as you can, will you?"

They exchanged telephone numbers, after which she said good-bye and left, Ian at her side. As they reached his car, an Alfa Romeo, he asked her whether she had any particular reason to hurry back to Blackheath. As she hesitated, he added, "I was wondering if you'd care to stay in town and have dinner with me."

She found him attractive and wanted so much to say yes, but she found herself hesitating still. He smiled. "I'd really like it if you would. Will you?"

She hesitated for only a moment longer, then, smiling back, she gave a nod. "Yes, I'd like that too."

They drove across London to a small Italian restaurant near Notting Hill where he was known by the proprietor. As it was still quite early there were not yet many other diners there, and the two of them were shown to a quiet table near the window. There, over the next two hours, as they talked and ate, Shenna felt her happiness and her sense of freedom burgeoning.

During the conversation she learned that he was one of the directors of a successful advertising company, his work at different times taking him to various parts of the world. She learned further that he had been divorced for three years, that there were no children from the marriage, and that he now lived alone in a flat off Knightsbridge. In turn, she told him about herself and her disenchantment with the opportunities presently available in Hollywood and her ambition to succeed with her painting.

It was almost ten when they left the restaurant and set off for Blackheath. Arriving at the flat some forty minutes later, she invited him in and he entered and stood before the easel, looking at the unfinished still life. She watched as he nodded his appreciation. He was impressed with her work, he said, and would like to see more examples of it. A little later, as they drank coffee, she took from a drawer the small album in which she had mounted the photographs of her paintings. He looked through it with interest and said, "If you like, I'll take this to Alfred first thing in the morning."

Twenty minutes later he got up to go, and she walked with him through the hall to the front door, where they stood facing one another. After a moment he said, "I was wondering—would you like to drive out somewhere tomorrow, see a little bit of the countryside. . . ?" Earlier, in the restaurant, he had asked her how much of England she had seen and she had replied, "Nothing." Now she smiled at his question and said, "Don't you have work to do?"

"Not till later in the day."

"Well—that would be wonderful. Where could we go?"

"Wherever you like. You have any place in mind? Maybe you'd like to go to Bath or Stratford-upon-Avon or somewhere . . ."

She said, "There is a place. . . ."

"Yes?"

"If it's possible, I'd like to go to Hinton Peeble."

"*Where?*"

"Hinton Peeble. You don't know it?"

"I've never even heard of it. Where is it?"

"It's in Wiltshire."

"What do you want to go there for?"

She hesitated, then said, "It was the home of someone my mother used to know."

"I see."

There was no curiosity in his tone, but she felt compelled to add, "A relative."

He nodded. "Okay."

A silence fell between them. She was suddenly aware that the wine and the evening had gone to her head a little. He smiled at her.

"Okay. If you want to go to Hinton Peeble, then I'll take you there."

"Thank you. That's very kind."

He frowned, still smiling. "Kind? No, not kind."

"Oh, yes." She smiled back at him. "And 'Ah have always depended on the kindness of strangers.'"

He laughed. "Yes, well, I'd be careful there, if I were you." Then he sighed. "Anyway, I'll go on home now and look up Hinton Peeble on the map—hoping it's *on* a map. I'll call for you tomorrow morning. Say ten-thirty. Can you be ready by then?"

"Of course."

"I'll call for you then."

He looked, smiling, into her eyes for a moment or two, then, putting his hands on her shoulders, kissed her lightly on the cheek. Then he turned and walked to the front gate.

5

With the sun shining brightly, it promised to be a perfect day for the trip, and Shenna was ready and eagerly waiting when Ian arrived just after ten-fifteen. When he had entered the flat he came to a stop in front of her, gazed at her with his keen blue eyes, and, raising his strong, tanned hands, gently laid his fingers on either side of her face. "Right," he said to her. "I dropped your photographs off with Alfred on my way here, and now the rest of the day is ours, providing I get back by nine in order to take a couple of phone calls. You all ready?"

"All ready."

They set off, leaving Blackheath and taking the South Circular Road to the M4 motorway. As they drove, Ian told her that he had looked up Hinton Peeble on the map and that it was some hundred and ten miles west of London, and that they should reach it in time for lunch.

The journey on the M4—part of which Shenna had taken before on the way in from the airport—lasted over an hour, and when they left it their route took them through the Wiltshire countryside, through small villages and golden fields where farmers were getting in the last of the harvest. It was close to twelve-forty when they saw the first signpost pointing the way to Hinton Peeble, and almost one o'clock by the time they got near the village itself. They approached it by a road that led between high banks on which trees spread their branches to meet in a green canopy overhead. Moments later, breaking through into the sun again, they saw before them, lying at the foot of the hill, the cluster of buildings that was the village.

"Oh, stop—please . . ." Shenna's voice sounded almost breathless, and she clasped her hands excitedly as Ian pulled the car to a halt near the grass shoulder. She got out and he followed and stopped beside her as she looked down the hillside. From where she stood she could see the village green, the church, and the narrow river that ran through the heart of the village. She had imagined the place to be small, but in reality it appeared even smaller. She could hardly believe it; she was here and it looked so much better than anything she had pictured in her mind. It was so perfect it was almost a cliché—like something dreamed up by Metro-Goldwyn-Mayer for some Greer Garson epic of days gone by.

Back in the car, they drove down into the village, parked at the side of the green, and got out, Ian with his camera around his neck. Then, moving past the little row of shops in the center, they entered The Swan, one of Hinton Peeble's two pubs, where several of the locals had gathered in the cool interior for lunchtime drinks. Shenna and Ian ordered salad, homemade pasties, and beer, which they carried outside into the garden, and there in the warm sun they ate while the birds sang and bees buzzed over the sunflowers.

Leaving the pub close on two o'clock, they made their way toward the church, and as they moved along in the warmth of the high summer afternoon Shenna suddenly became aware of her happiness. Almost in the same moment, Ian reached out for her hand and took it in his own. Gently, she pressed his fingers and relaxed in the pleasure of his touch.

They approached the church by a narrow lane shaded by birches and pushed open an old wrought-iron gate to enter the churchyard. Before them stood the small church, while on either side in the green grass lay the graves of Hinton Peeble's past inhabitants. Looking about her, Shenna felt almost overwhelmed by the sense of the rightness of things. On reaching the door of the little church, she saw that a notice had been pinned to the old wood. There, on a postcard, in neat block capitals in ball-point pen, now fading, was written:

DEAR FRIEND, KINDLY CLOSE THIS DOOR BEHIND
YOU ON ENTERING OR LEAVING THE CHURCH. IF IT
IS LEFT OPEN SMALL BIRDS MAY FIND THEIR WAY IN
AND SO PERISH.

The interior of the church was cool, and the sound of their feet and their low voices echoed in the stillness as they slowly walked around, looking at the memorial plaques set into the walls—plaques, like the gravestones outside, bearing the names of past villagers. After spending several minutes there they went back out into the warm sun, where Ian turned to her and said, "What's the name of the relative you're looking for?"

"Parnell."

He nodded, then turned and looked around him at the graves. "D'you want me to help you look?"

She shook her head. "No, I'll manage okay."

"Fine." He touched the camera suspended around his neck. "I think I'll go and take one or two pictures. I'll come back in a little while."

He moved away along the path to the gate. Shenna waited till he was almost out of sight, then turned her attention to the surrounding graves and began her search.

With the churchyard being relatively small, she had thought it would take no time at all to find the grave, but some minutes went by before she came upon it. When she did she came to a stop and just stood there.

The grave had a rather forgotten look about it. There was a dusty glass vase containing the remains of some long-dead flowers, while weeds grew around the headstone on which was carved:

TO THE MEMORY

OF

JAMES ALAN PARNELL
BORN 2 MAY, 1933, DIED 4 DECEMBER, 1962

She gazed at the words for a few moments and then, with a little sob, sank down onto her knees in the grass.

It was some little time later when Ian returned, and seeing him approaching through the gate, Shenna got to her feet. When he reached her side he saw the stain of tears on her cheek and put out a hand and touched his fingers to them.

"Were you that close?" he said.

"I—I never knew him." She shook her head. "Oh, I'm just being silly." Looking around, she gestured with a wave of her hand, encompassing the sky, the sun, the grass, the flowers. "Blame it on the beautiful day and—whatever else you like." She was silent for a moment, then she added, "He was my father."

Ian said nothing immediately, just looked at her. After a while they moved from the churchyard into the lane, where they walked in silence between the birch trees that grew on either side. At last Ian spoke. "I guessed it was somebody—special," he said. "Seeing how important the whole thing was to you, it was obviously no fifth cousin twice removed." He paused. "Why were you so reticent?"

"About saying who it was?" She shrugged. "Habit, I guess. My mother and I—we hardly ever talked about him, and I was positively discouraged from talking about him to other people. But he was always there—for me, anyway—whether we talked about him or not."

"Why didn't you talk about him?"

They had left the lane now and were moving along the village street. She said, "I guess it was because—well, it was too painful for her—my mother. It always has been. I was

54

all of fourteen when she told me that she and my father had never married. Till then it never occurred to me that they hadn't been."

"Was it a shock to you?"

"In a way, I guess. And I was a little upset at first—but not too much the more I learned about it."

"What was that—that you learned?"

She shrugged. "Well, about *them*. How they met, what happened to them. All that. And knowing it—well, it made everything somehow—okay." She turned to him and smiled. "Even so, that doesn't mean I was ready to go and talk about it to any stranger. In the business I was in, you have to be pretty careful what information you disclose if you don't want to see it splashed all over the papers, no matter how trivial it is."

He nodded.

"You know," she went on, "at one time I developed quite a fixation on him. It was really crazy."

"In what way?"

"Oh . . . I used to write poems about him, that sort of thing. And I used to make drawings of him—from the one photograph we had." She smiled. "I even tried to do an oil portrait of him—and all from the same old picture. I suppose it was because I never knew him. That's one of my greatest regrets. Although I feel I got to know him in a way, from what my mother told me—when I could get her to talk about him."

"What did he do?"

"For a living? He was a research scientist, working at some laboratory not far from here, I think. He met my mother when he was visiting New York in connection with his work. That was back in sixty-two. She was a student at Julliard then, studying piano. And—well—they met and fell in love." She smiled. "You know, the way it happens in all the best stories. Across a crowded room and all that."

He smiled in return, then said, "Nineteen-sixty-two—the same year as his death, according to the inscription on the stone. What happened?"

"They planned to marry, but first he had to return here to England to settle a few things, after which he was going to send for her. And after a little while he did, but then, just before my mother was due to leave, she got a letter from someone in his family—an aunt or a cousin or somebody like that—saying that—that he was dead."

"That's so sad. What was it? An illness?"

"One of those freak accidents. Some truck was driving through the village and got stuck on one of the narrow streets. It seems the driver tried to back up and turn. My father just happened to be passing by when—I don't know—something went wrong—the driver's foot slipped or something and—and the truck backed up too fast." She paused. "My father was crushed against a wall. He was killed instantly."

They had reached the village green and they walked across it and sat on a bench at the edge of the pond. On the bank nearby a mallard and his mate basked in the sun. "Why am I telling you all this?" Shenna said, and Ian answered, "I'm interested."

She nodded. "Yes, and I'm glad to talk about it, I guess. Maybe because I never get a chance to. To learn what I've learned from my mother over the years—it's been like pulling teeth." She sighed. "She still can't face it, even after all this time."

After a moment Ian said, "So what happened? Did your mother still come to England?"

"No. There was no longer any point, was there?"

"But didn't she want to see his family? Surely they would have wanted to see *her*—especially as she was carrying his child."

"He didn't have any *close* family—parents or brothers or

sisters. Anyway, my mother was proud, I guess. She's never had any contact with any of his relatives over the years."

"So she raised you on her own."

"Yes." She was silent for a few moments, then said, "You know, I realized something this afternoon. Seeing my father's grave there—it made me suddenly realize that he's one of the reasons I came here to England to study. I wouldn't even admit it to myself before, but—I guess it's been at the back of my mind for a long time. You see, this was his home, and it . . . well, I should have been born here—in this village. This should have been my home too."

She sat looking around for a second or two, then gave a sigh and turned to Ian. Changing the subject, she asked, "Did you take any photographs?"

"A few." He got up from the bench, stepped back, aimed the camera at her and clicked the shutter. "And one more," he said.

She took a photograph of him then as he sat on the seat, after which he took one of the pond with the mallards basking on its edge. Then he sat down beside her and they watched as the mallards stirred, got up, and moved down the bank and into the water. As the ducks swam together, Shenna said, "Mallards—I think they mate for life. Is that true?"

"I don't know."

"I think I remember reading it somewhere."

She fell silent, her eyes on the ducks as they moved smoothly over the water. Ian said, "What were the other reasons?"

"Mmm?"

"You said just now that your father was one of the reasons for your choosing to come to England to study. What were the other reasons?"

"Just one other reason, really—apart from my wanting to come here to study." She paused. "I came here to get away—to try to have a life of my own."

He said nothing to this. After a moment she went on, "I came to the realization that from the moment I was born my mother seemed to have invested everything in me. Everything. And who needs that kind of responsibility? I realized that I was all she had—me and whatever she could get through me." She shook her head. "I mean, it was because of me that she gave up the chance of a very promising career as a concert pianist."

"Really?"

"Oh, yes. She was really very talented. Apparently quite a few people thought she had a brilliant future ahead of her. When I came along, though, she gave up all thought of that and turned to teaching the piano—something steady and reliable that would enable her to bring up a child single-handed."

"She never thought of marrying again?"

"I don't think so, though over the years there've been a couple of guys who've been interested. I've often wished that she would return some of the interest, but she never has—never more than halfheartedly. So, most of the time it's just been the two of us. And still would be, if she had her way." She sighed. "It's all because of him, I guess—my father. If she hadn't lost him, she wouldn't have held on to me the way she has. And boy, she really has—held on, I mean." She gave a rueful little laugh. "I'm fond of my mother, don't get me wrong. But . . . I just felt that if I didn't get away from her and out on my own soon I never would. She's become so much more—dependent lately. I was beginning to feel stifled—that I'd never have a life of my own."

As she finished speaking she became aware that the sun-bright water of the pond had grown darker and that clouds had gathered. Now, suddenly, thunder growled in the distance, and a few moments later raindrops began to fall. Quickly, she and Ian got up from the bench and hurried over the grass. By the time they got to the car the rain was falling heavily.

They sat in the car watching as the rain pounded down, bouncing off the hood and washing down the windshield. After a while Ian said, "I'm afraid it doesn't look as if it's going to ease off for a while yet. I think we might as well go, don't you?"

Later, as they drove back along the motorway through the rain, Shenna thought of the village and knew that she would return.

They reached Blackheath just after six-thirty, and while Shenna made tea, Ian relaxed, sitting back in the easy chair and stretching out his long legs. They chatted of this and that, their talk easy, and she felt her comfort in his presence growing. But then, after a while, he said it was time for him to leave, and he rose. She walked with him to the door.

"Thank you," she said. "I had a lovely time. It meant so much to me."

He smiled down at her. "It meant a lot to me, too." He bent his head and lightly brushed her cheek with his lips. "Shall I see you tomorrow?"

"If you want to."

He nodded. "Oh, yes, I want to. I'll call you in the morning."

"Okay."

He kissed her again, more urgently, and this time on the mouth, his arms wrapping around her and drawing her to him. She had wanted the kiss, hoped for it, but now that it was happening she suddenly found herself tensing, as if about to resist him. With an effort, she pushed the feeling of resistance to one side and gave herself up to the embrace, to the kiss. Seconds later he was releasing her, stepping to the door and opening it.

"Good night, Shenna Preston."

He stood there for a moment longer, his tall frame silhouetted in the open doorway, and then he turned and was gone.

That night as she lay in bed, she thought back over the day, seeing again the village and her father's grave in the tiny churchyard. She thought of Ian coming to her as she had stood beside the grave; the way he had reached out and touched her cheek. And with the realization of her attraction to him, she remembered how, later, she had almost drawn back from his embrace. Another legacy from the lifetime of closeness with her mother. . . ?

She was eating toast and drinking coffee the next morning when the telephone rang. It was Alfred Carson.

"I'm calling to say that I was very impressed with the photographs of your paintings," he said, "and that I'd like to talk to you about them as soon as possible."

"Whenever you like."

"Could we meet this morning—here at the gallery?"

"Okay. I can be there by eleven-thirty."

After she had hung up she took a shower. While she was drying herself the telephone rang again. This time it was Ian. She had not expected him to call so early in the day, and she realized how happy she was to hear the sound of his voice. He was calling, he said, to ask her to have dinner with him that evening at his flat. She said yes without hesitation and, after getting directions, arranged to meet him around seven. After their conversation she finished getting ready and then left to meet Alfred.

She got to the gallery just after eleven-fifteen. Alfred greeted her warmly and, after leaving word with the receptionist where he could be found, took Shenna to a small coffee shop nearby, where they sat at a table on the sunlit pavement. As they drank fresh coffee he opened the photograph album and turned over the pages, commenting on the various paintings. When he came to the end he closed the book, looked at her steadily, and said, "You must have got some idea as to why I'm interested in your work, Shenna. The fact is, I'm mounting a new group exhibition early next year—at the end of January—and I'm looking for a third young painter. I've got two already." He paused for a moment, watching her keenly, then said, "D'you think you could have two dozen paintings ready by then? If so, the exhibition space is yours."

Shenna didn't know what to say. She had of course formed some vague idea as to why he was interested in seeing examples of her work; there could have been no other reason for his request. Nevertheless, to find, now, that that vague idea had become reality left her speechless for a moment. She had never hoped for such a chance so early in her painting career.

"I can hardly believe this," she said at last. "Do you—do you think I'm ready? Don't forget I'm only just getting started. Do you think my work is good enough?"

He was silent for a moment, then said, "You say you're only just getting started—and it's true, your work is primitive in certain respects—but in other respects it shows a very mature approach." He opened the album and pointed to two or three of the photographs. "Your paintings are fascinating, Shenna, and it's partly because of that rather raw, rather primitive approach you have that I want to show your work. I've seen hundreds of talented young painters with sparks of originality and I've seen so many of them get that spark snuffed out by tuition and by doing what they think they *ought* to be doing. I'd like to capture some of it while it's there."

Slowly, Shenna nodded. "And is that the reason—the real reason—you want to exhibit my work?"

"I don't understand you."

"I mean it's not because my name is fairly well known already, is it?"

He considered this for a moment, then said, "Well, let's put it this way: Your name will certainly help with attendance figures, and it might in the first instance help to sell the exhibition—and let's face it, we need all the help, all the publicity we can get—but in the end it's got to come down to more than that."

"Yes?"

"There's one thing you've got to realize and accept—and that is that what*ever* you do with your painting, at the start you're going to be Shenna Preston the film actress who's exhibiting her work. At the start you're not going to avoid that, so you might as well accept it and *use* it. Make it work for you." He smiled. "So, if you accept that face we might as well go ahead and use it now." He observed her steadily for a moment, then said, "So what's your answer? I'm offering you an exhibition of your work. Do you want it? And if so, can you get enough paintings?"

"Certainly I want it," Shenna said. "And I'm sure I can get enough pictures together. I'll have my mother pack up a load of my canvases and ship them off to me. Also I can get to work on some new things. I'll start right away. With over five months before the exhibition opens, I ought to be able to produce something worthwhile."

"So it's settled, then," Carson said, and Shenna nodded. Smiling together, they toasted the venture with more coffee.

On her return to Blackheath she wrote to her mother of the forthcoming exhibition and asked for certain paintings to be packed up and sent to England.

"You do that so well."

Holding her sherry glass, Shenna stood in the kitchen doorway of Ian's flat, watching as he expertly mixed a

French dressing and added it to the fresh, crisp salad he had just made.

He glanced around at her and smiled. "I've had to get in practice."

After a while Shenna slowly turned away and moved across the dining room to look out onto the quiet street through tall windows hung with silk drapes of pale champagne. Ian's spacious apartment was set in a graceful, curving Regency terrace just a stone's throw from Harrods. The furniture was mostly Georgian, the only concession to modern lines that she could see being the wide, comfortable, soft-leather couches that lined two walls of the elegant sitting room next door. Turning slightly, she suddenly caught sight of herself in a long mirror and became aware all at once of her presence there. So much seemed to have happened in such a short space of time. The days of her filming *Chain Letter* were only so recently in the past, yet they seemed to have happened so long ago. Her whole life was changing.

After a moment longer she turned and moved back to the kitchen door. Ian had finished preparing the salad and was now turning his attention to the steaks.

"Let me do something to help," she said. "I feel so useless just standing around."

"Okay," he said, "if you want to help you can set the table."

"Fine." Setting down her glass, Shenna followed his outstretched hand and went to the sideboard, from which she began to take the napery, mats, and silver.

When Ian came into the room a minute later he found her standing before the sideboard holding a framed photograph of a young woman in her mid-twenties. Shenna looked up guiltily as Ian approached.

"I'm sorry," she said. "I didn't mean to be inquisitive. I found it in the drawer beneath the napkins."

He shrugged as he came to a stop beside her. "It doesn't matter."

"Is she your wife?" Shenna asked.

"No, just a friend."

"She's very beautiful." The girl's face seemed somehow familiar. "I seem to have seen her somewhere before," she added. "Is that possible?"

"Yes, it's possible. She's a model."

With his words the familiarity of the face fell into place. It was a face that she had seen on the pages of various fashion magazines. "Of course," she said. "I remember now."

"Her name's Mary," he said. "Mary Carroll. She's American, too. From Maine, originally." He paused. "Once we were friends—or a little more than friends. But that's all in the past now."

She nodded, and he gently took the photograph from her hands and put it back in the drawer. "That's the place for that," he said, then he asked, smiling, "Is the table ready?"

"Just about, I think."

"Good. Then I think we're about ready to eat."

After they had eaten they washed the dishes together and then sat on the sofa and watched a videotape of *Casablanca*. When the movie was over he opened more wine, and as they drank it they talked of poetry and poets; he read G. K. Chesterton to her and she spoke of her own favorites, Whitman and Keats.

And then later, sometime later, the conversation was over and Ian was holding her in his arms and kissing her, and she felt his strong hands upon her breasts, cupping them, gently but firmly kneading them. Soon after that she was aware of him undoing the buttons of her blouse, and then she felt the touch of his warm hands on the bare flesh of her body. Moments later they both lay naked on the bed.

She had known it would happen, and she had tried to prepare herself, emotionally, for the event. She had also known that it was something she wanted to happen. She had had opportunities in the past, of course, but not with anyone of any importance in her life. Oh, yes, there had been the usual high-school petting sessions—experiences that were now only vague, detached memories of adolescent fumblings in the backs of parents' automobiles—and following those earlier times occasional dates with young men she had met who were involved in the entertainment business. But nothing had ever amounted to anything more than a few weeks of diminishing happiness. In any case, she had since realized that had any one of those young men been the right young man there would have always been her mother's presence to pour sand on the fire, to frown at any hint of commitment, and to urge her to wait, wait, wait. . . .

But that had been then; now was now. The time for waiting was past. Her mother was six thousand miles away, and this person beside her in the bed was no acned, inexperienced youth, but a grown man, a man of the world—and tall, handsome, warm, and exciting. Shenna had committed herself now to what was about to happen—gladly, totally, and, lying beside Ian's powerful, naked body, she willed herself to give herself completely to him as she felt his searching hands roaming, discovering, exploring. It would be all she had ever imagined it would be, she knew. . . . Feeling her excitement mounting to an almost unbearable pitch, she opened herself to his touch.

When it was over—so soon, it seemed—he lay beside her while his breathing gradually became calm again. "How was it for you?" he asked at last.

"Good," she said, "it was good." And next time it would be, she was sure.

"I'm sorry it was over so fast."

She laid a hand on his shoulder, bent her head, and kissed him. "It was good. It really was."

"I had no idea," he said. "I didn't know you were a virgin."

After a while he sat up, propped himself on one arm, and looked down at her in the soft light from the bedside lamp. With her head on the pillow she returned his steady gaze. "You remind me of somebody," she said.

"Oh? Who?"

"I don't know."

"Some past, discarded boyfriend?"

"Oh, no. I'd never have discarded anybody who looked like you." She smiled. "I can't think who it is. It'll come to me."

He was silent for a moment; then he said, "You know what *you* look like?"

"Tell me."

"You look about twelve years old, lying there like that."

"Is that good or is that bad?"

He smiled. "Not that you're much older than that, anyway."

"Oh, I don't know—nineteen is considerably older."

"Nineteen," he said with a note of disbelieving wonder. *"Nineteen . . ."* Then he added, "I'm thirty-four."

"So?"

"Yes, exactly," he said. "What's fifteen years between friends?"

The following morning Ian told her that he had to leave London a week later and wouldn't be returning till mid-October. His time away, he said, would be spent in Rome and New York, and then in San Francisco, where a new branch of the company was opening up. Over the coming months, he added, he would have to spend considerable time there; eventually he'd be moving out there altogether.

At the news of his impending departure Shenna felt disappointment well up within her. "Oh," she said, "do you have to go—so soon?"

He shrugged. "I'm afraid so." He smiled at her. "But we have a whole week before then."

That week leading up to his departure they spent together, almost every hour. Sometimes they stayed quietly around the flat, while at other times they went out into the city or beyond it into the countryside. They played tennis, visited art galleries and theaters and restaurants. They exchanged door keys, and on the two or three occasions he had to go out on business Shenna went to his flat and prepared dinner for the two of them. Often they made love. And with each time of their lovemaking she found increasing pleasure—a pleasure she had never experienced in her life before—and day by day she felt herself drawn closer to him.

On the last day before his departure they drove out of the city, to a village just outside of Rochester. There they stopped for dinner at a small country inn, where they sat facing one another across a candlelit table. Although there were other diners present, as far as Shenna was concerned they could have been light years away. She was aware only of Ian. She saw only him, heard only his voice.

They followed the opening course of prawns with lamb seasoned with rosemary, first drinking champagne, after which Ian chose a light-bodied Barbera. As she set down her glass, Shenna became aware of a light pressure on the side of her shoe and she glanced down and saw that he had surreptitiously put out his leg in order to touch her foot. Lightly she returned the pressure.

They touched whenever the opportunity arose, their fingers brushing at the slightest excuse, and then, when the waitress had taken away their empty plates, they stretched out a hand to one another on the tablecloth and let their hands rest there, fingers entwined.

She gazed at him as he gazed back at her. She watched as he took up his glass, silently toasted her, and then drank, a moment later winking both eyes together at her in a silent salute. Seeing just his eyes above the rim of the glass she said, "Of course—now I know who it is you remind me of."

"Oh, yes?"

"It's your eyes. Just your eyes. The photograph of my father . . . You have my father's eyes."

The next morning, as he got ready to leave, she stood in the doorway of the bathroom and looked at him. He was standing at the washbasin, a towel around his waist. She was dressed and ready to go—and putting off the final moment of separation until the last possible moment. He finished shaving, and she watched as he rinsed the soap from his face and then toweled himself dry.

"I don't want you to go," she said.

He turned to her, took her in his arms, and kissed her. "I don't want to go, either," he said softly. "But you have a lot of work to do, and so do I, and the time will soon pass."

"I suppose so." Her hands came up, fingers pressing into the firm flesh of his broad back.

"Of course it will. And we'll meet again soon—just as soon as I return."

She had wanted to hear him say that. "You promise?" she said.

"Of course. Do you feel you need to ask?"

She could feel his rising hardness beneath the covering of his towel and she pressed against him, without shame, glorying in the almost overpowering feeling that seemed to be taking her over. Time was against them, though.

When he was ready to leave he called a taxi, and on its arrival she went with him out onto the street and watched as he climbed in. He rolled down the window, and she reached out to him, and his hand came up and clasped her own.

"Look after yourself," he said.

"Yes. You, too."

"I will." He raised her hand to his mouth and lightly, so lightly, brushed the edge of his teeth over her knuckles. "I was wrong," he said.

"Wrong? About what?"

"I said the time will soon pass." He shook his head. "I don't think so. I have the feeling it's going to drag like hell."

The next day he telephoned her from Rome.

"I miss you already," he said.

Over the following days there were other phone calls, and a postcard that she put beside her bed, next to the photograph he had taken of the little Hinton Peeble church. There, too, on the bedside table—next to the picture of her father—was the photograph she had taken of Ian beside the village pond. She picked it up and gazed at it. She was in love with him, she knew.

The little time that was left before the start of the school term Shenna wanted to use in preparation for the coming exhibition. Although it was several months away, the time would pass too quickly. There were distractions, though— one of them being the post-sync recording for *Chain Letter* at a West End recording studio. It was tedious work at the best of times and now she found herself bitterly resenting the hours spent on it. At last it was finished, though, and she was free once more to get back to her painting. A few days before the start of the term she telephoned her mother for one of their brief, weekly chats. Shenna had said nothing to her about the visit to Hinton Peeble, but now, after having mustered the necessary courage, she asked where exactly in the village her father had lived.

After a little silence Doris asked, "What on earth do you want to know that for?"

"Well—I thought I'd like to drive out there and see where he lived."

Doris replied shortly, "I haven't got it now—not after all this time. I'm sorry."

"Oh, Mom, you must have it around somewhere. Couldn't you—"

Doris cut in. "Shenna, *I haven't got it*. For God's sake, it's been twenty years. And anyway, I can't understand why on earth you want to go there. Believe me, there's nothing to be gained from such a thing now."

Shenna, recognizing the warning signs, didn't pursue the matter any further. *Change the subject*, she told herself. "Well," she said after a moment, "well, I start school on Monday."

"Oh—really?"

"Yes. And I'm really excited, what with that and the exhibition. Everything's happening."

"Yes, well, that's nice," Doris replied. "I'm glad one of us is having a good time."

He wrote in his diary:

> *It won't be long now. The thought of being close to her brings me out in a sweat. My God, I can hardly wait.*

6

The term opened on a bright Monday morning in mid-September.

The early part of the day was taken up with enrollment and the allocation of lockers and various materials—drawing board, oil paints, brushes, and so on. This was followed by a talk from the vice-principal, Hirst, who welcomed the students to the school, urged them to make the most of their time there, and gave them advice and information to aid their studies and their settling in. There were over two hundred full-time students at the college, of whom about eighty were on the Foundation Course. Shenna soon discovered that she was not the only foreign student there—there were many others, among them Australians, Japanese, Israelis, Yugoslavians, and other Americans. Following Hirst's talk, the students, in roughly equal numbers of males and females, were separated into groups of three, which would remain together for the year. The various classes in the curriculum would in turn be made up of different groups, ensuring that over the weekly schedule each student would work with every other student taking the course.

Shenna found herself part of a group with two other girls, Margaret Henry, a short, rather stocky girl with a Yorkshire accent and a wide smile, and Hannah Carter, an attractive blonde from Kensington. Both girls recognized Shenna at once, but didn't dwell on the fact, and she, looking into their warm, friendly faces as she shook their hands, felt sure they were going to get along.

All of that first day's classes for Shenna, Margaret, and Hannah—as it would be each Monday for the rest of the term—were to be devoted to life drawing, the instruction taking place in one of the large studios up on the first floor, and after collecting drawing paper and charcoal from the supply cupboard the three girls, along with a dozen other students, made their way to the classroom. There they just had time to meet the instructor, James Trandell, a tall, rangy man in his forties, before it was time for the morning coffee break.

In the cafeteria they shared a table with some of the other students from the class and were soon engaged in a lively conversation. Among the others there, Shenna met Caspar Oliver, a homely young man with reddish-brown hair and deep-set dark eyes who looked to be three or four years older than the average student. She also met Colin Hunter, a very blond Australian; Brian Trent, tall, fair, and good-looking; and Jane Baxter, an extremely pretty dark-haired girl.

Sitting at the table, Shenna was well aware of the interest in her as someone a little different from the other students. Ever since she had arrived that morning she had been only too conscious of the glances of recognition that came her way. It was inescapable, she supposed. Many of the students would have learned from the newspapers that she was to be enrolling that day, and it would have taken only a very short while before everybody in the building knew she was there. She had prepared herself for that eventuality, though, and knew that the sooner it happened, the sooner she would be accepted along with everybody else.

As she sipped at her coffee, Brian asked her what she was doing giving up acting for a fine arts course, and in reply she told him of her longtime desire to study painting. She dealt with several polite, good-natured questions that came her way, and by the time she was due to return to class the conversation had moved on from herself to other subjects. Already, she told herself, she was ceasing to be a nine-day wonder.

Not everyone, though, it appeared, was ready to regard her as just another student. As she got up from her seat to follow the others into the hall, she noticed one of the cafeteria workers gazing at her as he stood holding a tray of cups and saucers and plates. As her eyes met his, he smiled and stepped toward her.

"I'm sorry," he said hesitantly, "I didn't mean to stare at you." He was narrow-faced and slim-bodied, with dark, thinning hair.

She smiled. "That's okay."

"I recognized you—from your films."

"I guessed as much."

She was about to move away when he said, dropping his voice to little more than a whisper, "I don't suppose you could let me have a photograph. . . ?"

She should have seen the question coming. Shaking her head apologetically, she said, "I'm sorry, but—look, I'm here as a student, not as an actress. . . ."

He nodded. "I shouldn't have asked you. I'm sorry."

"No, no, that's all right."

"I'm sorry."

As she began to move away he asked, "You think you're going to like it here?"

"Oh, I'm sure I am."

"Good. I hope you do."

The wry voice of the cafeteria manageress came from nearby. "Come on, Alan. Stand there much longer and you'll take root. His first day, look, and he can't get past coffee break without trying to chat up the students."

At the words he shrugged and smiled, then murmured a good-bye to Shenna and turned back to his task.

Upstairs, Shenna joined the other life-drawing students as they took their positions before the male model who, naked but for a black posing pouch, stood on a dais near one wall.

With his thin, pale body and round-shouldered stance he looked totally unlike any notion of a model she had ever had.

Sitting sidesaddle on her "donkey"—the four-legged wooden seat with attached drawing board support—Shenna worked hard at her drawing but found herself becoming increasingly frustrated with her efforts. She was glad when, at last, the morning class was over and she could leave the work for a while. She would do better in the afternoon, she told herself. When most of the other students had begun to move out into the hall she wandered around the room looking at the work on other drawing boards. When she came to Caspar Oliver's drawing she stopped and stood before it. Jane Baxter, who was moving by, came over to her side. Shenna glanced up at her and smiled. "Hi, Jane. How've you been doing?"

"Oh, okay, I suppose." Jane's speech had a somewhat nervous manner, and her hands moved in a slightly jerky way, her fingers fluttering. The smile she gave Shenna didn't reach above her mouth. "And you?" she asked.

"Oh, not too well, I'm afraid." Shenna turned her attention back to Caspar's drawing. He seemed to have achieved everything that she had been striving for all morning. After a moment she moved back to look disconsolately at her own efforts and sighed.

"What's wrong?" Jane asked.

Shenna shook her head. "I don't know. . . ." She sighed again. "After looking at Caspar's drawing I look at my own and realize just how far I've got to go. I wonder whether I'll ever get it right."

"Well," Jane said with a shrug, "it doesn't really matter, does it? For you, I mean."

"Doesn't matter?" Shenna frowned. "I don't get you."

"Well, somebody in *your* situation . . . you're never going to need it, are you? To teach or be an illustrator, or anything like that. You're never going to need to make your living from it. You don't have any kind of—hassle in front of *you*, do you?—not like the rest of us."

"What do you mean?"

"Well, you've got your *real* career to go back to, haven't you? Anytime you want."

Following afternoon classes there was an art history lecture for the Foundation Course students that went on till six-thirty, the time when all compulsory classes ended for the day. Afterward Shenna set off for her flat, thinking as she walked down Lee Road of Jane's words and their implication. They had hurt, and with the memory of them she became increasingly conscious of the limitations of her ability. How many other students had the same feelings about her? And what about the instructors? They were pleasant and helpful, but did they also believe that it was all something of a game for her, that she was merely killing time? That the whole thing was just a novelty from which the shine would soon disappear? Something which—as Jane had implied—she could abandon as soon as she got bored with it.

These first weeks, she realized, were going to be a time of testing. She was going to have to prove herself—to herself and everyone around her.

After some thought she decided to do some extra work, and the next day she enrolled for a Thursday night-school class in portraiture. If she didn't make it in her studies, it wouldn't be from lack of trying.

During coffee break on Thursday morning she was sitting at a table with some of the other students when she heard her name called. Turning, she saw the porter standing in the doorway looking about him. She got up, and as she drew near him he gave a little nod. "Oh, there you are," he said. "I wasn't exactly sure who Shenna Preston was, but I thought it might be you. Trouble is, there are so many students and it's impossible to get to know all their names." He added then that there was someone waiting to see her in the foyer.

"Who is it, do you know?"

"No, I don't; I'm sorry. By the way," he added as they walked into the hall, "I'm sorry I couldn't let you look round when you dropped in before the term began."

She smiled. "Forget it. Don't give it another thought."

They reached the foyer, and while the porter moved to his desk, a young man got up from a chair and came toward her. He wore cords and a sports jacket. After introducing himself as Geoffrey Ford, he told her he was a free-lance journalist. Shenna wanted at that point to end the meeting but she heard him out, listening patiently as he said that her enrollment at the art school and the change in her life were of interest. He told her he would like to write a piece on her, dealing with her first weeks in London and at the school— with, perhaps, some photographs. It wouldn't take much of her time, he added, and if she would agree, he would meet her anytime and anywhere that suited her.

She shook her head and told him that she couldn't even consider it. "That's something I'm getting *away* from," she said. "It doesn't have any part in my life right now. Please understand that all I want to do is get on with my work here, and something like this would only get in the way. Besides which, I really hate any kind of publicity. I always have, and I'm not about to change now."

Later, in the studio, she thought back over her encounter with the journalist. She had made the right decision, she knew. If Jane's attitude was anything to go by, half the school would be expecting her to cash in on any chance of publicity, and she had to make it clear at the start that she was here to study—not to increase whatever fame she already had as an actress.

Over lunch, Hannah and Margaret suggested going to see a film that evening, but to their surprise Shenna said she couldn't because of her night-school class. Later, seeing the two girls setting off together, she momentarily wished that she was going with them. The feeling didn't last, though; at the portrait class she felt to her great satisfaction that she was at last making some progress. Using conté on buff-colored paper, she worked on the head of a young woman who posed in a chair on the dais. To her added pleasure, the young instructor showed a real interest in her work, while at the same time looking at her without a flicker of recognition.

He had spent the evening packing, getting ready to leave in the morning. He'd get a taxi to his new home. He wasn't taking very much with him—just his clothes and whatever else was necessary for the kind of away-from-home existence he must temporarily lead. It wouldn't be for long, he hoped. Soon he would be returning to the house and bringing her with him. He couldn't wait for that time to come. Until then, though, he'd have to be patient—and careful. Yes, very careful.

That night, before he went to bed, he went through the house, making sure that it was secure. He hated the thought of leaving it unattended, but he had no choice if he was to be near her. All the locks on the doors he had had changed. He had done that right at the start; it had been a necessity. Sarah had keys to the house, and he didn't want her coming here in his absence and snooping around; not that he thought it likely. He hadn't seen anything of her since that Monday morning when she had come to the house to start her week's work. He had been waiting for her, and as soon as she opened the front door he had been there to give her her dismissal, along with a month's wages.

He could remember the way she had looked at him—the hurt and bewilderment in her watery blue eyes. "But I'm supposed to come in while your grandparents are away," she had protested.

He had been firm, though, not letting her get past the hall. "It's all changed now," he said. "I'm going away for a while, so you won't be needed."

She shook her head. "But for how long?"

He had shrugged. "I don't know. My grandparents will get in touch with you when they return."

She had looked lost and very unhappy as she had turned and walked away from the house. He didn't care.

He felt a sense of excitement now as he got undressed for bed. The adventure had begun. Tomorrow night he would be sleeping in his new, temporary home. Not that he would be away from here for any long periods. It wasn't that far away and he could return on the odd evening or at weekends to keep an eye on the place. He'd have to come back regularly, anyway, in order to get the place ready for when he brought Shenna back with him. There was a lot to do in preparation for that time.

As he thought of that day in the future, he looked at himself in the mirror above the wash basin and smiled. The tic on his temple started up and he put up a hand, feeling the faint, rhythmic pulsing beneath his fingertips. He hated it. He wanted so much to be perfect, for her.

Early Saturday afternoon, as Shenna returned to the house after doing some shopping, she found she had a new neighbor. Entering the lobby, she heard music—some opera or other—and then saw that the door of the flat opposite hers was open. As she looked toward it a man appeared in the doorway. He smiled shyly at her and she smiled back. He looked somewhere around thirty; he was just above average height, with light brown hair and pale blue eyes. He wore jeans and a checked shirt. Beyond his head she could see a couple of suitcases and one or two large cardboard boxes.

"You just moving in?" she asked.

He nodded, blinking. "That's right." Then, gesturing over

his shoulder, he added, "I get the record-player going first—to help me. With some familiar music I don't feel quite such a stranger."

She nodded, smiling. "Good idea." She recognized the opera as *Carmen*. "I wondered how long the apartment—the *flat*—would be empty," she added.

As she took her key from her bag, he turned down the music and then came into the lobby and introduced himself. His name was Kevin Brightwell, he said. She told him her own name, and although he made no sign of recognition, she could tell that he knew who she was. They chatted for a minute or two—somewhat awkwardly—until, telling him to knock on her door if he should need anything, she went on into her flat.

There was a postcard lying on the carpet and she picked it up and saw that it was from Ian. It had come from Rome. *See you in a few weeks! Love, Ian*, he had written. The picture on the front was of a detail of Michaelangelo's painting in the Sistine Chapel.

Shenna heard several times by telephone and the odd card from Ian over the next several days, and, happy in the knowledge of his affection, she settled more securely into her new life, working hard at her studies and spending whatever spare time she had on her paintings for the exhibition.

She found that she was able to work well in the flat. Apart from affording her space for her painting, it also gave her the peace and quiet she needed. She was never disturbed by her neighbors. With the widower Mr. Drake there were only occasional meetings in the hall, while of the presence of the elderly Miss Martin in the flat above there was rarely any indication, apart from the odd muffled sounds of her feet and the occasional faint murmur of her television set. Only Kevin from the flat opposite was regularly in evidence—Shenna sometimes meeting him in the hall or hearing the faint sound of his radio or his opera records as she passed by his door.

The only dark spot in her happiness was in her relationship with her mother. They talked briefly over the telephone regularly each week, but although several weeks had passed since Shenna's departure from California, Doris still seemed to have come no closer to accepting the situation. Her resentment was barely hidden. It seemed to Shenna that no matter what they talked about, the subject would eventually come around to her being in London and Doris being at home in Westwood.

The situation came to a head during Shenna's second week at the college, when she called her mother for a chat and, after a little while, began to speak of her work. Doris listened, then said, "I must say you surprise me."

"Surprise you? How?"

"Well, when I think of all your other—fads."

"My *fads?*"

"It's the only word I can think of." A pause, then Doris added, "You know what I'm thinking about. I mean all those other things—like your stamp collecting, your ice skating, your ballet classes, your tap lessons. All those nine-day wonders that were going to be lifelong passions. I'm just surprised this one's lasted a little longer."

"A little longer?"

"Shenna, why do you keep repeating everything I say? This line is perfectly good. Can't you hear me?"

"Yes, I can hear you"—there was quiet anger in Shenna's voice—"and I can hardly believe what I'm hearing. How can you do that? Belittle what I'm trying to do? My God, I'm insecure enough as it is without you adding to it."

Doris gave a short, humorless laugh. "*You're* insecure! How do you think *I* feel? You go off without a single thought for me, only thinking about yourself. Don't talk to me about your insecurities."

Shenna felt her anger building. She was silent for a moment, then said evenly, "Mother, I can't see any point in going on with this conversation, so I'm going to hang up."

"You're what?"

"Didn't you hear me? As you just said, Mom, this line is perfectly good. I told you—I'm going to hang up. I've had it." Doris tried to interrupt, but Shenna went on. "Every single time I call you you give me a hard time. And I don't need it. Each time I talk to you I end up feeling depressed and guilty and—"

"Don't blame *me* for your guilt feelings."

"Yes, well, that's it. No more."

"And what does that mean?"

"I'm just not going to phone you again for a while. I can't cope with it. I've got a lot of work to do here, work that's important to me. I need all the peace of mind I can get. I'll write to you, but I won't phone. I don't mind writing—you can't get at me so well that way."

"Fine," Doris said shortly. "Well, don't do me any favors. And if talking to me brings you so much misery, we'd better do something about it *now*."

Then she hung up.

During one of the breaks that allowed the model to rest during portrait class the next evening, Shenna exchanged a few words with two or three of the students sitting nearby her. Among them was a tall man, dark-haired, gray-eyed, who had smiled, saying, "Of course, you don't need to tell me who you are," and then had gone on to introduce himself. His name, he said, was Wesley Soames. After looking at her drawing and making some positive comments he went on to speak of the difficulties of the work. Shenna, glancing at the drawing pinned to his board, thought it demonstrated a certain ability, but that the ability was limited and obviously untutored.

When the class was over Shenna murmured her good nights and left the classroom to put her things in her locker. Going down to the lobby a few minutes later, she saw the young man, Wesley, waiting there, and as she moved to the doors he came toward her.

"I was wondering," he said, "whether you might like to go somewhere for a coffee. . . ." He looked at her with a slightly beseeching expression as he spoke.

Shenna regretfully shook her head. "I'd love to some other time," she said, "but right now I'm pretty tired. All I want to do is go on home and get some rest."

He nodded understandingly. Then he asked, "You have far to go?"

"No, not far. Just down the road—near Lee Green."

He nodded. "I live in the same direction. I'll walk with you if you don't mind."

She shrugged. "Okay. Why not?"

They left the school building and set off together. As they went, he told her, in answer to her questions, that he worked in an office in nearby Lewisham and lived in a small flat not far away. He seemed a little reluctant to talk about himself, though, and she didn't press him for information. Prompted by his own questions, however, she told him how she had given up her film work to become a student.

"You're very brave, I think," he said.

"Brave?"

"Giving up your work like that, to do something so completely different."

"Maybe. We'll just have to see how I get on. Time will tell whether I'm being brave or just exceptionally dumb."

"How do you mean?"

"Well, whether I'm good enough."

"And if you feel you're not?"

"Then it'll be very disappointing." She paused. "Though not to *everyone*."

"Oh?"

"I'm thinking of my mother." She shook her head. "Oh, forget it. Let's just say that I've got *several* good reasons for wanting to do well here. For one thing, I've got to prove that I can make it on my own—looking after myself and making my own decisions. I've got to start living my own life."

A few minutes later they reached Elm Court Road and the gate of number nineteen. Shenna thanked him for seeing her home and said, "You'll forgive me if I don't offer you any coffee, won't you? Like I said, I've just about had it." She smiled ruefully. "With tonight's class on top of everything, I'm already wondering whether I might be taking on a little too much—almost twelve hours straight. I must be crazy."

They chatted for another minute or so, and then she said good night. As she moved through the gateway, he turned and began to walk away along the street. A few moments later, as she opened the front door, she glanced back and saw him standing on the pavement. As she looked at him he lifted his hand in a wave. Smiling, she waved back.

The following Thursday he walked her home again. As they made their way the conversation got onto street markets. Finally he asked her if she'd like to go to the Portobello Road market that coming Saturday morning.

"Oh, I'd love to go there *some* Saturday," she replied, "but not this one. I'm afraid I can't." She explained that two Saturday mornings out of three she was expected to visit one of the London art galleries or go sketching outdoors. "And this Saturday morning I've arranged to go to the Victoria and Albert Museum," she added.

"Well, maybe some other time, then."

"Yes, sure."

They came to her front gate soon afterward and she turned to him to say good night. As she did so, he said, "Wait—just a minute," and took his portfolio from under his arm.

"A little something I've got for you," he said, smiling awkwardly as he opened the portfolio and took out a sheet of tinted cartridge paper. He held it out to her. "Here—for you—if you'd like it. . . ."

She squinted at it in the light from the street lamp and saw that it was a drawing of herself. It was not a brilliant piece of work, but nevertheless the subject was easily recognizable. "Why, Wesley—thank you very much," she said.

He shrugged. "I did it from a photograph from a magazine."

She nodded; she knew the photograph. "Yes, I can see."

He took a step away. "Anyway, do what you want with it. It was just something I thought of. . . ."

"Thank you," she said again.

They said good night and she went inside and looked at the drawing in the bright light of the living room. Then she put it aside. It bothered her, just a little, that he had gone to so much trouble to please her.

Saturday came, bringing a letter from her friend Amy, which she read over her coffee. Amy's letter was full of light chatter. She sounded happy. She had started her final year at UCLA and was looking forward to graduation, when she'd be totally free to pursue her acting.

A little later Shenna got ready to leave for the museum, and arriving there, she met Hannah and Margaret. They spent a couple of hours in the sculpture gallery, sketching and making notes. Afterward they separated, Hannah and Margaret going on to the West End and Shenna making her way to the museum shop. She had briefly sketched a copy of a Cellini angel in the gallery and was eager to get a good photograph of it. Looking at the array of postcards and prints for sale in the shop, she found postcards of two views of the sculpture, photographed from different angles. She bought one of each and put them in her sketchbook. A moment later she turned to see Wesley standing nearby.

"Wesley—what are you doing here?"

He smiled somewhat sheepishly as he came toward her. "You gave me an idea," he said, "saying you were coming here. I thought it was about time I paid the place a visit."

"Did you just get here?"

"No, I've been here a couple of hours."

"I didn't see you."

"Well, you were busy sketching. I saw you."

"Why didn't you come and say hello?"

"You were with your friends." He paused. "Where are you going now?"

"Back home, I guess."

"Would you like to go and have some lunch somewhere?"

She smiled. "Why not? I have to eat."

They found a little place nearby where they ate hamburgers, French fries, and salad, and afterward left for Charing Cross to catch a train for Blackheath. As they sat on the train, a woman passed by whose physical appearance reminded Shenna of her mother, and she felt a sudden stab of guilt. It had been well over a week now since she and Doris had talked.

"What are you thinking about?" Wesley asked.

"I was thinking about my being here—and my mother all those miles away."

"Are you homesick?"

She considered this for a moment. "No, not at all. I've been so busy. There's been so much to do. But my mother misses me a lot. That's the trouble. She's lonely without me—which doesn't exactly make me feel good. She's become so dependent on me over the years."

"What happened to your father?"

"He's—he's dead."

"Oh—I'm sorry."

"Thanks, but it was a long time ago. And I never knew him. He died before I was born."

"Maybe it would have been better for your mother if she'd married again."

Shenna nodded. "I agree. I think it's a shame she never found herself somebody else. I mean, she's attractive enough. But after my father died she just wouldn't look at anybody. I'm not sure it's such a good thing—to love that much."

Coming back from the launderette the next morning, she met Kevin near the front door as he returned from taking out the garbage. They exchanged good mornings and he asked her if she'd like to join him for a cup of coffee. In an effort to be neighborly, she said yes, she'd be glad to take a break. Two minutes later, after depositing her laundry, she was at the door of his flat and he was ushering her in.

As she entered, he went over to turn down his record player—*La Bohème*, she recognized—and urged her to sit down. She hadn't seen his flat since her first weekend in London, and now, as she sat on the sofa, she looked around with interest. He had hung two or three pictures on the walls, she saw, lined up a few books on the shelf above the gas fire, and put out one or two photographs. Even so, the place seemed to have lost little of its anonymity. Still, she reminded herself, he had only been there a couple of weeks.

He poured coffee and brought her a cup, placing it on the table at her side. Holding his own cup and saucer, he sat in the easy chair opposite. She had never realized just how shy his manner was. Often, she found, his pale eyes avoided her glance, as if somehow it embarrassed him—and she wondered why, if the meeting made him uncomfortable, he had suggested it. After a while, though, it seemed that a little of his shyness evaporated, and they began to talk a little more easily. She told him a little about her life in California, and he in turn told her a little about himself: after living in Nottingham with his parents for many years, he said, he had come back to live in London, where he had been born. His work, he added, was in the sales department of a small engineering company. All the while in the background the sounds of Puccini's *La Bohème* came from the stereo, filling in the gaps in their conversation.

They talked for twenty-five minutes or so and then Shenna thanked him and got up, saying she had to return to her own flat.

"I'm grateful," he said. "Thank you."

She smiled. "For what?"

He shrugged, his pale eyes flitting away from hers and coming to rest on her shoulder. "Well, for—for coming in for coffee. I know how busy you must be."

"Oh, not that busy."

"No? But somebody in your situation—you must have so many calls upon your time—so many friends calling you."

She shook her head. "God, no, it's not like that at all. It's not my social life that takes away my time, it's my work at school. And I don't have a load of friends pestering me for my time." She smiled and gave a little shrug. "I don't have a lot of friends here in London at all. Oh, I've made friends at school, but—well, don't forget that I'm like you in a way. I've only just arrived here—well, not that much earlier than you." She paused. "It takes time to build up relationships, doesn't it?"

"Oh, yes. It's not easy. And if you're like . . ." His voice trailed off.

"Like what?" Shenna prompted.

He shrugged. "I was going to say like me. I mean—some people naturally find it easy to make friends. I wish to God *I* did." He gave a rueful smile. "It's never been easy for me."

"No?"

"No." He laughed nervously. "In fact, it took quite a lot of courage to ask you over for coffee today."

"Really?"

"Really."

She gave him an encouraging smile then said, "Are you not used to being on your own?"

"No. I think that's part of the trouble."

She nodded understandingly. "Maybe you should get yourself a pet of some kind—a kitten, maybe. That would be company for you."

"Oh, no, thanks."

"You don't like cats?"

He shook his head. "Not much."

"Well, then you'll just have to cultivate some people, that's all."

He grinned back at her. "I suppose that's the only answer."

She returned to her own room and, after preparing some canvases for painting, had a light lunch and then put her sketching materials into her large beaded bag and left the flat to make her way up toward Blackheath. She planned to do a little sketching and then visit a small museum she had heard about in Greenwich Park.

The sun was bright and warm for early October, but she wore a heavy cardigan against the fresh breezes. When she got to the village she walked through it onto the heath where the wide expanse of green was dotted with people out getting the last of the sun—lovers, boys playing soccer, parents walking children and dogs. Finding a vacant bench, she sat down and began to make a drawing of the church, with the buildings of the village behind it. She concentrated totally on the work, ignoring the casual, curious passersby who walked slightly out of their way in order to see what she was doing. They didn't bother her. They weren't interested in who she was, but only in the drawing she was doing; with her hair scraped back and wearing her old jeans and cardigan, she was just another student.

When at last the drawing was done she put the sketchbook in her bag and set off across the grass in the direction of

Greenwich Park, on the other side of the heath. She went in through the main gates and consulted a large map just inside, then made her way to the museum building, which was set to one side of the grounds.

On two floors, the museum housed a number of paintings and sculptures that had once been the private collection of a local wealthy man who had left the pieces to the district on condition that they remain together. Now, many years after the bequest, the collection seemed to be all but forgotten. There were few other visitors there, and even the attendants—one elderly man on each of the two floors—seemed nothing more than tokens, gestures toward staffing the place. They remained where they were as Shenna moved past them, not even looking up from the comfort of their chairs.

Much of the work there was Victorian—a fact that, she thought, possibly accounted for some of its lack of popularity; certainly it was a period the average art student found unfashionable. For herself, though, who had for many years been drawn to the Pre-Raphaelites, its appeal was very great.

One painting that particularly caught her attention was by the Victorian painter Arthur Hughes. Entitled "Sunday," it depicted a group of people beside a grave. The grave was obviously a new one, for the earth on it looked recently turned, the flowers in the urn fresh, and the stone newly cut. At the graveside stood a young woman dressed in black, her lowered face shadowed by the folds of her veil. In one hand she held a prayerbook and a single carnation. Beside her, clinging to her arm, stood a boy of about fourteen. His tear-stained face was turned upwards, gazing at the woman, on whose other side stood a small girl, her shining eyes caught by the sight of a bright butterfly that had alighted on one of the flowers. In the background was an old, ivy-covered church.

Enthralled, Shenna was still gazing at the picture ten minutes later when one of the old caretakers approached to tell her that the museum was about to close for the day.

In her flat some time later she sat down on the bed and thought of the painting. The grave in it took her to thoughts of her father's grave in Hinton Peeble. And thinking of her father, her thoughts went automatically to her mother. After sitting there for some moments while her feelings of guilt grew stronger, she picked up the telephone and dialed the number in Westwood. There was no answer. Well, she said to herself, at least she had tried. And perhaps it was just as well that her mother wasn't at home, since it was doubtful that a phone call would get them very far. Perhaps she should write to her instead. With the thought, she took her notepad from her bag and began to write. She wrote steadily for a time and then closed the notepad and put her pen aside. She would finish it tomorrow.

The diary was open before him and he sat for long moments, pen poised in his hand. Then he wrote:

> *The picture of her stays with me. Each time I see her I find myself surprised. The blueness of her eyes, the dark lashes, the general look of her—I'm never quite prepared for it. She's more beautiful in real life than she ever looked on the screen. Sometimes when she looks at me I can hardly face her in return. It's all I can do not to look away. I love her so much.*
>
> *I've got to make her love me, too. Only when that's done shall I be happy. She'll be with me then, for always.*

He sat there thinking. He must start making preparations for that time, the start of their lives together. The house—it would have to be got ready.

Leaning back in the chair he gave himself up to his dreams.

7

After the evening art-history lecture Shenna, Brian, Jane, and Colin stood in the foyer, waiting for Margaret to come downstairs. They had arranged to go to Greenwich for a drink, followed by an inexpensive dinner. As they stood waiting Caspar came down the stairs, and Shenna went to ask him if he'd like to join them. He thanked her, but said no, he planned to go on home and get on with some work.

She smiled, saying, "As usual," then added, "You know, every Monday when we have life class I look at your drawings and—Oh, Caspar, I could hate you for it—having all that talent."

He frowned. "What do you mean? I just . . . struggle along like everybody else."

"Uh-uh. There are struggles and there are struggles—and I should be so lucky as to be struggling like you."

Over the past three weeks she had studied with interest the work of the other students in the course, and, looking at their work objectively, had placed herself in the top half as far as ability. However, one of those above her, she had realized at once, was Caspar. The reality of his talent was clearly evident in the little of his work she had seen—the life drawings and the beginnings of a few paintings. "Do you work a lot at home, in your flat?" she asked.

"A bit."

"Is that why you always disappear so quickly after class? You're usually gone like a flash."

He smiled. "Is that the way it appears? Well, it's one of the reasons. And there's so much to do—and not enough time for it all."

"Have you got much of your work in your flat?"

"A few bits and pieces. And it's not a flat. It's just a room."

"What's the other reason why you usually go on home when classes are over?"

There was reluctance in his voice as he said, "Well, I haven't got the loot to splash around in cafés and pubs."

After a moment she asked, "Could I come and see some of your work?"

He shrugged. "Yes, of course, if you want to. When?"

"What's wrong with now?"

"Fine, but I thought you were going to Greenwich."

"I am. But so are you. That's where you live, isn't it?"

"Yes."

"Well, I'll go with you and then I'll go on afterward to meet the others."

"All right."

Turning to the rest of the small crowd on the steps, Shenna said she'd forego the drink and would meet them at the café later on. Then she and Caspar set off together.

When they reached the house where he lived, set in a small residential street on the border of Blackheath and Greenwich, he unlocked the front door and led the way up two flights of stairs to the top floor. There he unlocked another door, switched on the light, and ushered her in. As she entered he said, "I'm afraid I can't offer you anything. I've got nothing in the place apart from some instant coffee. I've got to do some shopping."

"It doesn't matter." She looked around her as she took off her coat. She was in a very large room with a bed in one corner and a screen in the other, behind which, he told her, was what passed for his kitchen. The rest of the furniture consisted of a table, a couple of dining chairs, a Victorian sofa, and an armchair. She barely glanced at the furniture, though; it was the pictures that grabbed her attention. Apart from the canvas that stood on the easel in the center of the room, there were pictures all around the walls, original paintings and drawings, prints, and photographs torn from magazines. A great many canvases were stacked on the floor, standing face-in against the walls.

Nearly all of the works featured figures, often just a head or heads. In several instances he had taken classical themes and depicted them in modern settings or against very decorative backgrounds. The results were magical. The paintings seemed to be full of light, a light made even more vibrant and glowing by sharp contrasts with darker tones that were full of the richest color. The work was all so fresh and alive and original. In the past few weeks in class she had often observed his total involvement with his work and had been a little surprised by it. No longer, though. Now that she had seen the real evidence of his talent, his total involvement and his dedication were things she could understand perfectly.

She looked at the paintings for a long time, then she and Caspar sat and talked. After a while her thoughts went to her own paintings and the coming exhibition. So far, of her friends at the school, she had only told Hannah and Margaret about it, but now she found herself anxious to tell Caspar as well. When she had told him he congratulated her. "You must make the most of it," he said. "It could be a very important step."

"And what about you?" she said. "You should be exhibiting your paintings, too."

He nodded. "I think I'm getting a show next spring. That's what I'm working towards now."

Glancing at her watch, Shenna realized how much time had gone by and that she should be leaving. As she put on her coat her eyes moved to the marble mantelpiece above the gas fire, where some photographs stood in ornate frames. One was of a woman standing beside a gate with a small terrier at her side. "Your mother?" she asked. He nodded.

The second frame held two photographs—a larger portrait and a smaller snapshot tucked into the frame's corner. Both pictures were of the same man, good-looking, dark-haired, in his late thirties or early forties. Shenna turned to Caspar to ask who it was, but before she could speak he said simply, "A friend," then gazed at her for a moment and looked away.

Downstairs at the front door she said, "Can't I persuade you to come and eat with us?" but he shook his head.

"No, really, thanks all the same."

"Okay. I'll see you tomorrow."

"Yes. Have a nice time."

She left him and made her way to the café, where she found the others had just arrived and were giving their orders to the waitress. They ate pizzas and salad. After three weeks of working together, a camaraderie had developed and the conversation was easy and lighthearted. Shenna sat between Margaret and Colin while on the other side Jane leaned close to Brian, her hand on his arm. He had made a conquest where she was concerned, everyone knew, and the way she wouldn't leave him alone had become a source of quiet amusement among them.

It was after eight-thirty when they paid the bill between them and got up to go, and outside Shenna and Margaret said good night to the others and set off together toward Blackheath. The sky above was very clear, and when they reached the top of the hill, the wide expanse of the heath before them was bathed in moonlight. "Let's walk on the grass, okay?" Shenna said. "It's so beautiful and I wouldn't dare do it on my own—not at this hour."

They left the narrow road and made their way on the springy turf until they came to a park bench, and there they sat and looked out over the moonlit landscape. As they sat talking, an old man came by wheeling a bicycle, and coming to a stop near the bench, he propped up the bicycle and took some old records from a carrier at the back. Shenna saw that he had an old, portable windup phonograph strapped over the rear mudguard and she watched as he wound it up and put a record on the turntable. She and Margaret turned to one another and grinned, and the old man caught the grins and joined in. Margaret said, smiling at him, "Before you really get going, I'd better tell you we've got no money." The old man just shrugged, raised his eyebrows, and smiled even more broadly. "He's just a gentle nutter," Margaret said under her breath, and Shenna whispered back, "Right," and watched as he carefully adjusted the needle in the sound box and lowered it onto the record. The old 78 sounded worn, but then above the hissing came the voices of a soprano and a tenor. "*Madame Butterfly*," Margaret said. "The love duet . . ."

Shenna gave the old man a smile of appreciation and then gazed casually about her at the scene. Suddenly the sweep of her glance was halted. The moon's light was almost hidden by clouds, but as she peered into the gloom she saw, some distance away, in the shadow of the church wall, the solitary figure of a man. And even as she saw him and registered his presence, he was stepping back, vanishing. She shivered.

"What's up?" Margaret said. "What's the matter?"

"Nothing, nothing. . . ." Shenna stared into the dark for a second or two longer, but now she could see no sign at all of the figure. She looked back at the old man as the music flowed on. The moment of pleasure was gone, though, and she got up from the bench. "Shall we go?" she said. "I'm getting cold." They moved off across the grass, while, behind them, the sounds of the opera faded.

They had just reached the village when Shenna said suddenly, "Oh, *no!*" and, clapping a hand to forehead, came to a sudden stop.

Margaret looked at her in surprise. "What's up?"

"My bag—I left it by the bench."

Turning, they went back onto the heath. When they

reached the bench, there was no sign of either the bag or the old man. Shenna swore. "And my key's in it. The key to my flat. And my sketchbook and other things."

"Have you got a spare key?"

Shenna nodded. "Yes, in the *flat*." The only other key was with Ian, she remembered. "But how the hell do I get into my flat without a key?"

After leaving Margaret, Shenna returned to Elm Court Road, where she rang Kevin's bell and told him of her predicament—adding, however, that she thought her bathroom window, which opened onto the backyard, was unlocked. Getting a flashlight and a chair, Kevin followed her into the yard, where, looking at the window, he said he reckoned he might just about get through. She watched as he climbed up, pushed the window open, and, with difficulty, struggled through. As his feet disappeared from view, she called to him dryly, "Thank God I left it unlocked—but remind me to lock it in the future. If you can get through, so can others."

Later, lying in bed, she thought of the missing bag. It had held her purse, containing a little money—five or six pounds—but apart from that, there had been nothing that could be worth anything to anyone else. Her sketchbook and some pencils and pens had been in it, along with a paperback she had been reading and a small bag holding cosmetics. Also, there was the unfinished letter to her mother. The rest was just odds and ends. Perhaps the old man with the phonograph—or whoever had found it—would return it. It shouldn't be difficult—after all, her address was in both her sketchbook and the letter.

In his room he put the beaded bag on the table and settled himself before it in his chair.

He pictured her carrying the bag, as he had seen her do over the past days. Yes, and in one of her films, too; he recalled that she had used it in *Child's Play*. Who would ever have dreamed that something of hers—something so personal—would be here in his hands? He could hardly believe his luck—for it had been just that, luck; it could have been anyone who had picked up the bag.

Thinking back over the whole strange incident, he remembered how she had turned and seen him there as he had stood in the shadow of the church wall, and how for that one moment it seemed that she had looked right into his eyes. Had she seen him clearly? No, he felt sure she hadn't. He had moved so quickly, dodging back out of her sight and then swiftly moving round to the other side of the church.

When he had returned just moments later, keeping quietly to the shadows, he had seen that she and her companion were walking over the heath, away from the crazy old man with the bike and his windup gramophone. Watching the old man, he had seen him stoop and pick up the bag from beside the seat and look at it for a moment, as if bewildered and wondering what to do, and then replace it on the grass once more. That done, the old man had packed up his records and ridden away. It had been the easiest thing then to stroll over and pick up the bag. . . .

And now here it was. *His*. His to do with as he chose. He sat unmoving before it a little longer, savoring the moments, then reached out and pulled it toward him.

One by one he took out the items inside—a paperback of Hemingway's *For Whom the Bell Tolls;* a smaller bag containing lipsticks and creams and things; a wallet containing money, credit cards, various union membership cards, and two or three snaps—one of Shenna with an attractive dark-haired woman in her forties. There was a sketchbook, too, and he opened it and looked at the drawings.

Toward the back of the sketchbook he found a couple of postcards of a statue, photographed from two different angles. An angel holding a sword. There was a drawing of the

same statue in her sketchbook. He put the cards back between the pages, closed the book, and then took a notepad
from the bag. After that he scooped up several pencils, pens,
and erasers that lay at the bottom, along with a key ring and
keys, and other odd items—a couple of buttons, a roll of
peppermints, and some loose coins. He put the whole collection in front of him on the table and sat and gazed at it.

There was nothing there that seemed to be of any importance. They were all things that he could imagine any other
student carrying around. He was glad. Somehow the very
ordinariness of it all made her seem less unattainable, less
remote.

He took up the notepad and flicked through it. There were
some loose pages inside it, folded over. Opening them, he
saw that they were covered with handwriting—*her* handwriting. A letter. Beneath her address, telephone number, and
the date, October 3, was written:

Dear Mom,
  *I just tried to call you but got no answer—so I'm writing instead.
And I really must admit that writing to you is far easier than
calling you on the telephone. Why, when we talk to each other—and
over a distance of so many thousands of miles—do we end up
fighting? It doesn't get us anywhere, does it? Except farther apart.*
  *Please, try not to be unhappy or lonely. I know it's difficult for
you to understand, but believe me, if you could see me you would
agree that I've made the right decision and you'd share my happiness.
Sometimes I can hardly believe I'm here. It's a different life for me,
totally. Sometimes when I've been going about my work I've pictured
myself as I was perhaps a year ago—and I can hardly recognize
myself. Covered in paint or clay, or going off to the art supply shop
and coming back loaded down with materials; sitting sketching in the
most unlikely places—I don't feel the same. I feel different, and it's a
wonderful feeling, a wonderful difference.*
  *When I get the chance I work at my paintings for the exhibition. I
only wish I had more time. Still, I'll manage somehow. I guess my
paintings from home will be here soon.*

Yesterday morning I looked around the Victoria and Albert museum, where I sketched some of the sculptures. One in particular I was very taken with—by Cellini, of an angel; I managed to get a postcard of it, which I'll put in with this letter. Then this afternoon I visited a little museum in Greenwich Park. It houses a collection of Victorian items and has one of the most appealing paintings I've seen in a long, long time. It's by Arthur Hughes, entitled "Sunday." I'll go back and look at it again soon. I stood before it thinking how much I'd like to wake up every morning and see it hanging in my room.

I've made several friends, as I've told you, and I've realized how nice it is to get to know people who aren't part of the acting business. I hope you'll meet some of my friends here someday soon. They're nice people—and are far more interested in me as a person than as an actress—which is the way I want it to be. To them, I'm just a fellow student. I do the same things they do; I go for drinks with them at the school bar, go out to eat with them at the same cheap restaurants, and travel with them by bus, subway, and train. I've become very money conscious lately. Of necessity. I guess in the past I had it all too easy (Yes, you were right!), but having allowed myself just a certain amount for the year it's harder for me; but that's part of the whole thing. I know I could call on greater financial resources if I wanted to, but I don't want to. Nearly all the students here have to watch their pennies and that's the way it should be for me, too, I feel. Who was it who said that "nothing of value is created out of comfort"?

This city has so much going for it, and I'd love it if I could take advantage of all it has to offer. There are several things I'd like to see at the theater: Cats, *and a new production of* As You Like It. *Oh, yes, and* Keats—*which is about the poet's last days in Rome. I'd like to go to the opera and the ballet, too. I'll get to some of it on what my allowance allows, and what I can't, I'll do without. It's no terrible hardship. Besides, I've set my mind on getting a little secondhand car, which I've decided I* must *have. That will enable me to get out into the countryside a little. I thought how terrific it would be to be able to get a little house in the country someday. Someplace I could go to on weekends. Ah, well, I can dream, can't I?*

When he'd read it through he opened his diary, took up his felt-tip pen, and carefully copied the letter into it. Beneath it he wrote:

I can't get over finding her bag. What a gift!

He looked through the items several times, afterward re-placing them carefully in the bag again—all except the keys. There were three keys on the ring; one was obviously a door key and the other two looked like keys to suitcases. He looked at the door key long and hard. He would get a copy of it made tomorrow.

That night he slept with the bag on his bed, close to his pillow.

8

On Tuesday evening after classes Shenna returned to the flat to find that a card had been left by a company called Mercury Shippers, briefly stating that their deliverymen had tried to deliver goods from California that morning, but had found no one at home; it then asked her to telephone to arrange a suitable time for delivery.

After she had made herself a supper of soup, followed by some pâté and toast, she relaxed for a while and then, to a radio accompaniment of Bizet's *The Pearl Fishers*, got to work at her easel. An hour later the telephone rang. It was her mother.

The guilt Shenna felt over not calling sent her voice up a couple of tones. "Mom—*hi!* How are you?"

"That's some question. Do you care?"

"Mom, what kind of talk is that? Tell me—really—how are you?"

"Well, I don't mind admitting I've been pretty unhappy since our last conversation. That's why I'm calling now."

"Aw, Mom, listen," Shenna said. "I got upset. You think I like fighting?"

"Yes, well, anyway—let's not start the whole thing again now."

Shenna stopped herself from commenting further and, instead, said that she had started writing a letter, but that she had lost it along with her bag. Then, on a brighter note, she added, "By the way, my pictures have arrived. The shipping company tried to deliver them today while I was at school. I've got to make arrangements with them tomorrow."

"Good," Doris said, obviously trying to sound enthusiastic; then, "And how's school going? You still enjoying it?"

"Oh, yes, very much." Shenna wanted to tell her about it, but instead she asked after Doris's work with her piano students. In answer, Doris complained about them and went on to complain about the house. "It's too big now that I'm here on my own," she said, and Shenna realized that, in spite of their brief estrangement, nothing had really changed.

Autumn was well and truly here. On waking that morning he had been aware of a cold snap in the air, and at once he became concerned about the lack of heat in the house at Kew. It had no central heating and in winter it got so cold; his grandparents had always regarded the idea of central heating as an unnecessary luxury. There was nothing he could do about it now, he told himself, but later on he would have a proper heating system installed; he couldn't expect Shenna to live in a cold house, not when she was used to the warmth of California.

At lunchtime he slipped out to a nearby locksmith, where he had Shenna's door key copied. In the evening, when he returned to his small flat, he put the master back with the other things from her bag.

Sitting at the table, he spread the items out before him and carefully, lovingly, dwelt on them, one by one touching, caressing, putting them up to his cheek—the wallet, the keys, the sketchbook, the postcards of the angel with the sword, the letter to her mother, the little makeup bag with its lipsticks, creams, pencils, and tiny brushes. This, the makeup, he didn't really approve of. Still, once she was with him she would have no use for such things.

Half an hour later all the items were wrapped up together—that way they wouldn't rattle around—and put into the bag, along with a note. After that he carefully wrapped the whole thing in brown paper, neatly secured it with tape, and wrote her name and address on the front. He would post it to her the next day.

Shenna called the shipping company during coffee break the next morning and asked them to leave her paintings in the hall outside her flat. They would be perfectly safe, she was sure, and she didn't want to lose time from school waiting for them.

Going on into the cafeteria, she bought a cup of coffee and carried it over to the table where Margaret and Hannah had joined Jane, Caspar, Colin, and Brian, who, part of a different tutorial group, were spending the day painting in oils. As Shenna sat down, she found Jane carrying on about the school, and giving every appearance of being generally disenchanted with everything connected with it. "I should have gone to Chelsea," she was saying, "or maybe St. Martin's or Camberwell. One thing I'm sure of, and that's that this place was one hell of a mistake."

While some of those present remonstrated with her, saying that it was too early to start making such judgments, Brian remained silent, and as Shenna watched him she became aware that since joining them at the table she hadn't seen any communication between him and Jane. Their previous closeness seemed to have vanished.

"Well," Jane said, "I know what *I* think, and I think this place is a dump." She shook her head. "God knows how I'm going to stick it out for the rest of the course. But who knows, maybe I'll decide not to."

Shenna felt sorry for her. "Oh, come on, Jane," she said. "This is just a phase you're going through; a little—period of adjustment, that's all. You'll get over it soon, you'll see."

In response, Jane slowly turned cold, disdainful eyes upon her. "Oh, yes? And what the hell d'you know about it?" Her lips curled in a sneer. "Oh, I see—you've conquered the entertainment world; you're in the process of taking over

London's fine arts, and now you're starting up in psychology as well." She shook her head witheringly. "What makes you think you know so much, Miss Superstar? Why don't you just shut up and attend to your own business?"

Silence fell around the table while Shenna felt the color rising in her cheeks. Then, in the embarrassed quiet, Jane was suddenly rising to her feet, flouncing from the table, and moving toward the door. When she had gone from the room Shenna gave an awkward, forced little laugh.

"Tell me," she said, "did I say something wrong?"

"Forget it," Margaret said. "Take no notice."

After a few moments Margaret looked up at the clock and, saying it was time she left, got up from her seat. Together, she and Hannah went from the room, followed a few moments later by Caspar and then Colin. Shenna remained there while Brian went to get more coffee for himself and for her. When he came back he put the cups down, sat at the table again, and lit a cigarette. He blew out the match and, shaking his head, said, "I hope you weren't too upset by that."

"By Jane?" Shenna shrugged. "I just don't understand it. Though I am aware that she's never cared that much for me."

He said nothing to this, and she added, "She doesn't, does she?"

He shook his head. "No, I suppose not."

"But why?"

Shrugging, he said, "I think at the start it was just that she regarded you with—well—with envy. To her, you seem to have everything. I mean, Jane's a pretty girl, but you have so much else going for you. And perhaps you seemed in a way—complacent."

"Complacent?"

"Well, having so much—being a very successful actress—a

film star, no less—and not being content with it. Giving it all up to come here and study."

"Is that how you see it?"

"No, of course not." He paused. "And, of course, added to that, you're a much better artist than she is. That's another thing she resents."

"I can't win with her, can I?"

He gave a rueful grin. "Well, it'll be difficult, I'll grant you that." A brief silence fell between them, then he said, "But she's not happy here, that's for sure."

Shenna nodded. "So it seems. But like the others said, it's early days. For God's sake, it's only been three weeks. She needs to give it a little more time."

"Maybe." He paused. "It's not really the course, though, the school . . ."

"No?"

"It's us. Or perhaps I should say *me*."

"Well, these things happen."

He nodded. "Anyway, we haven't known one another five minutes. It's ridiculous her getting so uptight."

"Look, I wouldn't worry about it. It'll probably be all right again."

"Maybe."

"You sound as if you don't *want* it to be all right. Don't you?" Then, before he could reply, she added, "Don't answer that. It's none of my business and I don't want to know."

As she finished speaking, she glanced around and suddenly saw that Jane had returned and was watching them from the doorway. Brian, following Shenna's gaze, turned, and after a moment nodded awkwardly to her. Jane didn't acknowledge the gesture. She just stood there for a moment longer, then turned away and moved off out of sight. Brian sighed. "I'd better go," he said. "I don't want to aggravate matters."

"Meaning what?"

He got to his feet. "I mean my sitting here talking to you. She's pissed off enough already as it is. I don't want to make it worse."

"How can that make it worse?"

He smiled. "That's another thing she has against you. She thinks I fancy you. I made the mistake of saying one or two complimentary things about you one day. That was enough."

Jane didn't join the group for coffee as usual the next day, but sat at another table with other students. She was obviously doing her best to keep out of Brian's way, Shenna thought. Later in the day she passed Jane in the hall and paused to smile and ask her how she was. In reply, Jane just said, "Fine, thank you," without the slightest hint of any warmth. Shenna shrugged at the cool reaction and went on her way.

That evening, after the night-school portrait class was over, Wesley walked back with her to Elm Court Road. She wished him good night and hurried indoors, anxious to see whether her paintings had arrived.

Entering the hall, she was surprised to see no trace of them, but on going into her flat she found a note from Kevin saying that her things had been delivered and that he had taken them in for safety. An unnecessary step, she thought, but kind of him, nevertheless. When she had taken off her coat she rang his bell, and he opened the door and invited her in. As she went in, she saw several wooden crates standing just inside the sitting room.

"They were taking up so much room in the hall," Kevin said. "I was afraid one of the other tenants would fall over them."

Shenna nodded. "Of course, yes." She thanked him, and together they carried the crates into her own flat, where he took a hammer and screwdriver and began to open them. They were in the midst of the work when the doorbell rang, and Shenna, her arms loaded down with canvases, said to him, "Please, Kevin—just see who it is, will you?"

As she carefully set the canvases down, Kevin opened the door, and then she heard a girl's voice asking, "Is Shenna here?" She recognized the voice at once. A moment later she reached the door and saw Jane standing on the threshold.

"Jane . . ."

As Kevin moved away from the door, Shenna, smiling, invited the girl in. Jane, not returning the smile, said simply, "No, thanks. I've only come to ask if you know where Brian is."

"Brian? How should I know where he is."

Jane smiled now, but it was a smile without humor. "Aw, come on, Shenna, don't try to kid me."

Shenna stared at her for a moment, then said quietly, "Jane, I have no idea what you're trying to say. I don't know where Brian is, and actually I'm not that interested."

They stood facing one another for a few seconds, and then Jane gave a surly shrug and turned away. Moments later she had opened the front door and disappeared from sight.

Shenna remained for a minute, just standing there, then closed the door and came back into the room. Kevin, who had clearly heard everything, looked concernedly into her face, trying to read her expression. Smiling at him, she shook her head. "Weird," she said with a shrug. "Really weird. God knows why she decided to come round *here* looking for Brian." Then, doing her best to dismiss the incident, she said, "Well, there's no point in my trying to make sense of it all. It's beyond me."

She got back to the paintings then, taking them from the packing and stacking them face-in against the walls. Kevin, who had finished opening the crates, had begun to make some tea. When it was ready he handed her a cup, and with a nod toward the stacked canvases, said, "Aren't you going to look at them?"

"Not tonight."

Later, when Kevin had gone back to his own flat, she took a couple of the canvases and studied them. She had been nervous about looking at them before—afraid of what she would find—that they wouldn't be as good as she had remembered them to be, that they wouldn't be good enough for the exhibition. Her brief time at the art school was making her examine her work in ways she had never done before.

The postman brought a package the next morning as she was getting ready to leave for school, and moments later she had opened it up and found her bag and all its contents.

There was a note there, too, and she unfolded it and read the typewritten words:

Dear Shenna,

I'm so happy to be able to return your bag to you—which you carelessly left behind. On looking through your sketch-book I was fortunate enough to find your address. At least I hope it's *your* address—otherwise I'll be sending it to the wrong person. Anyway, here it is, all intact. Lucky for you it was found by *me*,

A Friend

No name; just that: *A Friend*. She picked up the brown-paper wrapping and saw from the postmark that it had been posted in Greenwich.

There was no sign of Jane during the morning coffee break, and when Shenna asked about her Brian said she hadn't turned up. Shenna just nodded; she had decided to say nothing to him about Jane's visit to her flat the evening before.

At lunchtime she took her mother's letter from her newly

recovered bag, added a few last lines to it, put it in an envelope, along with one of the angel postcards, and mailed it off.

Monday, October the eleventh.

The start of a new week—the week Ian was due back in England. Before he'd left—ages ago now, it seemed—he had told her that he'd be back by Wednesday, the thirteenth, at the latest. This week. But she had heard nothing from him in so long, it seemed. There had been the cards and the phone calls from Italy, then a couple more after his arrival in New York—and then nothing. He was busy, she knew that, and he had told her he would be, and, she said to herself, she was foolish to have expected daily correspondence. Even so, she had hoped . . . But, anyway, this week he would be back. By Wednesday. She was bound to hear something from him before then. She could only wait.

On Tuesday morning she received an envelope containing two theater tickets in the mail. They were for two stalls seats for the play *Keats*. She didn't understand. She stood staring at the tickets for a while and then unfolded the typewritten letter that had come with them. She read:

Dear Shenna,

In searching for your address when I found your bag, I couldn't help but see the letter you had begun—and from this, of course, I learned that *Keats* was one of the plays you wanted to see. And now you can. I'm enclosing two tickets for you for this coming Saturday—I chose Saturday as I didn't want it to get in the way of your art studies. I'm sure you won't have any difficulty in getting one of your girl friends to accompany you. I hope you enjoy it.

Your Friend

From him again, the person—it had to be a man—who had found her bag.

Reading the letter through once more, she recalled that, in

the letter to her mother, she had written about the play, *Keats*, and how much she wanted to see it.

What should she do about them? she wondered. She couldn't send them back. And simply to ignore them, not use them, would just be a waste. After a minute she put the tickets into her bag. Ian would be back any day now. Who knew, perhaps on Saturday he'd like to go to the theater. . . .

In his diary he wrote:

> *I enjoyed sending her the tickets. I keep trying to imagine her face when she opened the envelope and saw them inside. I see her smiling a little, wondering who this friend, this benefactor can be. One day she'll know—when I reveal myself. Not yet, though; I've got to wait until the time is right, and that time isn't yet. At the moment she must be rather puzzled. Such feelings will pass, though, and she'll learn to trust me and be grateful to me. Then, from that trust, love will spring.*

He paused for a few moments, felt-tip pen in his hand, then he added:

> *She didn't know who I was that night when I watched her from near the church. When I look into her eyes there's not the faintest glimmer of recognition there.*

He smiled at the thoughts that ran through his mind; all of them were about her, Shenna. Some of them were concerned with what he would do for her, while others brought images of the two of them together. He read through the lines he had written and gave a little nod. Yes, from her trust in him love would spring. When that happened he could come in out of the cold.

There had been no word from Ian. With each mail delivery and each phone call that came during the week, she had hoped it would be from him. But there had been nothing.

When Friday came Shenna remembered that she had theater tickets. She went to Hannah and Margaret and, without saying how she had come by the tickets, asked whether either of the girls would like to go with her to the play. They were both busy, though, and so she went to Caspar. Would he, she asked, like to go and see a play about Keats the following day? After a moment's hesitation he said yes, he'd like to, very much.

Early the next evening Caspar arrived at Shenna's flat on his bicycle, which he chained to the railing outside the front door. A few minutes later the two of them made their way to Blackheath station, where they took the train to Charing Cross and then walked to the theater on Shaftesbury Avenue.

The play, beautiful and moving, was set in a small apartment overlooking the Spanish Steps in Rome, and covered the last days in Keats's life. After the show they stopped in a pub for a drink; then they set off for the station.

On their return to Shenna's flat she made tea and they sat talking of the play and of Keats's life and poetry. Shenna had just gotten up to pour second cups for them when Caspar, turning to the window, said, "There's somebody at your front door."

Shenna stood and listened for a moment. "I didn't hear anything." Then she shrugged. "Well, it was probably just one of the neighbors."

As she turned back to her task, Caspar got up from his chair. "I think I'll just go and see if my bike's still there. I can't imagine anybody being desperate enough to steal it, but you can't be sure."

While Shenna finished pouring the tea he left the flat and went out into the hall. When he came back a minute later he was shaking his head. "I couldn't see anybody around. And my bike's still there."

They drank the tea and went on talking for another half

hour or so until, at almost twelve-thirty, Caspar got up to leave. Shenna followed him outside and watched as he bent to unlock the chain that secured his bicycle.

"Oh, *no!*" he muttered.

"What's up? What's wrong?" Shenna stepped closer and watched as he took a small flashlight from the tool kit at the back of the saddle and pointed it downward at the wheels.

"There *was* sombody out here," he said. "Look at my tires." He reached down and prodded them with his fingers. "Would you believe it? Somebody's gone and slashed my tires."

9

Shenna stood in the open doorway, watching as Caspar wheeled the useless machine along the street. Then, closing the door and turning, she suddenly became aware of Kevin standing in the hall behind her. She started and clapped a hand to her heart.

"Oh, for God's sake, Kevin!" she said. "You scared the life out of me, hovering there like that!"

"Sorry—I didn't mean to scare you, but I heard voices and I came out to see what was up." He stood in his doorway wearing a plaid dressing gown over his pajamas.

"I'm sorry if we woke you," she said.

"I was already awake."

She told him about the damage to Caspar's bicycle and asked whether he had heard or seen anyone tampering with the machine. No, he said. Shenna shook her head. "I can't understand how anybody could do something like that."

Later, lying awake in bed, she thought of the incident involving Caspar's bicycle. The whole evening had been spoiled by the senseless, malicious damage.

Lips grimly pressed together, he wrote in his diary:

> *Sunday morning. 17th October.*
> *It's almost three o'clock. Everything is so quiet. I can't go to bed yet, though, not while she's so much on my mind. God, but she makes me angry. I thought I made it clear in my letter that she was to take a girlfriend. And what happens?—she takes* him—*that ugly, red-haired specimen. She had no idea, of course, that I could see them, or that I was anywhere near—not that she would have seen me sitting up in the dress circle.*

I wonder whether she enjoyed the show. I couldn't tell. I didn't—not really. I was too preoccupied with them. *I didn't stay till the end, either—I was so anxious to get back and see that she arrived home safely. And I have to confess that when she didn't return by the time I expected her to I began to get worried. But then there she was—there they* both *were. I thought he'd leave then, on his bicycle, but he didn't. Still, by the time he did go he found out he'd stayed too long. He was lucky that it was only a couple of slashed tyres.*

I think I might write her a letter. We'll see. She's got to learn. Though it was probably only thoughtlessness on her part. I know as well as I know myself that essentially she's a good girl. It's one of the main things that drew me to her right at the start, the feeling—no, the knowledge—*that she's not like other girls her age—those girls who only have one thing on their minds. They disgust me.*

He closed the diary. Yes, he would write a short letter to her. Not just yet, though. He had other little surprises in mind for her—if he could arrange them. . . .

Shenna was painting at her easel with BBC Radio 4 in the background when Caspar phoned to thank her and to say again how much he had enjoyed the play. When they got onto the subject of his damaged bicycle he said, "Can you imagine it?—some creep doing a thing like that? There were no half measures, either. I had a good look at the tires in daylight this morning, and whoever it was did a thorough job. I can't repair them; I'll just have to get new ones."

After Shenna had hung up she went back to her easel and took up her brush again. She was working on a painting of a garden seen through a tracery of intricate wrought-ironwork. The scene was one she had discovered on one of her excursions around London and that she had tried to capture in a drawing in her sketchbook. Now, standing back to study the painting, she suddenly saw in it the influence of Caspar's work. Some of the colors she had used were his colors; his influence also could be seen in the dramatic contrasts and the rich shadows set against the light.

She worked quickly, and the painting was close to completion by midafternoon. Then, after standing before it for a long time, she took it from the easel and placed it beside another recently completed painting—one of a graveyard, based on the one at Hinton Peeble, aided in its composition by Ian's photographs. And that canvas, too, she saw, bore signs of Caspar's influence.

She realized as she looked at the paintings that they were both better than any of those she'd had shipped from California. Since their arrival she had studied them at different times and her disappointment in them had grown into something immovable and inescapable. Examining her reactions, she realized that the California pictures had been painted in comparative isolation from external influences. Since then she had begun working at the art school and, although she had only been there a short time, its effect had been dynamic. Apart from the concentration of her own efforts, she had been steeped in the influences of other students, some of whom—Caspar in particular—displayed a brilliance that she was forever contrasting with her own talent, making her continually reassess her ability and its development. Her standards were changing—and along with her standards, her rate of development, her style, and her technique. Now, very much aware of those changes, she began to feel that the paintings she eventually gave to Alfred Carson for the exhibition were going to be rather different from the ones he was expecting.

After a while she put the paintings aside and lay down on the bed. When she turned her head she found herself facing the photograph of Ian, the one she had taken by the pond in Hinton Peeble.

And still there had been no word from him.

On Tuesday evening she had just returned to the flat after classes had ended when the telephone rang. She picked up the receiver.

"Yes? Hello?"

"Shenna."

"*Ian!*" She hadn't dared to hope the voice would be his. She felt happiness surge through her. "Where are you?" she asked. "Are you in London?"

"No, not yet. I'll be getting in tomorrow afternoon."

"Where? Heathrow?"

"Yes."

"Would you like me to meet you at the airport?"

"No, no. Thanks all the same. No, I'll call round for you tomorrow evening if you like."

"If I like? Of course." What a question.

"Good. We'll go out and eat somewhere."

"Fine. What time shall I expect you?"

"Oh, between six-thirty and seven. How will that be?"

"Perfect." She was all smiles.

"You're okay, are you?" he said.

"Yes, I'm okay."

"No problems?"

"Only one, now."

"What's that?"

"How'm I going to get through the time till tomorrow evening?"

She threw herself into his arms as soon as he came through the doorway of the flat just after seven-fifteen the next evening. Having him there at last, she would have liked just to sit beside him, to touch him, to hear him talk, to be alone with him, but after a little while he looked at his watch and said they'd better be going to the restaurant; he had reserved a table for them at seven-thirty, and they were already going to be late.

He took her to a small restaurant in Kensington, and as they ate he told her that he had to fly back to San Francisco on the following Sunday and would be away for several weeks.

"But you've only just come back," Shenna said. "Can't you stay longer?"

"I'm sorry. I'd hoped I'd be here for a longer time but—" He shrugged. "It just didn't work out."

She gave a little shake of her head. "Was it like this when you were married?"

"Worse. I suppose you can understand my wife getting fed up. Still, within a year it'll be better."

"You mean your going to live in San Francisco?"

"Yes. I shan't do any traveling then—or very little. I'll be staying put."

"Your wife should have held on a little longer."

"Perhaps."

Afterward they went back to his apartment. "Stay with me," he said as they lay in bed. "Don't go back tonight. Go back in the morning."

She should have said no, she knew; she didn't want to start the day dashing around for trains and fighting the rush-hour traffic. Nestled into his warmth, though, such reasons seemed petty and unrealistic.

"Yes," she said. "I'll stay."

They spent the following evening together, too, and again she stayed overnight. "But I have a late class this evening," she told him as she prepared to leave the next morning, "a portrait class. So I guess I won't be able to see you." She waited, wanting him to ask her to give up the class, just for that night. When he said nothing she added, "Not that it'll make any difference if I skip the class just once."

"No," he said. "If you've committed yourself to the class then you should go to it."

His words made her feel like a child; moved by whim, irresponsible. "But the class isn't really an important one," she protested with a little laugh. "It's only an extra one I took on by myself."

"It was important enough to you to decide to do it in the first place, wasn't it?"

"I guess so."

"Well, then. Come on, now." He put his arms around her. "You go on to your class and I'll see you tomorrow, all right?"

"Okay." Then, after a moment, she began to protest again. "But you're here for such a short time."

"I know, but it won't hurt us not to meet just this one time. And you'll feel better if you go to your class and work hard. After all, isn't that the reason you came here to England?"

"You've got an answer for everything."

She left him soon afterward and went back to her flat, where she changed and got ready for her classes. She kept thinking of Ian, though, as the hours went by, and gradually she made the decision to see him that evening. To hell with the portrait class. She couldn't wait until tomorrow to be with him again. Besides, she told herself, he would be leaving once more this weekend and she wouldn't be seeing him for some time.

There was no answer when she telephoned him on her return to the flat, but, undeterred, she began to get ready. Later, when she was all set to leave, she dialed his number again. Still no answer. She waited impatiently for another ten minutes and dialed once more. Still no answer—and precious time was going by. Eventually she decided she couldn't wait any longer, and, putting on her coat and slipping his door key into her pocket, she left the flat.

The journey took an unusually long time that evening, but at last it was over and she made her way from the Knightsbridge underground station to the street; from there to Ian's flat was just a couple of minutes' walk.

She caught sight of him the second after she turned the corner.

He was wearing a white raincoat and was standing outside a shop. Breaking into a smile, she hurried forward, raising her hand to greet him. But then she saw a tall blond girl stepping to his side. It was the girl whose photograph she had seen in his apartment.

Coming to a halt, Shenna shrank back into the shadows and watched as Ian and the girl walked away along the street.

Ian was due to call at the flat the next evening, and Shenna was ready well before the appointed time. When he got there, putting his arms around her and kissing her, she sought some sign of coolness in his manner. She could detect nothing.

They left soon afterward to go to a fringe production of a new play in a large room above a Hammersmith pub. It was a disappointment, though, and during the intermission they crept out and headed for Notting Hill and the Italian restaurant where they had first eaten together. Then they went back to Ian's flat.

During the evening they had talked of many things, but had never touched upon the one thing that was uppermost in Shenna's mind. So much she wanted to ask about his relationship with the girl, Mary Carroll. *What does she mean to you now?* she wanted to ask. *Couldn't you spend one night on your own without me? Why did you see her? Was she the real reason you encouraged me to go to my evening class?* But she kept silent. And if she kept silent long enough, she told herself, perhaps the questions would fade.

Saturday morning. As he moved toward the mailbox with the letter to her in his hand, a large tabby cat left the shelter of a doorway and sauntered into his path. He froze, waiting for the creature to go safely on by while he glanced down around him, looking for some likely missile to help the loathsome animal on its way. There was nothing handy. Anyway, there were too many people about.

In another few moments the cat had walked on out of sight around a corner and he continued on to the mailbox. When he had posted the letter he began to wander about, looking in the shop windows. He was bored and restless. He was just killing time, he knew—killing time while he waited. All his waking hours seemed to be spent doing that—waiting—waiting for the time to arrive when they would be together.

But then something happened that dispelled his boredom and restlessness, and in their place gave him excitement and a compelling, immediate purpose. His wanderings had taken him browsing among some antique shops in Richmond, and it was while gazing into one of the windows that he had seen the thing that fired his enthusiasm.

Peering between the shelves of decorative plates and silverware, he glimpsed, in the more shadowed area of the interior beyond, a statue of a figure. It was an angel holding a sword. *She* had had postcards of a similar figure in her bag—a figure by Cellini, in the museum—she had written of it in the letter to her mother.

Entering the shop, he stood and gazed at the figure. The angel was on one knee, his face lifted to heaven, while in his clasped hands he held, pointing upward, a broad, heavy-looking sword of bronze. Behind him, great wings swept down in a graceful curve. It was not exactly like the Cellini on the postcards, but it was very similar. From the base to the tip of the sword, it measured about eight feet; it appeared to be cast in concrete.

"Sir, can I help you?"

At the words, he turned from his study of the angel to see the assistant moving toward him. After a brief pause he gave a little nod and said, "Yes—this statue—can you tell me how much it is?"

That night in Ian's bed, after they had made love, Shenna lay with her arm across him, feeling the rise and fall of his chest. It had been a busy day. That morning as they had eaten breakfast she had talked about her wish to get a small car for herself, and Ian had offered to go with her and help her find something suitable. She had left him after breakfast to go to the Victoria and Albert Museum to spend a couple of hours making notes and sketches. Then, when she was through, Ian had driven her to several car showrooms and eventually, under his watchful eye, she had picked out a neat little two-year-old white Renault 5.

The car was now parked in the street just outside the apartment. She would be driving home in it in the morning. Lying there beside Ian, she thought of the coming morning and of his departure.

"I wish you weren't going tomorrow," she said softly, and he lifted her hand to his mouth and kissed it. "I wish it, too," he said. "Still, I'll be back next month." They made love again later on. Afterward, when he was in the bathroom, she got up and poured herself a glass of water. Sitting up in the bed, she sipped from the glass. It seemed that she could still feel Ian's hardness inside her, the warm touch of his hands on her body, his breath on her face, his mouth on hers. . . . She was aware now, suddenly, that she felt so much more relaxed. For most of the day, she realized, she had felt tense and a little depressed. She knew the reason why, of course. It had been because of seeing him with Mary Carroll last night. Now, though, after spending most of the day with him and having just made love with him, so many of her unspoken fears seemed to have vanished. Any that remained she thrust impatiently to one side.

She sighed, drank the last of the water, and reached out to put the glass down. As she did so, setting it down beside the lamp, she saw a paperback novel on the bedside table and recognized the American cover of a current best-seller. Obviously Ian had brought it over with him. Idly, she picked it up, opened it to his marked page, took out his paper marker and glanced at the text. She found very quickly that it was of no interest to her, and after reading just a couple of paragraphs she put the marker back. She was just about to close the book when she realized what the marker was: the carbon duplicate of his plane ticket. Taking it from between the pages again, she looked at it closely.

When she heard Ian come back into the room a minute later she was lying facing away from him, with her eyes closed, as if asleep. She was not asleep, however, and she wondered as she lay there whether she would ever sleep that night. She lay still as he got in beside her and, molding his body to hers, put his arms around her. She didn't respond. All she could think of were the figures she had seen on the airline ticket. Very clearly, without any doubt at all, it showed that he had arrived back in London on the thirteenth. Yet when he had called her that Monday just past, he had told her that he was arriving the next day. And he had already been back almost a week. Why had he lied?

In the morning, as he made coffee, she covertly studied him. And she could see nothing at all about him that showed that he thought any the less of her than she had assumed he did.

"Penny for them?"

"Mmm?" She realized suddenly that she had been staring at him and she hastily dropped her gaze and looked away.

"You're miles away," he said.

"Oh . . ." She shrugged. "Was I?"

"Is anything wrong?"

"No."

He set a cup of coffee down before her as she sat at the kitchen table. They were both dressed to leave. These were their last minutes before parting. She picked up the cup and, as she did so, his hand came out and gently touched the top of her head. "Don't be sad," he said, "I'll be back before you know it." Dumbly, she nodded.

"And I'll write to you in the meantime," he added.

She nodded again. She didn't dare look at him. She just wanted to weep.

In her newly acquired Renault she drew up outside 19 Elm Court Road, switched off the motor, and sat there, arms crossed over the steering wheel, eyes staring unseeingly into space. She could feel her depression settling about her like a thick fog. She had looked forward to Ian's return so much. She had never questioned the feeling that it would bring her only happiness. Instead, however, it had brought her only unhappiness, uncertainty, and confusion.

After a while she got out of the car, locked it, and went into the flat. She sat down and eventually gave herself up to the tears that had been threatening for so long.

Later, when her weeping had stopped and her tears had dried, she tried to look objectively at the situation.

She should have asked him about Mary Carroll, she told herself; she should have told him that she had seen the two of them together. And she should have asked him why he had lied about the day of his return to England. She should have asked all these questions. Of course—and she was angry now that she hadn't done so. Had she done so, then he would have surely explained everything—whatever there was to explain—and put her mind at rest. For she had no doubt, the more she thought about it, that there was some perfectly ordinary and acceptable explanation for what had happened. Oh, if only she had mentioned it to him! Yes. Yes!—his explanation would, she felt sure, have left her feeling foolish and immature, but at least she would have *known*. And now it was too late and he was gone. There was nothing she could do about it but wait for him to come back and, in the meantime, try to put the whole thing out of her mind and get back to her work, back to her routine.

She got up and changed her clothes and then, stirring herself to make the effort, began to prepare materials for painting.

It was about fifteen minutes later when the telephone began to ring. She spun, moving quickly toward the phone. Perhaps it was Ian, calling her from the airport. When she put the receiver to her ear, though, there was only silence. After a while she hung up.

The phone rang again a little later and once more she heard only silence. Angrily, she slammed down the receiver.

He stood in the house at Kew with the receiver to his ear. He had made the call in the excitement of getting the statue; he had wanted to hear her voice.

After replacing the receiver he left the house, moved out into the front garden, and stood looking at the statue. By paying extra he had been able to have it delivered that morning. The seller had seemed eager to accommodate him; probably anxious to get rid of it—after all, it couldn't be everybody's cup of tea. It had come from the garden of some large house whose effects had recently been sold, the man had said. And now here it was, in the garden at Kew.

Close to the wall of the house at the front was a little arbor, a paved area surrounded by a rock garden and a bank on which rose trees grew. He had told the deliverymen to place the angel right in the center. It was made for it. He would spend the rest of his time there today clearing away the weeds. At the moment it was untidy and overgrown. Next spring he would prune the roses and replant the rock garden.

In time it would be beautiful—a perfect setting. She would love it, he knew.

A letter came for her on Monday morning and at once its familiar appearance registered in her mind. It was from *him*—the man who had sent the theater tickets.

Looking at the postmark on the envelope, she saw that it had been posted locally the previous Saturday morning. Tearing it open, she read the typewritten letter inside.

My dear Shenna,

Did you enjoy *Keats*? I hope so. I found the whole thing a little too sad and depressing, but if *you* enjoyed it, that's all that matters.

I have to say that at first I was a little cross with you for taking that young man to accompany you, but since then I've thought that perhaps you didn't have much choice, so don't worry about it.

So he had gone to the theater that night, too. He had been there all the time—watching her. She became suddenly aware of the beating of her heart. After a moment she went back to the letter.

I'd hoped to write to you before this, but there wasn't much point. I wanted to arrange another little surprise for you—which I couldn't do just at a moment's notice. Anyway, it's done now, as you can see by the enclosed tickets. I hope you're able to use them and that you enjoy the performance. It's the best I could do at fairly short notice.

And who will you take with you this time? Someone I approve of, I hope.

I'll be in touch again very soon. Till then you can be assured of my constant love and affection.

Always,
Your devoted
Friend

Opening the envelope, she dipped into it and brought out

two tickets for the Royal Opera House, Covent Garden. The tickets were for the twenty-seventh, this coming Wednesday. She was bewildered. Why had he sent her these tickets? And then she remembered that in the letter to her mother she had mentioned how much she would like to go to the opera or the ballet. And now he had moved to grant her wish—as he had with the play.

When she left the house she stopped at a newsstand and bought a paper. The program for Wednesday at the Opera House was a ballet—Prokofiev's *Romeo and Juliet*.

She had thought that when she got to school she might ask Margaret and Hannah whether they would like the tickets, but when the time came she said nothing. She realized she was becoming increasingly disturbed about the whole thing; it hadn't really bothered her so much having the *Keats* tickets sent to her—after all, during her career people had often sent her little gifts. It was the thought that this man, whoever he was, had sat in the theater to observe her. It was a disturbing thought, and it stayed with her.

At lunchtime she left the studio along with Hannah and Margaret to go to the cafeteria. As they emerged into the foyer she saw Harry, the porter, talking to a young man who stood near the main doors. She recognized the young man at once and, before he had a chance to see her, she dodged to the right and slipped through the open doorway of Harry's office. A few moments later Harry himself came in. Finding her there, he raised his eyebrows and said in a low voice, "I was just about to put out a call for you. You've got a visitor. He's waiting out there for you. I don't know what he wants. He wouldn't say."

"I know what he wants," she said. "He's a reporter."

Harry nodded. "Ah, yes. He was here to see you before, wasn't he?"

"Right. Please, Harry—can you get rid of him for me?"

He nodded and turned back to the door. "Well, I'll see. I'll have a word with him."

As he went out into the hall, Shenna waited in the small office, its starkness relieved somewhat by the addition of little personal touches—family photographs on the desk, a framed child's drawing of a house with flowers on either side. After a couple of minutes Harry was back. "He's gone," he said, "so you can relax. I told him you didn't want to see him and that he was wasting his time."

She thanked him, started toward the door, then came to a stop. "Harry," she said, "do you like the ballet?"

"Ballet?"

"Yes, ballet. You know—all that dancing around in tights and tutus."

He smiled suddenly, his usually grave expression brightening. "Yes," he said. "We'd often go, my wife and I."

Shenna turned to one of the photographs on his desk; it showed a woman in her twenties sitting on a gate beside two small girls. "This is your wife?" she asked.

He nodded. "Janet. Yes."

"And these are your daughters? They look so cute sitting there."

"Yes." He nodded again; his face was turned away.

"How old are they?"

"They would be five and six now."

They would be. As the realization dawned on her, she looked at him and he shrugged. "Time heals all wounds, they say. . . ."

There was a brief, awkward silence, then Shenna said, "Do you—have anyone now who . . ." Her voice trailed off.

"You mean have I got a lady friend?" He smiled and nodded. "In a way I have, yes. Her name's Sally. It's nothing serious but—she's nice company."

"It's important."

"I think so, yes." He paused. "Anyway, why were you asking. . . ?"

"I asked because—well, as I was saying—the ballet . . ."

"Ah, yes."

"*Romeo and Juliet.* Prokofiev."

"What's all this about?"

"Oh, I have a reason for wanting to know." Fishing in her bag, she brought out the tickets. *And who will you take with you this time?* her benefactor had written. *Someone I approve of, I hope.* Well, she wasn't going to take anybody. "Here, Harry . . ." She put the tickets into his hand. "I've got these tickets and I can't use them. Can you? They're for *Romeo and Juliet*, on Wednesday at Covent Garden. It'd be a shame to waste them."

He shook his head. "But—why me? You must have lots of friends who'd like to go."

"Harry, it's a complicated story. But just believe me—I want you to have them—if you'd like them. I know it's short notice, but . . ."

He said uncertainly, "How much do they cost? I—"

Shenna broke in quickly. "Don't be silly. I don't want anything for them. Just take them—take Sally out for the evening."

After a moment he nodded. "Thank you. Thank you very much."

"Attaboy. Good old Harry."

He smiled again. "Good old Harry—that's what they all say. Not so old, though." He looked at the tickets. "You're quite sure about these. . . ?"

"Quite." She glanced at her watch. "Hey, I'd better go and get my lunch." In the doorway she turned back to him. "And you should smile more often, Harry. It suits you."

The next morning she was moving toward the stairs at school when she heard her name called and turned to see Harry coming toward her. Seeing his expression, she said, "What's up?"

He held out his hand to her and she saw that he was holding the tickets. "Don't you want them?" she asked.

He shook his head. "It's not that. It's not a case of not wanting them."

"Then what's the problem? Can't you get someone to stand in for you?"

"Oh, no, that's no problem either. The trouble is, Sally can't get away from her job early enough—and there's nobody else I can ask on such short notice."

"Well, why don't you go on your own?"

"No, I don't think I'd care to do that. Besides, I think it would be better if you could find a *couple* to use them." He shook his head. "Shame, but"—he took her hand and put the tickets into it—"thanks anyway."

Shenna watched him as he moved back across the foyer. After a moment she went after him. "Harry?"

He turned to face her again at his office door.

"Would you really like to go?" she asked.

"Well, yes, but—"

"Well, suppose *I* go along with you—would that be all right?"

She had expected him to agree immediately, but he didn't. "I don't understand," he said. "No, you ask one of your friends. You don't want to go with me."

She nodded emphatically. "Yes, I do. I do want to go with you. So—what d'you say?"

"Okay. Yes." He was beaming now. "Yes, I'd like that very much."

Shenna had arranged with Harry to leave just after six, and with this in mind she hurried back to Elm Court Road to change her clothes in the hour before the Wednesday lecture began. Harry, she saw, had gone home at lunchtime and returned wearing a new-looking suit and a fresh shirt and tie.

The lecture ended at about five to six and the two of them caught the train for Charing Cross. It would be easier going by train, they had decided; there'd be no rush-hour traffic to fight and the opera house was only a short walk from the station.

Their seats were in the dress circle and after they were settled Shenna took the opportunity to look around her. She was sure that the sender of the tickets would also be there and she was hopeful of seeing him. As it was, though, she recognized no one and saw nothing unusual. As she turned back in her seat from looking around her, she was aware of Harry's curious glance. "You looking for somebody?" he said, and she smiled. "No, just being a little curious, I guess."

When the performance was over and the final curtain call had been taken they made their way to the exit, Shenna still taking what opportunity she could to look about her. There were many who, recognizing her, looked at her curiously—and where men alone were concerned, there was no way of knowing what was behind those stares; any one of them, she supposed, could be the sender of the tickets. But then she and Harry were outside and she was no wiser than she had been at the start of the evening.

When they got back to Blackheath Harry walked with her toward her car, which she had left near the school. As they reached it, she tried to persuade him to allow her to drive him home, but he wouldn't hear of it. It wasn't far, he said, and he would enjoy the walk.

"I shall see you in the morning," he told her. "Right now I shall go on home and sit and think about this evening. I know it may sound corny to you, but it was one of the best evenings of my life. I shan't forget it."

*   *   *

Later, lying in bed, Shenna's glance found its way to Ian's photograph—as it always did. He had gone away last Sunday morning and here it was, Wednesday night, and there had been no word at all from him.

In an effort to dispel the disturbing thoughts, she let her mind wander back to the ballet she had just seen, allowing the music to run through her head. And then she thought again about *him*, her benefactor. Had he been there, too?

The letter finished, he sealed and stamped the envelope, then turned to his diary and wrote:

> *Wednesday, 27th Nov.*
>
> *It was hard to tell whether she really enjoyed the evening or not. By what I could see she seemed somewhat preoccupied—the way she kept turning around in her seat so often. Trying to see me, probably. I would like to have made myself known to her, but I couldn't, of course.*
>
> *Thinking about the ballet, I have to say that I hated it. But I expected to. I always have loathed it—right from those times when my grandparents used to drag me to it or make me sit and listen to their records of Tchaikovsky and their Rimski-Korsakov and what-have-you.*
>
> *And she made me angry again. Really angry. I know I didn't spell it out to her in so many words but she knew very well that I intended her to take a girlfriend along with her. And she didn't, of course. Oh, yes, she might well have thought that her choice was no threat to me, but that's not the point. I couldn't tolerate it when she took that red-haired student and I won't tolerate it this time either. It's the principle that's involved here. I wonder—is it an example of a willful streak in her nature? But she'll learn. It's got to be me and only me—as and when I eventually present myself to her.*
>
> *But as I say, she'll learn. She's going to get some unexpected news tomorrow, and I'd like to see her face when she hears it.*

When Shenna entered the foyer the next morning, she was surprised not to see Harry at the reception counter. Instead, an older man sat working the tiny switchboard. As she moved toward the desk, he flicked a switch, hung up the phone, and smiled at her. "Morning, miss."

"Good morning," she said, and then, "Where's Harry?"

The man shook his head. "Not coming in this morning, I'm afraid. I've come in to take over for him."

"Why? What for?"

"You didn't 'ear what happened to 'im last night?"

Shenna shook her head. "No . . ."

He curled his lip in disgust. "Seems somebody had it in for him—some yob. Apparently, as he was going home last night somebody attacked him and beat him up."

10

When Shenna left the cafeteria after lunch she found Harry back behind his desk, his left arm bandaged and in a sling. As she looked at him, tears welled in her eyes.

"Oh, Harry—what a terrible thing."

He nodded, lips set. "Well—I'm just thankful it was no worse. At least it wasn't my *right* arm. Besides, if it hadn't been my arm it would have been my head."

"What happened? Or would you rather not talk about it?"

"It's okay. . . ." After a moment's pause he told her that he had been walking to Lewisham after seeing her to the car when, just as he was nearing his home in a darker part of the dark street, someone had jumped out behind him. "I suppose he wanted my wallet," he said, "though he didn't get it." He shook his head. "He just—just hit out at me. There was no warning at all. Luckily I heard him come up behind me and, as he struck out at me, I—I raised my arm." He closed his eyes briefly, turning his head away, and Shenna saw that he was shaking. She reached out and put a hand on his shoulder.

"Oh, Harry . . ."

He gave a weak smile. "I'm all right." Another little silence passed, then he said, "After he hit me he just—ran off. Didn't even stop to see whether I had any money with me, just went."

"Did you get a look at him?"

He hesitated. "No, I'm afraid not. It all happened so quickly."

Seeing the hesitation, she said, "There is something. What is it?"

He frowned. "Oh, I'm sure it's just my imagination, but—well, afterward I was left with the impression that—that there was something *familiar* about him. Yet when I think back there's nothing I can put my finger on. It's just a vague impression. All I can really feel sure of is that he was fairly young." He shrugged. "He was gone so quickly . . ."

Shenna gazed at him, then said, "You know you ought to be at home, Harry. Why on earth did you come in this afternoon? You think they can't manage without you?"

He shook his head. "It's better for me to be here—to be busy. What good would it do, staying at home? I'm much better off here with something to do."

Shenna paused. "Does your arm hurt much?"

"On and off. It was pretty badly gashed. I don't know what he hit me with—some metal bar or something, I should think. At the hospital they gave me some painkillers when they put in the stitches." He smiled at her. "I'll live, don't worry."

"Did you report it to the police?"

"Yes, of course. Not that it'll do any good. I mean, I couldn't give them anything to go on. Not even a description. I'm afraid they don't hold out much hope of finding the culprit—not that I expected them to." He frowned. "I still don't understand why he didn't take my money."

Following an evening session of life drawing, Shenna was faced with the portrait class. She didn't feel like it, though, apart from the fact that she had an art history assignment to work on. After some deliberation she decided to skip it. Later, in the flat, while she was going through her notes, the doorbell rang and she peered through the peep hole and sat the tall form of Wesley standing in the hall. She opened the door. "Wesley—well, hello."

With a gesture of awkwardness, he raised a hand and ran his fingers through his dark, curling hair. "When you didn't turn up for the class again I wondered how you were—if you were okay."

"Oh, I'm fine," she said. "Come on in for a minute." When he had entered, she added with a shrug, "I just didn't feel like staying on for the class, that's all. It'd already been a long day and I had other work to do."

"Oh." He nodded, then paused. "I hope you don't mind me calling. . . ."

"No, not at all. I'm glad for the excuse to take a break."

He sat down at her invitation, and while she made coffee she told him of the visit to the opera house the night before and of the subsequent attack on Harry as he had gone home afterward. They discussed the incident for a while and then, after about half an hour, Wesley got up to go. Shenna followed him through the hall to the main door, where he turned to her and asked, "Will you be at portrait class next week?"

"I really don't know. I think maybe I bit off more than I could chew when I took that on. Perhaps it's better that I stay away all together than just go in occasionally."

"Oh, don't say that."

She shrugged. "Well, I'll have to see how things work out. But anyway, we can still meet for a drink or something if you want."

"Yes?"

"Of course."

He smiled then, and with his smile she realized how somber his mood had been on his arrival. She said good night and he murmured a good night in return and moved toward the front gate. As he did so she looked at her watch and saw that it was still not quite nine o'clock. "I thought it was later," she said. "The class doesn't finish till nine. How come you left so early?"

Turning back, he looked at her for a moment then said, "I didn't feel like staying on either."

*   *   *

A letter came the next morning, Friday. She opened it and read:

My dear Shenna,

When I sent you the tickets for the ballet I said I hoped you would take with you someone of whom I approved. I meant, of course, that you should take one of your girlfriends. But you didn't. You must learn to take a more responsible attitude, and remember that it is not always you who must take the consequences of your actions. Surely what happened to your friend's bicycle must have taught you that.

Anyway, enough of that. Did you like the ballet? I have to say that it wasn't my cup of tea. I suppose I'm just not the ballet type. It always seems to me that the more desperately those dancers spring about trying to get off the ground, the more earthbound they appear. Still, as long as you enjoyed it. I would like to have got you the very best seats, but I'm afraid it just wasn't possible. But just know this: Anything that I can do for you I will. I have your interests at heart. Remember that.

With regard to other matters, there is still much to do—as you will discover. In the meantime there will be further pleasant surprises for you. Till then, I urge you to be patient. You'll soon hear again from,

Your devoted friend

Shenna's heart was thudding as she read the letter again. *It is not always you who must take the consequences of your actions*, he had written—and he had underlined the *you*. And then he had written: *Surely what happened to your friend's bicycle must have taught you that*. The bumping of her heart grew stronger. Was he saying that he had damaged Caspar's bike for going with her to the theater? And had he also been responsible for the attack on Harry after the ballet?

Sitting on the edge of the bed, she wrapped her arms around her chest, clutching herself. He was mad. She looked down at the letter again. *With regard to other matters there is still much to do*, and then: *there will be further pleasant surprises for you*. And, just as he had been at the play, so during the performance of the ballet he had been watching her. . . . She gave a little choking cry and got up, moving swiftly to the gas stove. There, her hand trembling, she ignited one of the burners and put the letter to the blue flame. When it was burning she dropped it into the sink and watched as it was reduced to ashes. After that she turned on the tap and washed every trace of it away.

As soon as she got to school she stopped to see Harry and ask how he was feeling. He was much better, he told her. She asked him how he was managing for himself at home, to which he replied that he was coping quite well. "Sally comes round," he told her, "and she'll get shopping in for me and things like that."

"Good." Shenna nodded. The responsibility she felt for what had happened to him was like a weight. "Is there anything I can do?" she asked.

"No, no." He shook his head and patted her hand. "No, really, I'm fine, thanks. I'm touched that you're so concerned, but I shall be all right."

On Saturday morning she met Kevin coming from his flat, and voicing an idea that had been on her mind for some time, asked him if he would consider sitting for her while she painted his portrait. He agreed at once, and they arranged to start that afternoon. If it went well, it would be one more painting for the exhibition.

When he rang her bell at two o'clock she was ready and waiting. He had brought with him some of his opera records—a recording of *Manon Lescaut*—and after Shenna had set up the pose she put the first disc on the stereo and got started on the painting. He proved to be a good model, both interesting to paint and patient in his sitting. She had him sit against a wall, having first pinned up a backcloth of a length of fabric she had recently bought. The design was of sun-flowers; large, bold splashes of color against a blue ground. Against the strong colors and shapes his light brown hair, light blue eyes, and rather pale complexion made an interesting contrast. She felt, in fact, that the boldness of the pattern behind him in some way diminished his rather slight figure even more, but still the effect was good. It was the kind of background that Caspar might have chosen, she realized, and contributed to the kind of effect that he might have tried for.

With the occasional break to allow Kevin to rest, they worked for over three hours, by which time the opera was finished and the painting was progressing well. Shenna, standing back to study the canvas, couldn't escape the fact that, as with her other recent works, it showed Caspar's influence. Apart from the background, it was there in the clean lines of the face, the look in the pale eyes, and the crisp rendition of the white of the shirt.

Kevin left just before five o'clock, having agreed to sit again the following morning. Shenna packed away her materials and relaxed with a bath. When she was out and drying off the telephone rang. She picked up the receiver.

"Hello. . . ?"

Nothing—just the sound of the pips telling her that the call was coming from a public phone booth. And then, with a click the call was disconnected and the dial tone was purring in her ear.

After replacing the receiver he stood unmoving in the phone booth, then picked up the two heavy shopping bags, pushed open the door, and set off for the house. As he drew near it he saw, coming toward him, an old woman walking her dog. He recognized her as Mrs. Medlin, a lonely old woman who lived a little farther along the street and who could be seen out with her dog in all winds and weathers. Now, as she approached, she beamed at him.

"Good evening."

He smiled back. "Hello, Mrs. Medlin."

"Your grandparents still away, are they?" Her ugly little Yorkshire terrier came to sniff at his shoes and he stepped back a pace. He hated dogs almost as much as he hated cats.

"Yes, they're still away," he said.

"And having a good time, are they?"

He nodded. "Yes, they are—if their postcards are anything to go by." He moved toward the gate. "Well, I must get on. These bags are breaking my arms."

"Oh, then I mustn't keep you. Bye-bye."

"Bye."

He opened the gate, went through, and closed it behind him while she passed on along the street. As he walked up the path he looked over to the little arbor where the concrete-winged angel knelt on one knee, face uplifted, bronze sword pointing to the darkening sky. Behind it, the house, with its shuttered upper windows, stood like a ghost with cataracts.

He let himself into the hall and switched on the light. Then, setting down the heavy bags, he scraped up the mail from the mat and went through it. There was nothing there of interest and he tossed it aside on the hall table, picked up the bags again, and carried them upstairs.

He went to a room on the second floor, just above his own. This was to be *their* room, his and Shenna's. It was the best room in the house. When he had set down the bags he took from them several tins of paint. He had chosen the colors carefully, learning her favorite shades from the clothes she wore and various notes he had found in her sketchbook. He set to work.

Next morning, close to ten-thirty, Kevin came over and Shenna resumed the painting, working steadily on it until lunchtime, when she called a halt. Just one more sitting and it would be finished, she said.

After lunch she put her sketchbook and pencils into her beaded bag and set off, walking toward Blackheath village. She might do a little sketching, she thought, and perhaps later wander over to Greenwich Park and have another look at the Arthur Hughes painting.

When she got to the village she saw the familiar figure of Brian Trent emerging from the station. She smiled at him, and he came over and asked if she'd like to go and have coffee somewhere. She said yes and they went to a nearby café, where in the course of their conversation the subject of Jane came up. "Is she all right?" Shenna asked. "She's been missing so many classes lately."

Brian nodded. "I think she's okay—I mean, I don't think she's sick. What *is* the matter with her, though, I don't know. She's acting so strangely. And now that she's missing classes I—well, I feel partly responsible. But it's not my fault. She just expected too much of me. How could she build some great affair out of something that only lasted a couple of weeks?"

Shenna shrugged. "It seems that she has."

"I never made any promises. She just won't see it for what it was—which really wasn't much, I can tell you."

They left the café soon afterward and made their way across the heath to Greenwich Park. There, as they wandered leisurely between the neat, wide patches of green, Shenna said that she wanted to go and look at a painting in the museum. Brian said he'd like to go with her, and they set off back in the direction of the gates. They were just drawing near the museum entrance when Shenna was aware of Brian suddenly faltering in his step and, following the direction of his gaze, she saw Jane coming toward them.

"Christ," Brian muttered, "this is all I need."

At Jane's side walked another girl whom Shenna had seen around the school. They were also heading for the museum, it appeared. As Shenna stopped at Brian's side, Jane—who had clearly seen them—passed by without a glance, all the while talking to her friend. Moments later they had gone into the museum, out of sight.

Looking after them, Brian shook his head. "I bet I haven't heard the last of that," he said.

Putting the museum and Jane behind them, they left the park and headed back to the village, where they parted, and Shenna continued on alone to Elm Court Road. Some minutes later, as she let herself into the flat, she heard her telephone ringing. It was Wesley. He was just calling to say hello, he said, and to see if they could get together for a drink or something. After a brief conversation they agreed to meet the following Wednesday and go to the movies. He would call for her at eight o'clock, he said.

She was later than usual getting to school the next morning, and barely had time to call out a greeting to Harry as she hurried by his desk. Upstairs, she signed the attendance register, got together her life-drawing materials, and made her way to the studio where the model—an overweight, elderly man—was being posed. As she positioned her donkey, she exchanged silent good mornings with the other students, noticing at the same time that Jane was absent again.

When coffee break came around she stopped at Harry's desk in the foyer and he looked up and smiled.

"I wasn't sure if that was really you earlier on," he said, "dashing past as if you were being pursued."

She nodded. "I was so late. How's the arm today?"

"Oh, it's much better." He went on to say that it was causing him no trouble, apart from the inconvenience, and then said, "Oh, I'm forgetting—there's a package here for you."

"A package?"

He bent slightly behind the counter. "It was delivered a little earlier this morning. I was away from the desk for a few minutes and when I got back it was here." He straightened and, one-handed, took up a large, flat, rectangular, brown paper-wrapped package. "Can you take it from me?" he said. "I can't manage it so well with one hand."

"Yes, of course. Sorry . . ." She took the package from him and looked at it. There was nothing on it, apart from her name, printed in felt-tip pen in block capitals. "You don't know who brought it?" she asked.

"No idea. As I said, I was away from the desk when it was left." He paused. "You're not expecting it?"

"Not at all. I've no idea what it is."

He began to clear a space on the counter, but she shook her head. "No, that's okay, Harry, I'll take it upstairs and open it later."

"Aren't you curious?"

"Well, yes, but—"

"*I* am."

She grinned. "Don't worry, I'll let you know what it is."

Upstairs, she put the package on the floor beside her locker and tore off some of the brown paper. Then, exposing part of the object inside, she saw what looked to be the corner of a painted canvas. Why would someone send her a painting? Pulling more of the paper off, she exposed more of the picture and realized that the colors were the green of grass and the gray of what looked to be large, rectangular stones. And then she realized what she was looking at. She froze. It was the Arthur Hughes painting, *Sunday*, that she had seen in the museum.

11

"What's the matter?"

Hearing Caspar's voice, she looked up across the edge of the package and saw him and Brian coming toward her, carrying between them a heavy bag of clay.

"Nothing . . . nothing . . ." She quickly covered up the canvas, all the time aware of their curious eyes upon her. As they drew even with her, she pushed the package into her locker, turned the key, and then straightened, waiting as they walked past. When they had gone she started off toward the stairs. As she reached the foyer, she met Harry going by with a stack of books beneath his unbandaged arm. After a moment's hesitation she said, "Tell me, Harry—that package that came for me this morning—do you have *any* idea who it could be from?"

He shook his head. "I haven't. As I told you, I was away from the office for a little while, and when I got back it was there, leaning against the counter."

"Do you remember seeing anybody hanging around? A stranger?"

"No. Why? Is something wrong?"

"No, I'd just like to know who the guy who brought it is. You didn't see *anyone* who might have brought it?"

"No. But with all the students pouring in here at that hour it's hardly surprising, is it? Nobody would notice just one more. At that time of morning it would be easy for anybody to come in and leave something and—" He stopped and looked more closely into her face. "Why are you so concerned? What's happened?"

"No—it's okay." She forced a smile. "It's nothing. Really, it's nothing."

"It's *something*. I'm not blind." She remained silent and he gave a shrug. "I'm sorry. I don't mean to be nosy. It's just that—well, just let me say one thing: If you're in any kind of trouble, and there's anything I can do—*anything* at *all*—I'd like to help. Believe me."

She smiled. "Thanks, Harry. You're very kind."

"No, not kind. It's just that—well . . ." He shrugged, looked away, and added gruffly, "I don't forget kindness shown to me. Anyway, just remember what I said."

"I'll remember. And thank you."

She left him and moved off toward the cafeteria. There was a line at the counter, as usual, and she got in it behind the other students.

"Yes, miss?"

As the voice got through to her consciousness, she became aware that she had been miles away and that the tall, slim, young canteen assistant, Alan, was smiling expectantly at her from behind the counter. "You were dreaming," he said.

She nodded. "Yes, I guess I was."

When she'd got her coffee she carried it over to the table where Brian sat with Caspar, Hannah, and Margaret. There was still no sign of Jane.

Sitting at the table, she tried to contribute to the light chatter going on around her, but her preoccupation made it difficult. It had been a mistake coming down here, and now all she could do was wait for the remaining few minutes to pass so that she could be alone again. And then, at last, the break was over, and she made her way back upstairs. There, however, instead of continuing on to the life-drawing studio with the others, she went to her locker and took out the package. After relocking the door she turned and made her way down the stairs and across the foyer to the main doors. A moment later she was outside and walking down the steps to the pavement.

When at last she reached the flat and was safely inside she leaned back against the door, closing her eyes and sucking in air. Against her ribs she could feel her heart thumping. After a moment she put the package down on the bed and ripped off the remaining wrapping. Although she knew what was inside, there was still a slim chance that it might be something else. But no, there it was, the Arthur Hughes painting, *Sunday*. She had written in the letter to her mother how much she admired it, how much she would like to own it, and now here it was.

She noticed then that amongst the wrapping paper she had discarded was an envelope. She picked it up and tore it open. Inside was a brief, typewritten note:

My dearest Shenna,

I hope you like your little gift. Quite a surprise, yes? And there are more still to come.

I can't stop for more now as I want to get this off—and also I have to choose carefully my time of delivery. Wouldn't do to give too much away at once, would it? There's a right time for everything and that time isn't just yet. However, as I'm sure you must be wondering about me, I'll tell you something. I'll tell you that I've been a friend of yours for a very long time now—before you ever came to England. Do you remember John Cosgray who used to write to you? That's right. You guessed it.

That's all I have time for now. So, till next time . . .

With love,
Your friend,
John

John Cosgray. Yes, she remembered the name from the past, and as she searched her memory she remembered also how he had begged her to write—and how she had torn up his letter. . . .

Picking up the telephone directory covering the letter *C*, she searched for his name. There were no Cosgrays listed at all.

She sank down on the carpet and leaned against the bed.

Then, drawing the painting toward her, she noticed that its wooden stretcher was new and that the edge of the canvas was freshly cut. Cut out of its frame as it hung in the museum?

She propped the painting up against the table leg, lay down on the bed, drew up her knees, and hugged herself. She didn't know what to do. Should she take the painting to the police and tell them what had happened? But such an act would bring to her all the publicity she had so far carefully managed to avoid, and right now she needed all the peace she could get. Then what? All she knew was that she wanted the painting gone.

After a while she left the flat and went to Lee Green, where she bought two national newspapers. Then, returning home, she sat on the bed and searched the pages for a report of the painting's theft. She could find nothing. But perhaps the robbery was not deemed important enough to warrant coverage in a national paper—and anyway, even if it was, it might well have been in the edition of some previous day; she had no idea when the painting had been stolen. She tossed the papers aside. What did it matter whether or not the theft had been reported? Its acknowledgment in a newspaper wasn't going to alter anything. The important fact was that the picture was in her possession.

After sitting there for almost an hour she got up, tore up the brown wrapping paper that bore her name, and carefully wrapped the picture in the newspapers she had just bought. That done, she sealed the package securely with scotch tape and put it in the closet. Looking at her watch, she saw that it was only eleven-twenty. She didn't feel like going back to class, but she couldn't think of anything else to do. She couldn't stay in the flat; shut up here she'd go crazy. After a while she got her things together and let herself out.

When she got to the school she went up to the studio, where the life-drawing class was still in progress. She moved to her abandoned donkey and got back to her drawing. As she began work, James Trandell, the tutor, came to her and murmured, "Everything all right, Shenna?" and she nodded and replied quietly, "Yes, thanks, James."

After lunch, she found the time dragging so much that she thought the afternoon would never come to an end. After tea break there was the art history lecture to attend, but at last it was over and she could make her escape. When she got back to the flat she took the package from the closet. She still had no idea how she was going to get rid of it. She needed someone to tell her what to do. If Ian were there, he would have the answer. He was not, however, and he might never be again. The problem was one she'd have to solve on her own.

After she had sat there for almost two hours she got up and put the painting back in the closet.

She went through the next day's classes only half occupied with her work, and as soon as she was free, she returned to the flat. Then, when darkness had fallen, she took the painting from the closet, hurried out to the car with it and drove away.

She headed for the Lewisham area, where, after driving around for twenty minutes or so, her attention focused on an empty telephone booth. She parked close by in a side street and turned off the motor, then took a large pair of glasses from her bag and put them on. That done, she picked up the package and got out onto the sidewalk.

Turning the corner onto the main street, she hurried toward the telephone booth, went inside, stood the package on the floor, and picked up the receiver. She stood there for seemingly endless seconds with the receiver to her ear, trying to give the impression that she was making a call, while all the time she watched to see if anyone approached. Then, just as she was about to replace the receiver and leave the booth, she saw a woman appear around the corner, walk toward the booth, and come to a stop outside. Shenna could feel the sweat damp on her palms. She couldn't leave the package now. After a moment she replaced the receiver, picked up the package, and stepped outside. A minute later she was back in the car, her nerve gone, and heading back to Elm Court Road.

She entered the house just as Kevin emerged from his flat. Coming face to face with him so suddenly, she started violently and clutched the package more tightly to her. He grinned apologetically. "Sorry," he said, "I didn't mean to make you jump." Then, gesturing to the package, he added, "More paintings?"

She gaped at him. "What?"

He gestured again. "More paintings, I said. From California, I mean."

"Mmm? Oh—no. *No.*" She could feel the desperation in the smile she gave him as she wrapped her arms even more closely about the package. For a moment she was aware of him looking from the package to her face, and then she was stepping past him, wishing him good night, and going into the flat.

Throughout the next day thoughts of the painting continued to prey on her mind. She remembered that she'd be meeting Wesley that evening, but she had no idea how she was going to sit through a movie with him, knowing that the painting was still in her possession.

When the art history lecture ended at six-thirty she hurried back to the flat, where she took a shower, dressed, ate a sandwich, and then sat waiting for Wesley. The time crawled by. All of a sudden she could stand the waiting no longer, and she got up, went to the closet, took out the package, and ran from the flat.

Stepping from the front door, she almost collided with Wesley, and came to an abrupt stop before him. It was like her meeting the day before with Kevin. For a couple of seconds she stood staring at Wesley while she grasped the package tighter in her hands, feeling so guilty that she could almost sense the blood rushing to her cheeks. And then she was pushing past him and hurrying across the sidewalk to her car. Moments later she was driving away along the street.

As she slowed to take the corner she looked over her shoulder and saw Wesley standing on the sidewalk, looking after her.

It was a long time before she finally got up the courage to carry out her plan, but then at last, after driving through unfamiliar streets in strange, distant areas, she stopped the car, put on her dark glasses, and, with the package under her arm, got out and went into a telephone booth. There, as before, she placed the package on the floor and went through the motions of making a call. After only seconds, she was putting down the receiver and stepping out onto the sidewalk again. A minute later she was back behind the wheel of the car and driving away.

It was after eleven when she got back to the flat, and as she entered she found a note that had been pushed through her mail slot. It was from Wesley. In blue felt-tip he had written: *I am concerned about you. I waited for you to come back till 9:30 and then gave up. Are you all right? Or is it something I've done? I'll be at the portrait class tomorrow if you decide to go. Yours, Wesley.*

She sat on the bed. Then, after long, agonizing moments of indecision she looked up the local police station in the telephone directory and, with her hands trembling, dialed the number. A woman answered.

Doing her best to hide her American accent, Shenna began by saying, "There is a painting—it was taken from the museum in Greenwich Park. . . ." Her heart was beating hard and her palms were wet. "It's a painting by Arthur Hughes. It's called *Sunday.* . . ."

On the other end of the line the woman's voice was calm and measured as she said, "Could you give me your name, please, miss." Shenna ignored the question. "The painting," she said in the assumed, clipped accent, "it's in a—it's in a telephone booth, in Streatham—at the corner of Marchmont Road and Oakdale Terrace." She repeated the names of the streets and then asked, "Have you got that?"

"Could you give me your name, please," the woman said again, but Shenna wordlessly shook her head and replaced the receiver.

Afterward she began to shake.

He kept seeing her face. There had been such anguish there—and he was the cause of it.

He got up from the table and began to pace the room. He thought back to how he had got the painting; how he had walked into the museum and, unobserved, cut the canvas from its stretcher and walked out with it. The old man in the chair had barely looked up as he had gone past, and certainly hadn't looked at him long enough to gain any reliable memory of him. But even if he had, it wouldn't have mattered. No one would have recognized him wearing the false beard and wig, and the old coat. It had all worked perfectly, much more smoothly than he had ever dared hope.

Now, though, it was all spoiled. All his efforts, all the risks he had taken—they had all gone for nothing. In the letter to her mother she had said how much she would like to own the painting, and he had believed that in giving it to her he would make her happy. Instead he had made her miserable. All he had thought of was getting the picture for her. He hadn't realized what such an action might do. He put his head in his hands and sighed. How could he have been so stupid?

After a while he closed the diary again and sat thinking over it all. He would make it up to her somehow. Some chance would present itself. And when that chance came he would make sure he did right. He wouldn't make another mistake.

And then another thought came to him. With the painting,

as with the theater and ballet tickets, she knew it had come from him. And perhaps that was a mistake, too. Yes. If he should do anything else, then perhaps he should do it without her knowing that he was responsible—and then he could choose whether or not to tell her.

Harry wasn't at his desk when she went by first thing the next morning, but at lunchtime, when she went through the foyer, she saw that he was back. She went over to him and he lifted his arm to show that the sling and the bandage were gone. "I was at the hospital this morning," he said. "They took the stitches out."

"Oh, poor Harry. How does it feel now?"

"Fine. It's left quite a scar—but I'm told it'll fade in time." He started to pull back his sleeve. "You want to see it?"

She shook her head and shuddered. "No, no—please. It's bad enough hearing about it."

When he laughed she couldn't join in.

As the time went by, though, she found to her great relief that she was beginning to feel safer and calmer. She had gone through three days of fear, but now the worst of it was over and she could think about her work again. And the feeling of security grew, the only dark spot in the day coming from Jane and the sneering look she threw at her when they passed one another during the lunch hour. Shenna shrugged it aside. It was nothing to the torment she'd just gone through.

It being Thursday, there was a portrait class in the late evening. Shenna had no intention of attending it, though; she'd just wait around for Wesley to show up, apologize to him for last night, and then go on home.

Later, in the break before the portrait class, she went out to a newsstand and bought an evening paper. Back at the college, she looked through it. And there on page three she found what she was looking for. Under the heading STOLEN PAINTING RETURNED, she read:

The stolen painting entitled *Sunday*, by Victorian artist Arthur Hughes, has been recovered, police say. The painting was stolen some time during last Saturday, October 30, from the Chivers Collection in the Greenwich Park Museum, when the canvas was cut from its stretcher and removed. There were no witnesses and apparently local police had no leads, but then yesterday evening an anonymous phone call from a woman informed police where the picture might be found. The painting was subsequently recovered from a telephone kiosk in South West London. The painting, it is understood, is somewhat damaged and experts are to examine it to determine what can be done to effect its restoration.

Shenna read the piece through once again, then folded the paper and thrust it aside. And, please God, that would be an end to it.

In the foyer she sat on a bench near the door, waiting while the students moved back and forth. She had no idea what excuse she was going to give Wesley for her behavior. She certainly couldn't tell him about the painting. In the end she realized there was nothing she could do but simply apologize and leave it at that.

As she sat there, Brian and Colin came by on their way to the bar and stopped to ask her what she was doing. She replied that she was waiting for a friend to show up. As she spoke, she glanced over to her right and saw Jane standing just a few feet away.

Jane gave a brittle little laugh as she looked from Shenna to Brian. "It makes a charming scene," she said. "If I had the time and the interest I'd try to capture it for posterity."

At Shenna's side, Brian colored. "Okay, Jane, knock it off," he muttered. "It's unnecessary."

Jane merely smiled contemptuously. "I knew all along there was something going on between you two. Not that I care much anymore." With her last words, she turned away and went out to the street. Brian looked after her with a shake of his head, then said, turning back to Colin, "Come on—let's go."

Soon after they had gone Shenna saw Wesley enter by the main door. As he came to her side, she smiled hesitantly at him and said, "Are you in a hurry to go to class?"

"I gather from that that you're not coming."

"I've decided not to, but to go on back home instead. But first I thought we might have a drink together for ten minutes—if you can spare the time."

He nodded. "Fine. It won't matter if I'm a bit late for class."

In the bar she bought a shandy for herself and a Coke for Wesley. Looking through the crowd, she could see Brian and Colin over on the far side talking to other students, and she led Wesley to a small table on the opposite side. When they were seated she told him how sorry she was for what had happened the previous evening. He shrugged. "I just couldn't make out what was going on."

"No, of course you couldn't. And I'm afraid I can't go into it right now. But please—just accept that I was doing something I had to do. I'm only sorry it ruined your evening."

"Doesn't matter about that. Of course I was disappointed, but more than that I was concerned. I don't mind telling you that you had me worried—seeing you like that. Still, as long as you're okay now."

"Yes, I am. And thank you."

"For what?"

"For not asking a load of questions—and for being understanding."

He shook his head. "I haven't done anything." He fell silent for a moment, then he said, "Anyway, I might as well tell you—well, that you're—you're very important to me."

Shenna didn't know what to say, and then suddenly a voice cut in sharply behind her, saying, "Well, if she's important to you, just join the queue."

Shenna turned briefly in astonishment at Jane's words, then said to Wesley in a low voice, "Take no notice. Ignore it."

"Yes, ignore it," Jane said. "Is that the way you cope with all your difficulties?"

Shenna turned to her again. "Jane," she said, "would you mind telling me what I've done to upset you? It's a mystery to me."

"A mystery! Hah!" Jane shook her head. "You're pathetic, you really are. You put on that innocent-little-girl act and expect everybody to be taken in. But it doesn't always work, I'm afraid."

"Fine—so now you've got that off your chest, would you mind leaving us alone? We're trying to have a quiet drink, and if it's all the same to you we'd like to do it without your paranoid ravings."

"I don't have to take that bullshit from you," Jane hissed at her. "So don't talk to me like that."

"Jane," Shenna's tone sounded infinitely patient, "I don't want to talk to you at *all*. So please go away and leave us alone." Then, turning back to Wesley as he sat tense and pale, she said, "Would you like another drink? I'm going to have one."

He answered hesitantly. "Yes, okay." He got to his feet. "I'll get them. The same as before?"

"Thank you." Another drink was the last thing Shenna wanted, but the ritual helped in her pretense of calm. She watched Wesley move toward the bar, pushing a way through the throng, and all the while she could feel Jane's eyes boring into her skull. Then Jane spoke again, placing her hands on the table and leaning forward.

"I had something good going with Brian," she said bitterly, "until you did your little bit to ruin it."

"Jane, I didn't ruin anything," Shenna said. "This is something you've built up in your own mind. It has no basis in truth, so why don't you accept that? What is it you want from me?"

Jane laughed. "From *you?* What do I want from *you?* Christ, you must be joking." She turned and said laughingly to no one in particular, "What do I want from her? she asks." She shook her head pityingly. "Jesus."

Shenna forced herself to remain calm. "Jane," she said, "I'm not standing in your way with Brian. As far as I'm concerned, you can have him."

"Now that you've finished with him, you mean? No, thanks. I don't want your rejects."

Shenna got to her feet and shook her head. "Are you going to keep this up? Because I don't mind telling you I'm getting tired of it all."

"Yes? Well, that's too bad about you." Jane smiled, a hard, thin smile, without a touch of humor. "You think because you've done a few films and have made something of a name for yourself it entitles you to do whatever you want. Well, I've got news for you. It doesn't. You come over here and try to take over. I'm sorry, but we do things differently here."

Shenna became aware suddenly that all around them a hush had descended. Then Wesley was at her side, holding the drinks. As he held out Shenna's glass, Jane said to her, "Oh, you want your drink, do you?" And snatching the glass from Wesley's hand, she threw its contents in Shenna's face.

12

Shenna was so shocked that for a moment she found herself gasping for breath, and then, as she recovered, she became aware that the room was deathly silent and that every eye in the place was focused on herself and Jane. As she stood there with her face the color of chalk and the liquid from the glass running down her face and dripping onto her sweater, she saw Jane turn and, with a sob, rush from the room. A second later she felt a touch on her elbow and she turned to see the young canteen worker, Alan, standing there with a towel in his hand.

"Here . . ."

He held the towel out to her, and she took it from him and touched it to her face while she nodded her thanks; she was unable to trust herself to speak.

"Are you all right?" he asked her and she nodded again.

Frowning, he gazed off in the direction Jane had taken, then turned back to look concernedly into Shenna's eyes. "That was a terrible thing to do," he said.

Shenna dabbed feebly at the front of her sweater and handed the towel back to him. Looking to her right, she saw Wesley standing motionless, shocked and pale-faced, and as her eyes met his he stepped closer and she noticed that his eyes were shining, as if he himself was on the verge of tears. Then, before the remains of her control vanished, she brushed aside his hand and, with the curious spectators breaking aside for her, hurried from the room.

At the foot of the stairs she stood floundering, as if not knowing what to do, while surprised eyes stared in her direction. She turned from them, vaguely aware as she did so of

Caspar's voice calling to her. She took no notice, but ran to the door and dashed outside.

Wesley caught up with her at the end of the street and she slowed her pace. They walked in silence. When they got to the house he followed her into the hall, where she squeezed his arm and said, "I won't ask you in if you don't mind, Wesley. I think I just want to be on my own." She spoke stiffly, afraid of losing control.

"Are you sure? Is there anything I can do?"

"No, really, thanks. I'll be okay."

He sighed. "I feel so useless. And back there in the bar—I just stood there like a stump."

"You couldn't have done anything."

"Even so . . ."

"Anyway, it's done—and I've no doubt I'll survive." She smiled weakly. "Thank you for walking back with me. I'm afraid your portrait class is half over now."

He shrugged. "It's not the same without you, anyway."

Awkwardly, she fumbled in her bag for her keys, head bent, avoiding his glance.

"Listen," he went on, "don't let her upset you. She's not worth it." She didn't answer and he added, "I can't leave you like this."

"Please. I'll be better on my own."

"Are you sure?"

"Yes. It's not only her, anyway, Jane. There are other things. Sometimes—you know how it is—things just get too much and just—get you down."

"Yes." He nodded reluctantly and moved to the front door. "Well—good night. . . ."

"Good night, Wesley, and thanks again."

"Good night."

He left then, backing hesitantly out onto the path, and she heard the sound of his footsteps as he walked to the front gate. Then, bending her head, she once again fumbled in her bag for her door key. The tears suddenly welled up in her eyes, blinding her in her search; tears so long kept back, now spilling over and running down her cheeks, and she leaned against the door and sobbed.

When she lifted her head a moment later she became aware that Kevin was standing in the open doorway of his flat. She jumped, startled. "Kevin!" she moaned, "what are you trying to do? Give me a seizure?"

"I'm sorry." He came toward her. "I heard voices and I—I looked out and saw you crying." He peered closely at her and she turned her face away. "What's happened?" he said.

"What's happened?" she said. "What's happened is that I can't find my damn key." She wiped a hand across her eyes. "And I'm making a lot of fuss about nothing." And then her door key was in her hand and she was fumbling, all thumbs, at the lock. He watched her for a moment, then reached out, took the key, inserted it in the lock, and opened the door.

"Thank you." She pushed past him into the flat and he followed her in and closed the door.

Dropping her bag on the carpet, she sank into the easy chair, put her head on her arm, and wept. He stood gazing down at her. "Don't," he said. "Please, Shenna, don't cry." He stepped forward, bent to his knees, and awkwardly put an arm around her. She continued to sit there sobbing, the tears streaming down her cheeks.

It was only after some minutes that she was calm enough to tell him what had happened, and when she had finished he nodded and said, "I remember her—Jane. I remember how she came round here to your flat upsetting you." He looked at her for a moment longer, with anger in his eyes, then got up and turned away. "I'll make some tea," he said, moving to the kitchen.

When she lay in bed later she realized how alone the incident had made her feel. She needed someone *close* to turn to at a time like this. What had happened to Ian? He had been gone almost two weeks now and there had been no word from him.

The diary was open, and in it he wrote the date, *Thursday, November 4th*. Afterward he sat there for some minutes, his pen in his hand. Then he wrote:

I couldn't bear it—to see the anguish, the hurt in her face. The look of her stays with me—and I never loved her more than when I saw her there, so vulnerable. That girl isn't fit to clean her shoes.

It was after midnight when Jane left the Friday night disco. She could smell in the air the scent of dozens of bonfires and the faintly acrid smell of fireworks. Of course, tonight, the fifth, was Guy Fawkes night. Not that the night's festivities would have been noticed beneath the pulsating music and flashing lights of the disco. She walked on. The night was warm and she stepped out smartly, keeping to the curb edge of the pavement, as far away as possible from the shadowed doorways. She could still hear the music of the last record she had danced to, the sounds going round in her mind. She had left her friends, Julie and Cass, still there. It was a long way home, but she'd pick up a taxi without too much trouble, she was sure. She didn't mind going alone. Besides, the one person she would have liked to accompany her—the biology student, David Marshall—was already tied up for the evening.

She thought of his face as he had looked at her in the flickering strobe lights. The quick, careful looks he had given her—and often over the head of the girl he was with, the blond student from Humanities. From those looks and the odd whispered words, Jane knew that she would soon meet him again.

She kept seeing his face as she walked; it gave her a glow,

and she hugged the feeling to her and looked forward to Monday. It was what she needed, to meet someone else; that was the only way to exorcise Brian. It was a pity she had planned to go away with her parents tomorrow; otherwise she might have arranged something with David for the weekend. But it was too late now to cancel her arrangements, and he would still be there on Monday.

There was hardly anyone about now. At the end of Carmer Street she crossed over and turned left onto Wilton. It was darker here, and some of the street lamps weren't functioning. She quickened her step.

She had just turned from Wilton Street onto the road that fringed the housing development when she heard the sound of footsteps behind her. She felt suddenly afraid.

And then, all at once, the footsteps were right there.

Even as she whirled to face her pursuer, he struck. She hardly had time to cry out, the sound abruptly breaking off in her throat as the heavy, metal object smashed down onto her skull. "*Bitch*," he muttered, the word a breath through his drawn-back lips. She staggered under the blow, stunned, one arm lifting weakly for protection and waving drunkenly in the air. It didn't help her. "Bitch . . . *bitch* . . ." The second blow smashed the bone of her forearm so that it hung useless at her side, and she staggered again, blindly, bumping against him. Roughly he pushed her away and brought down the weapon again. This time her knees gave way, buckling under her weight, all her strength gone. The next blow that crashed down on her skull shattered the bone, and she fell to the ground. Seconds later, when he stood over her prone body to deliver a final, smashing blow to the back of her broken head, she was already dead.

Standing before the mirror, he looked at himself. He was spattered with blood—his face, his hands, his clothes. Thank God no one had seen him; he felt reasonably sure that no one had. At his temple the tic began; he could see and feel it—a light pounding just beneath the skin. He put up a blood-stained hand and felt the rhythmic beating against his finger-tip.

When he was out of his clothes he washed himself. In the morning he would burn the clothing. No one would ever know.

Later, in his dressing gown, he sat down at the table, pulled the diary toward him, and began to write.

The early hours of
Saturday, November 6th

It's done. And I find that my hand is still shaking a little—and I don't think it's from fear. I think it's the excitement. I feel a great sense of achievement. I would love to go to her now and say I did this for you, but I can't, of course. Who knows?—perhaps she will never know. Perhaps I will never tell her. Perhaps this is to be one of those secrets that I must keep with me forever—even when we are together. But then I tell myself that when that time comes—the time of our being together—there will be no secrets between us. We shall know everything there is to know about one another. And the more we learn of one another, then the stronger and deeper our love will grow. Until that time comes I shall continue to do everything in my power to make her happy.

I shall sleep well tonight. I've taken a great step forward. There can be no looking back now—not after this. Something as momentous as this can only bind us more strongly together.

13

Jane Baxter's body was found in the early hours of the morning. The evening papers carried reports of the killing and the popular Sunday papers next day made all they could of it. There was nothing quite as good for selling newspapers as a sensational report of the brutal murder of a pretty young girl.

With the discovery of Jane's empty purse farther along the street, it seemed fairly certain that robbery was behind the killing. Nevertheless, the police searched for other motives and, in their pursuit, came to the college to talk to the dead girl's classmates. There, in a room on the first floor, over the following week they spent many hours interviewing various students as to their relationships with her and their movements at the time of her death. Among those questioned at length was Brian Trent, who stated that at the time of the killing he had been alone in his room. Without any discernible motive for his involvement, though, he was eventually eliminated from the investigation, and the police found themselves settling for their original reasoning—that Jane had been struck down simply for the few pounds she had carried in her purse.

The murder seemed to cast a shadow over the school, and in the strange hush that descended on the place Shenna was miserable, depressed, and uneasy. Apart from her natural unhappiness over Jane's ugly death, it was one more dreadful happening in a series of dreadful happenings. There had been the injury to Harry—also by some unknown attacker—and then the business of the painting, and now this terrible thing. And though she didn't consider that the incidents had any connection with each other, she was aware that in one way or another she had some connection with each one. It was a disturbing realization and she tried to put it out of her mind.

She had other problems, too. From early Monday morning, while the police were inside asking their questions, reporters were there also, trying to get what information they could from anyone who looked in any way promising. Drawn also by the knowledge that Shenna Preston was one of the students there and, furthermore, by the news that she and Jane had been at the center of an angry scene shortly before the girl's death, the copy was even more promising. The reporters hung patiently around the school entrance, hoping to catch Shenna as she entered or left the building, and for several days she was forced to run the gauntlet of their questions as she hurried past. She never spoke to them, though, and in the end they gave up, but not before they had made as much as they could of it all in their reports.

On Tuesday evening her mother telephoned, and it was clear at once just from the way she said, "*Shenna?*" that she had read of the murder.

"Mom," Shenna said, "I was going to call you."

"My God, what's happening there? Are you all right?"

"Yes, of course I am."

"That terrible murder. It's even in the American papers."

Shenna spent the next few minutes trying to reassure her mother that she herself was fine and in no danger, but by the time the conversation came to an end Doris didn't sound any closer to being convinced.

Ian phoned ten minutes later.

Hearing his voice, Shenna felt such a feeling of relief that she thought for a second that she might burst into tears. She wanted to cry out to him but a constraint born of his long silence stayed her, and after a moment she simply said, softly, "Hello, Ian." Then, "I thought you'd forgotten all about me."

"What's this?" he said. "Reproaches straightaway?"

"What?—oh, no, of course not. It's just that you took me by surprise. I wasn't expecting to hear from you."

"Listen," he said, "I said I'd write to you, and I haven't, I know. I'm sorry. I don't blame you for being angry."

"I didn't say I was angry, Ian."

He paused. "Listen, I've been reading in the papers about the murder. The student at your college. What an awful thing."

"Yes."

"I had to call you. How are you coping with it all? Are the newspapers giving you a hard time?"

"Oh . . . I'm managing okay."

"Good."

There was a softness in his voice, and it destroyed her defenses. She found herself saying, "It's good to hear your voice, Ian. I've missed you. You can't imagine how much."

"Ah, Shenna, I've missed you, too."

"Really?"

"Really."

She was silent for a moment, then she said, "At a time like this—I really wanted you here with me." She paused. "Will you be coming back in a couple of weeks, as you said you would be?" Then the silence was back, and she said into it, "Ian? Are you still there?"

"Yes, I'm here."

"I thought for a minute we'd been cut off."

"No, no." He paused. "Listen—about my coming back at the end of the month . . ."

He was about to tell her something she didn't want to hear. "Yes?" she said.

"I think it's going to be a little difficult for me to get back just yet. Well—*very* difficult, I should say."

"I—I see."

"I'm sorry, Shenna, really I am. But I'm up to my eyes in it here and I just know I'm not going to be able to get away. We've got new accounts coming in, and what with the few teething troubles we're having—well, this would be a bad time for me to leave."

"I see."

"I hope you understand."

"Of course, yes. . ."

"But, naturally, if I find I can get away, then I'll let you know at once, all right?"

"Yes."

"Try not to be too disappointed, okay?"

"Yes." A pause. "When *do* you think you'll be coming back?"

When he spoke she could hear in his voice the faintest note of irritation, and she felt suddenly cold. "Oh, Shenna, please," he said, "don't pin me down, sweetheart. I don't know yet when I can make it. But as soon as I've got a date, I'll tell you. And I'm afraid we're going to have to leave it like that. Okay?"

"Yes, all right."

"Okay?"

"Yes, I said, yes."

"Good. You do understand, don't you?"

"I think so, Ian."

"You *think* so?"

"Yes, I understand . . ."

"Are you all right?"

"Yes, I'm fine."

"Okay." He sounded slightly awkward and at the same time a little relieved. "Well, I'll be in touch soon then. . . ."

"Fine."

For another thirty seconds they spoke in platitudes, and

then the conversation came to an end and she replaced the receiver.

The inquest on Jane's death brought in a verdict of MURDER BY PERSON OR PERSONS UNKNOWN. The funeral that followed brought a change in the atmosphere among the students and staff; it seemed to bring, with its finality, a sense of freedom from the subduing constrictions of the tragedy, and although the police seemed no closer to finding the killer, things began to get back to normal and the school relaxed again.

Almost two weeks after the funeral Shenna, seeing the date—November 25—suddenly realized it was her mother's birthday. She had forgotten all about it; she hadn't even sent a card. When she got back to the flat she rang the Westwood number, hoping to catch her mother as she began work for the day, but there was no reply. She tried at intervals throughout the rest of the evening, but still there was no answer. When she got up the next morning she tried again. Still no answer. She began to be concerned, and her concern grew with the passing time.

The thought that some harm had befallen her mother took root and grew stronger as the morning progressed, and she determined that if there was still no answer when she called that evening, she would telephone the Westwood police and ask them to drive to the house and check that everything was all right.

She was at work painting later that afternoon when a message was relayed that she had a visitor waiting in the foyer. Shenna hesitated as she moved to the door, a little uncertain in case the visitor should be someone from the press. When she got to the foyer she came to an abrupt stop. Then she said, "Mom—for God's sake, what are you doing here?"

Doris came toward her. "What am I doing here?" She gave a nod. "That's nice. Whatever happened to 'Welcome'?"

*　　*　　*

In the flat Shenna put on the water for coffee while her mother sat in the easy chair and looked around her, unimpressed. "So this is it," Doris said, "where you live."

"That's right." As Shenna followed her mother's gaze around the room, she began to wonder what she herself had ever seen in the place.

"Yes," Doris said, "it's very nice."

"Well, I know it's small, but—"

"Yes, it is."

"Still, it suits me all right."

"Well, that's the main thing, isn't it?" Doris turned from her survey of the room and smiled at Shenna. "Anyway, I didn't come six thousand miles to see your apartment, I came here to see *you*." She sighed. "I can still hardly believe I'm here."

Shenna felt the same way. After the initial shock of finding Doris in the foyer of the school she had gone back to her class and told the instructor of her mother's unexpected arrival. Afterward she had brought her to the flat.

Now, withdrawing her hand, Shenna said, "I'm sorry I seemed so unwelcoming back there, but that was quite a jolt you gave me. You were the last person I expected to see. Not to mention the fact that I've been trying to call you—and not getting any answer. I was worried sick." She shook her head. "And all the time you were on your way here."

Doris smiled. "That's right."

On their walk to the flat Doris had told her that she had arrived just that morning and had checked into a hotel near Marble Arch in the West End. Now, watching Shenna's face, she asked, "Are you pleased to see me?"

"Oh, Mom, of course I am. It just came as one hell of a shock."

"Yes, I guess it must have. But I just felt I had to come.

All that terrible business about that poor young girl and everything. . . ."

"Yes, poor Jane—but I don't understand why you felt you had to come here. I mean, it was an awful thing. Terrible. But it's over, and *I'm* not in any danger."

"Maybe not," Doris said disbelievingly, "but there are other things apart from your being in danger. I mean, what about all that coverage you were getting in the papers? I knew how upset you must be, how unhappy about it all, and—well, I just thought you might need me. I know it sounds corny, but people need friends. And that doesn't exclude mothers and their daughters."

"No, of course not. But I'm fine, Mom, I really am. I'm glad to see you—but why didn't you call me first? Tell me what you had in mind?"

Doris hesitated before answering, then she said, "And if I had, what would you have done? You'd have stopped me coming, and I was set on it. Anyway," she added, "I thought I'd surprise you."

"Yes, well, you sure did that. But if you'd told me we could have—arranged it a little better, you know?"

Doris frowned. "No, I don't know. Arranged what? What's to arrange?"

Shenna shrugged. "I guess what I'm trying to say is—it's just a shame you didn't time your trip for a little later."

Doris stiffened slightly. "Look," she said, "let's get one thing straight—I'm not about to be in anybody's way. If you want me to leave, I'll leave. Just say the word."

"No, no, of course not. Don't be silly." Shenna reached out and grasped her hand. "Come on, Mom. I'm not saying that, and you know it. What I mean is—well, right now I'm trying to get my paintings ready for my exhibition, and in a couple of months it'll all be done—it has to be—and after that time I'll be able to relax a little and take things easier. Until then, though, I'm not going to be much fun, I'm afraid. I'm going to be very busy. That's all I'm trying to say."

"I see." Doris nodded. "Anyway, don't worry about it. You get your paintings done or whatever. I'm not in any hurry to get back."

"How long are you staying for?"

"I just *said*—I'm not in any hurry to get back." Doris was silent for a moment while Shenna stared at her, then she said brightly, "As a matter of fact, I've closed up the house."

"You've what? What do you mean?"

"I mean that I've put the valuables in storage for safekeeping, and that the whole place is shut up for the winter."

"But—" Shenna shook her head. "I don't understand."

"What's so difficult to understand?" Doris smiled. "You know, you're not the only one who needs a change of scene. And I decided that was exactly what I needed. So—here I am. I plan to stay a little while. Maybe into the spring. I hear the spring in England is a lovely time."

Shenna said lamely, "But your students—what about them?"

"What *about* them? I put them off. Maybe they'll be there when I get back, and maybe they won't. Tell you the truth, I don't really care."

Shenna could feel something like panic rising within her. "When did you decide on all this?" she said. "How did you arrange it all so quickly?"

"Oh, it wasn't so quick. Sorting things out at the house and putting them in storage—that took a while."

"Then you've been working on it for some time."

"Well, yes, you could say that. Now listen, don't worry—the house is perfectly secure. No harm will come to it, I promise you."

"Mom," Shenna said, "I just wish you'd told me you planned to do all this. Don't you think it would have been smarter to have let me in on it?"

Doris didn't answer for a moment, then she sighed and said, "I already explained that to you." She paused. "This attitude of yours, Shenna—it's not at all what I hoped it would be. I wasn't quite sure what to expect—knowing you—but whatever it was I certainly didn't reckon on sitting here and getting the third degree."

"Oh, Mom, I'm sorry, but you're throwing one surprise at me after another. How else do you expect me to react? I just don't understand what's going on. First you arrive out of the blue and now you tell me you're planning to stay over here till next spring. What are you going to *do* while you're here?"

"Do? I'm not going to do anything—except take it easy maybe. Try to enjoy myself."

"But where will you stay?" Shenna moved a hand, taking in the room. "As you can see, there isn't room here for the two of us."

"I already told you, I'm not about to be in your way, so don't be afraid of that."

"Well, where will you stay? In your hotel? You hate hotels. You always have. And anyway, it'll cost you a fortune."

"Don't worry. I don't intend staying at the hotel. I've got other plans."

"Oh?"

Doris looked at her for a few moments, then reached into her bag and brought out a key, which she laid on the table.

"What's that for?"

"It's the key to a little place I've found in the country."

Shenna looked at her, bewildered. "To a little place you've . . . Mom, what are you talking about?"

"I've taken a little furnished house in a village in Kent called Hallowridge. A very small place—near a town called Sevenoaks. Do you know it?"

"No." Shenna shook her head.

"It seems to be very nice, the village, going by what I was

told by the agents. And the house, too—the cottage—it sounds charming. It's on the edge of the village. I move in this weekend. Tomorrow if I can. I've taken it for six months."

Shenna could hardly believe she was hearing correctly. She sat there dumbly for a few moments, then she said, "How did you arrange all this?"

"Oh, it wasn't difficult. And at this time of year you can take your pick of properties."

Shenna nodded. "You've been even busier than I imagined. But I don't understand why you've done it—come here to bury yourself in the country."

Doris clicked her tongue. "I'm not burying myself in the country. The cottage is no distance at all from here. And I'll hire or buy a little car. Oh, it'll be fun; it really will. All these years I've worked so damned hard, putting money aside. And for what purpose? I never went anywhere. So I figured I might as well spend some of it this way. At least I'll be getting something I want."

"*Is* it something you want?"

"Yes. And it's what you want, too, isn't it?"

"*Me?*"

"Don't you remember what you wrote to me—not long after you got here? You wrote you'd like to have a place in the country. Well, that's what I've got for you—for us. A place you can come to at weekends—or during the week as well, if you want. It's certainly close enough for you to commute. I made sure of that. Anyway, it's a place you can relax in—a place where you can bring your friends. A home." She gestured at the room. "Not like this. Oh, Shenna, just think—a little place in the country that'll be all our own." She gave a little laugh of excitement. "I thought maybe tomorrow we could drive out there. What do you think?"

Shenna found herself nodding while her heart sank. With

every word she heard all her newfound freedom and independence were going out the window.

The next morning Shenna received a postcard and a letter in the mail. The postcard was from Ian—the first word from him since his telephone call following Jane's death three weeks before. The picture on the card was a reproduction of a still life by Andrew Wyeth. On the back was written: *Hope to see you very soon. In the meantime don't give up on me. Love, Ian.* She looked at the brief message for a long time. Perhaps, after all, everything was going to be all right. . . . *No, Ian,* she murmured, *I won't give up on you.*

The letter was from her friend Amy Michaels in North Hollywood. It was a long letter that, after all the news and chat, asked Shenna how things were going and told of her own studies and her wish to get back to her acting career.

Shenna wrote a short reply to Amy at once. To Ian, though, she wrote nothing. She could think of nothing to say.

She posted Amy's letter on the way to the Tate Gallery, where she spent some time sketching, after which she went to meet Doris at her hotel.

They went to a nearby restaurant for lunch, and as they ate Doris talked animatedly about the cottage. Shenna, only half listening, wondered how she was going to get out of the situation. She had no wish to go and live with her mother—not even on weekends. It had been difficult enough to gain what freedom she now had; she couldn't give it up so easily—especially not now, when it was beginning to work for her.

As Doris went on speaking brightly of England's attractions and the things they could do together, Shenna's mind turned over the problem before her. She looked at Doris's smile, heard the happy sound in her voice; her mother had got what she wanted, but what about herself?

After a while Doris moved from the subject of the cottage to speak of Jack Tanner, Shenna's agent who, she said, had called two or three times.

"What about?" Shenna asked.

"Oh, this and that. For one thing, he wanted to know whether you had any plans to return soon."

"Well, he knows I haven't."

"Yes. Apparently the producers of *Chain Letter* are hoping you'll help publicize it when it's ready."

Shenna shrugged. "I don't think I'll be in a position to."

"That's what Jack thought."

"What else did he want?"

Doris was silent for a moment, then delving into her bag, she pulled out a paperback, which she laid on the tablecloth. Shenna recognized its title. It was *Bridges Are for Burning*, a current bestseller, the story of an ambitious politician's relationship with a girl many years his junior. "Have you read it?" Doris asked.

"No."

"You should. Really. It's good."

"I don't have much time for reading right now, Mom. Not novels, anyway."

"You should find time for this one."

"Why? What's so special about it?"

"Because it's going to be a big movie, that's why. And don't look like that. It'll be made in the spring, apparently; the screenplay's being written now. According to Jack it's going to be one of the major productions of the year. They're talking really big names for the male lead." She paused. "Jack wants to put you up for the girl. He says you're perfect for it, and he feels sure you've got the best chance of anybody."

Shenna smiled. "You don't give up, Mom, do you? I'm sorry, but you'll just have to tell Jack there's no way I can consider it. I just can't—not with what I've got to do."

Doris sighed. "I told him what I thought your reaction would be. Well, I tried, anyway."

After lunch they drove the few miles out of London to the town of Sevenoaks, and then just beyond it to the small village of Hallowridge. There on its outskirts, in a secluded lane, they came to the cottage Doris had rented. And seeing it, Shenna's spirits fell. She had been hoping it would turn out to be a disappointment—in which case perhaps her mother wouldn't want to stay. Not so. The cottage stood in a well-kept garden, set back among the trees, charming, picturesque, and inviting, and if the interior was anything like the exterior, then it couldn't fail to be a success.

Inside the house she followed her mother from room to room. Built at the turn of the century and unexpectedly spacious, the cottage had been carefully and tastefully modernized, and the furniture in it looked comfortable and cared for and was in keeping with its setting. It must have been everything her mother had hoped for. As Shenna stood there, Doris reached out and took her hand. "Come with me," she said. "There's something else for you to see."

Obediently, Shenna allowed herself to be led back across the hall and into a room on the other side. "This room's for you," Doris said, "for your work." She gestured to the window. "With a north light, look. You see, I remembered how important that is to a painter." She put her arms around Shenna. "I just want you to be happy," she said.

Shenna, held in Doris's embrace, said to herself, She's thought of it all. She's thought of every single thing.

They spent the rest of the afternoon shopping in Sevenoaks, after which Doris got busy in the kitchen, preparing dinner for the two of them. Shenna stayed at the cottage that night, sleeping in the second bedroom, and then in the morning drove Doris to the hotel. After Doris had checked out, Shenna took her back to Hallowridge with her luggage.

When Shenna prepared to leave the cottage after lunch Doris suggested that she bring her easel to the cottage and set it up in the room across the hall. No, Shenna told her, she couldn't consider that yet—not until she had finished her pictures for the exhibition. She was stalling. She knew that once her easel was in the cottage she might just as well move in completely; such action, she was sure, would spell the end of her freedom.

They had no contact the next day, Monday, but on Tuesday evening Doris called to say that the telephone had been connected and to ask when Shenna would be coming back to see her. Hiding her reluctance, Shenna replied that she would be there the next evening.

During class on Wednesday she was reminded that the coming Saturday was the fourth of December, the anniversary of her father's death. Months ago she had decided that when that day came around she would drive out to Hinton Peeble and visit his grave again. And now the time was here. But what about her mother? Should she tell her of her intentions—or would that be the last word in insensitivity? In the end she decided not to mention it.

She had just finished getting ready when Wesley telephoned to ask if she planned to go to the portrait class the following evening. No, she told him, she had too much work to do, in addition to which her mother had arrived unexpectedly from California. She felt guilty where he was concerned; she always seemed to be letting him down. Then, just as the brief conversation was about to come to an end, she thought again of her planned trip to Hinton Peeble and after a moment's hesitation she asked him if he would like to go with her and then go on somewhere for dinner. He said yes at once; he needed no second invitation.

Shenna left the flat soon afterward, reaching the cottage some forty-odd minutes later, where she found the dining table set for dinner and some of her favorite dishes prepared. A little later she sat facing her mother across the table while Doris spoke enthusiastically of the village and of how well she was settling in. She spoke also of what she would do in the coming months, and all the while Shenna heard implicit in her words the understanding that she, Shenna, would be a part of that time. She felt increasingly depressed. With each passing minute it seemed she was becoming more deeply entrenched in a growing problem that already seemed to be insoluble.

While Shenna turned the problem over in her mind, Doris said, "I hope it stays fine over the weekend. I thought maybe we could drive out somewhere. You could show me something of the countryside you were raving about. What do you think?"

Shenna shook her head. "I can't, I'm sorry. I'm already going out."

"Oh." Doris paused. "Somewhere exciting?"

"I'm driving out with a friend of mine."

"I see. It all sounds very mysterious."

Shenna was silent, then after a moment Doris said, "Well, obviously you're not going to tell me."

Shenna had no choice then, and with a shrug, she said, "I wasn't going to mention it, but I'm driving to Hinton Peeble."

Doris looked down at her plate. "Why do you want to go there?"

"*Why?* Mom, it's the anniversary of Dad's death. Have you forgotten?"

"No." Doris spoke sharply. "Of course I haven't forgotten. But what's the purpose of your going there? What d'you hope to gain?"

"It's just something I want to do. I thought you'd understand that."

Doris said nothing. Shenna went on, "I didn't mention it to you earlier because I didn't want to upset you. I've arranged to go there with a friend of mine. We plan to drive on somewhere afterward for dinner. But, listen—why don't you come with us? Would you like to?"

Doris replied in a low voice, "No, thank you."

"Are you sure?" Shenna reached across the table and touched her mother's hand. "I know how you feel, Mom, believe me, I do. But it's been a long, long time. Maybe now you'd feel differently. Think about it, okay?"

Doris shook her head. "I don't need to think about it, Shenna. I don't want to go, and let's leave it at that."

During the rest of the week Shenna resisted her mother's invitations to the cottage, saying that her work commitments wouldn't allow it. When they spoke on Friday evening Shenna asked her again if she would like to go to Hinton Peeble the following day, but still Doris refused, and Shenna didn't press the issue any further. As the call came to an end, Doris asked, "Will I see you on Sunday?"

Shenna hesitated. She had planned to spend Sunday working on her paintings. "Okay," she said, "I'll come on Sunday."

As soon as the shops were open the next morning, Shenna went out and bought some white roses and an earthenware pot to put them in. Then, back in the flat, she had breakfast and got ready for Wesley's arrival. As she waited for him she took the pot from its wrapping of newspaper and brown paper and looked at it. It would look fine on the grave. Pleased with the purchase, she began to wrap it again. And as she did so she saw on one of the pieces of newspaper a photograph that stopped her in her tracks.

The photograph was one of three showing guests at a nightclub party following the opening of a new Broadway musical. Ian was not in the forefront of the picture, but slightly in the background, and wouldn't have been immediately noticeable to just anyone who happened to glance at it. He was shown standing talking to an actress, while to one side of him and holding on to his arm stood the blond girl Shenna had seen him with, and whose photograph was in his apartment. Mary Carroll.

Her eyes moving to the top of the page, Shenna saw that the newspaper was dated two days earlier.

She stared at the photograph for a long time, and as she did so other images came swarming into her mind, scenes from the days she had spent with him, scenes that moved and flickered in her brain like a montage in some badly edited movie.

As she sat there she heard the ringing of the doorbell. Wesley had arrived.

They set off together soon afterward, and after a stop for gas headed for Hammersmith and the M4 motorway.

For the first part of the journey she remained silent until, becoming aware of Wesley looking at her with concern in his eyes, she made a positive effort to break out of the mood and be better company. They made good time, getting to Hinton Peeble at close to three, when, as they got out of the car beside the village green, Wesley said, "Look, you don't want me with you right now. I'll just wander around for a while and look at the place."

She smiled. "Fine. I'll see you back here in half an hour or so, okay?"

"Right."

She remained still for a moment, watching as he moved off along the narrow village street toward the row of shops, then she turned and, carrying the roses and the earthenware pot, made her way in the direction of the church. Her shoes scattering the dead leaves, she moved along beside the old church wall, her coat collar drawn up against the keen wind, all the time seeing in her mind's eye the newspaper photograph. Reaching the gate, she passed through and then paused to look at the scene before her. Now, in winter, it was very different from when she had seen it last in the summer. After a moment she moved on until she came to the grave.

There was something different about the grave, too, she saw at once. When she had been here before it had had an uncared-for, almost abandoned look. Now it bore fresh flowers. Pink roses. She stood there looking down at it for some seconds, then moved away and filled the pot at a tap. Then, back at the graveside, she set the pot in the earth and carefully began to arrange the roses in it. She had just finished when she heard a voice from somewhere behind her.

"Hello."

Turning, she saw a woman standing there, middle-aged and smartly dressed, and gazing at her with curious eyes.

"Hello." Shenna straightened and smiled, and the woman nodded toward the grave and said, "Your roses—they're very pretty."

Shenna nodded.

The woman looked at her steadily. "Did you know him?" she asked.

Shenna, hearing the question echo in her mind, thought of all those times in her past when she would have been too afraid to truthfully answer such a question. Now she was not. The reasons she had had then didn't matter anymore.

"No," she said, "I never knew him. I wish I had." She paused. "He was my father."

And then she saw the woman's expression change and she became suddenly afraid.

14

The light was fading as she moved toward the car. When she got there she found Wesley standing beside it, hunched up against the cold. As she reached his side he said, "I was wondering where you were."

"I'm sorry for keeping you hanging around." She unlocked the car. "I was walking."

"Walking? Where?"

"Oh," she shrugged, "round and about."

They got inside and she sat forward over the wheel, gazing off along the darkening village street. He frowned. "Are you okay?"

She started slightly, as if coming out of a dream. "Yes," she said, then, "Wesley, would you mind very much if we went straight back to London?"

"Now?"

"There's something I have to do. It won't take long, and we can find somewhere to eat afterward. It shouldn't be too late. Would you mind?"

"No, of course not. Where d'you want to go?"

"To Hallowridge—to see my mother."

He peered at her. "Has something happened?"

She hesitated before answering. "Maybe I'll tell you about it sometime. Not now." She inserted the key in the ignition and turned on the motor. "Right now all I want to do is get away."

They drove mostly in silence and when eventually they got to Hallowridge Shenna parked the car outside the front gate of the cottage. "Would you mind waiting here?" she said. "It'll only take a minute."

"Okay."

She got out of the car and went up the path to the front door where, without bothering to search for the key Doris had given her, she rang the bell. Doris opened the door almost at once. "I thought it must be you," she said. "I couldn't think who else it might be." Then she stood aside as Shenna, with nothing more than a nod, stepped past her into the hall.

Doris followed her into the lounge. "I thought you were going to have dinner with one of your friends," she said. "Did you change your mind?"

"We'll be eating later." Shenna, tight-lipped, could hear the coldness in her tone and see it mirrored in her mother's expression.

"Where's your friend now?" Doris asked.

"Outside, waiting in the car."

"Well, bring him in. I've eaten, but I can get something for the two of you."

"No, thanks. We'll go off and find a restaurant in a minute or two."

Doris frowned. "Shenna, are you all right?"

"Do you care?"

Doris gave a little shake of her head. "What does that mean?"

Shenna, feeling her rage growing stronger, kept silent. Doris stared at her. "There's something wrong, isn't there?" she said. "I knew it as soon as I saw you at the door." She paused. "Did you go there—to Hinton Peeble?"

"Yes, I did."

"What's wrong, Shenna? Tell me."

Shenna just stared at her for a second while her anger fused with all her recent hurt and resentment of the past and came boiling to the surface. *"What's wrong?"* she said, almost spitting out the words. "I'll tell you what's wrong. You lied to me, that's what's wrong."

"Lied to you?"

"Yes, *lied*. For years and years. All my life. And today I found out the truth. I met someone today in the cemetery at Hinton Peeble. I wasn't the only one to visit my beloved father's grave on the anniversary of his death. Somebody else had the same idea. There was a woman there. She had traveled from some town nearby. We said hello and—and in a moment of idiocy I told her."

"Told her what?"

"That he was my father."

A brief pause. "Go on."

"I told her. And in return she told *me* a few things. Little things, for instance, like how well she'd known him. And she knew him very well. She ought to." She looked at Doris through narrowed eyes. "Don't you want to know who she was? No? I'll tell you. She was his wife—his widow, I should say."

As she spoke Shenna saw in her mind the woman at the graveside; saw the growing anger and bitterness in her expression as they had faced one another. She heard again the woman's words as, like water bursting through a dam, they had poured out. Horrified, Shenna had asked her, "Why are you telling me all this? Why?"

"*Why?*" And tears had started in the woman's eyes. "Why? Because if he was your father, then for a start you should know a little about him. You should know the truth. You're old enough. The truth—it might do something about that look of blind pride on your face when you speak of him."

"And she told me the truth about him," Shenna said now. "And he wasn't the way you portrayed him all these years. He wasn't that kind, caring man who thought only of you in your state of pregnancy. He wasn't that lovely loving man who couldn't wait for you to join him here. He was a lousy shit who never gave a thought for anybody—least of all for you or your unborn kid."

While Doris stared at her, eyes wide, Shenna went on, her anger unabated, "All these years you let me believe he was some kind of saint. You encouraged me to believe it. Why? Why did you?"

"I thought it was better," Doris answered at last in a low voice. "I thought it was better you had good thoughts about him than the bitterness I've had. Better you believed a lie than know the truth."

"You really believed that?"

"Yes. I still do. If you hadn't met that woman you would have gone on quite happily."

"In my ignorance, right?"

"If you like."

"But I *did* meet her and I heard what she had to say. At first I didn't believe her. It didn't seem possible she was talking about my father. Not my *father*. There had to be a mistake, I thought. No. No mistake." She paused. "You weren't the only one, did you know that?"

Doris shrugged and turned away. Shenna watched her for a moment then went on, "Oh, no, you weren't the only one. There were others—in different places, at different times. You were just one of several. And what happened after you told him you were pregnant? All that crap about your planning to come here to England to join him. He never did send for you, did he? He didn't want to know, did he? That's more like the truth, isn't it? And what about your meeting with him in the first place? What was that in reality? I always imagined I was born out of some wonderful, starry, romantic love affair. What was it in truth? Just some tacky little one-night stand?"

"Please, Shenna, *don't*." Tears welled up in Doris's eyes. "For God's sake, leave me with something."

"Leave you with something? What about *me*? How do you think *I* felt—learning what I did? You knew the truth. . . . I didn't. You brought me up believing he was the most wonderful person who ever lived. My God, I used to write poems about him; I used to copy that photograph of him till I knew every line of his face, every hair on his head. When I dared to I used to boast about him to my friends. You fed me a fantastic fairy story and I believed it." She paused. "And not only that, you used it to get what you wanted."

"Used it? What do you mean?"

"I mean the way you kept me with you all these years. That was all part of it, wasn't it? You knew how I thought of you when I was growing up—when I was becoming aware of things. I saw you as someone who'd had a bad deal from life—a really bad deal. I saw you almost as some tragic heroine, I guess. You were a woman who had loved just once—finding for a while a really great, powerful love in a relationship with a marvelous man—a man who was taken from you by what I thought of as the—the cruelest trick of fate." She paused. "You feel like laughing? It's pretty pathetic, isn't it? But that's the truth. That's how I felt. And with him gone—that wonderful man—that love of your life—you were left alone to raise me—me—the child of that *great union*. And growing up with the knowledge of how you'd loved him I knew what I stood for. I felt that I was all that was left of him—so how could I ever let you down? I couldn't, could I? Never. My God, that was a responsibility I didn't need. I suppose by those means you thought you'd keep me with you forever."

"No," Doris said, "that's not the way it was."

"No? You know, I felt so sorry for you, always. And of course I realize now that that's what you've been trading on all this time—my sympathy. No more, though. From now on you'd better get used to being on your own. Because I'm not responsible for you. I refuse to be. That's a responsibility I refuse to let you force on me any longer."

"Shenna—please—"

"Let me finish. You wasted your time coming here to England. I didn't have the nerve to say it before, but now I have. It's knowing about *him* that's given me the courage. You never told me the truth, but now I'm going to tell it to *you*. Mother, *you* are one of the reasons I came here to study. Although I was laden down with guilt at what I was doing, nevertheless I came here to get away from *you*. And now, just when I've started to get myself sorted out, you follow me here and try to disrupt my life again. No more." She waved a hand at the room. "You've taken this house—for what? Because you thought I'd come back and live with you again—so that things would be just the same as they were before. No. I'm afraid you've wasted your time. I'm not that romantic, impressionable little girl you could con into believing what you wanted. Not anymore. I've learned a few things now, and I'm my own person and I've got my own life to lead." She turned and stepped toward the door. "Mother, go on back to California. There's nothing for you here. I'll come and visit you when I can, but I will never live with you again."

She turned and went into the hall, opened the front door, and walked down the garden path. As she neared the gate she heard behind her the sound of Doris's voice, "Shenna, Shenna . . ." She ignored it and walked on. As she got into the car Wesley frowned, turning curious eyes upon her, and said, obviously puzzled, "Is that your mother there at the gate?"

Without turning, Shenna nodded. "Probably." Then she put the car in gear and drove away.

She didn't speak until they got back to London, to the bottom of Lee Road, where she pulled the car over to the curb and braked. Then she said, "I'm sorry, Wesley. I've spoiled it all. I couldn't go and eat now. I'm sorry."

"Don't worry about it."

"I've got no appetite—and the way I'm feeling, I know I wouldn't be very good company."

"Forget it." He reached out and touched her hand. "I don't know what's happened, but if there's anything I can do to help . . . Tell me if there is."

"Thanks, but—it's all right."

"What are you going to do now?"

"Just go on back to the flat, I guess."

"You want me to go with you?"

"No, thanks. I'll be better on my own for a while." She paused. "I'll drive you on home first."

"No. I'll get out here and walk."

As he moved to open the door, she reached over and pressed his hand. "I'm really sorry. I didn't mean for it to turn out this way."

"Of course you didn't."

"We'll talk later in the week, okay? Then maybe we can have that dinner."

He smiled. "Maybe."

"No, really," she said with false brightness, eager to make it up to him. "Let's see—Wednesday—how about Wednesday? That's usually a fairly easy day for me, and everything will be okay by then." It would be; it had to be; she had to get on with her life.

"Wednesday's fine—if you can manage it."

"I'll manage it."

"Right. I'll call for you, shall I?"

"All right. Say seven-fifteen? Seven-thirty?"

"Seven-fifteen. I'll be there then."

"Good." She forced a smile. "We'll get that dinner *some*time."

He smiled at her, opened the door, and got out and walked away along the street. Shenna watched his diminishing figure for a couple of seconds, then put the car in gear and drove off in the direction of Elm Court Road.

As she lay on the bed her eyes lighted on her wristwatch. It was almost eleven. She had been lying there for over two hours. Pushing herself up from the rumpled cover, she stood up and looked at herself in the glass. Her hair was awry and her eyes were red from her weeping. She had been crying for so many things: the loss of her father, the loss of Ian, the scene with her mother.

Turning away from the sight, she moved to the kitchen and made herself a cup of coffee. Then she sat on the bed again while the coffee grew cold beside her on the table. The words she had said to her mother kept repeating in her mind, and she was numbed with shame. Could she have been so cruel? She thought of how her mother had come after her down the garden path, and of how she had ignored her, and with the thought a sob burst from her throat and she picked up the telephone and dialed the Hallowridge number.

When there was no answer she hung up and dialed again, but still the ringing tone just went on and on. And then, at last, she heard the sound of the receiver being lifted at the other end of the line.

"Hello? Mom, are you there?"

There was no answer for many seconds, but then there came her mother's voice—but strangely slow, halting and slurred; it was almost unrecognizable. The next moment the voice had gone and she heard what sounded like the receiver falling. After that there was only silence.

"Mother. . . ! Mother. . . !" Shenna cried out. "Mother, answer me, *please!*" She listened for a moment longer, then slammed down the receiver, ran to the door, and threw it open. On the threshold she spun in panic, turning full circle, then dashed back into the flat and snatched up her keys. Hurrying back to the hall, she saw Kevin appear from the open door of his flat. "What's the matter?" he said.

She burst into tears. "Kevin, it's my mother. I think something terrible's happened to her."

"Oh, come on," he said, infuriatingly calm, and she flapped her hands distractedly and cried out, "I *know* it! I just know it. I must go to her."

He nodded then. "I'll come with you. Just let me get my coat."

They reached Hallowridge at half past midnight. It was a bitterly cold night, and as Shenna led the way up the garden path, the biting wind was like ice against her face. The only light in the house was in her mother's bedroom window. Quickly unlocking the door, Shenna entered the hall, switched on the light, and called out, "Mom. . . ? Mom. . . ?"

There was no answer. "Wait here a moment," she said, and started up the stairs.

She found her mother lying across the bed; on the carpet below her outstretched hand the telephone receiver lay where she had dropped it. On the small bedside table stood a glass with an inch of water in it and, next to it, a pharmacist's pill container, empty. All this Shenna took in in one glance, in the moment before she bent over Doris's limp form and found her still breathing. The next moment she was rushing from the room and onto the landing. "Kevin!" she cried out. "We must get an ambulance! Hurry!"

15

In the hospital waiting room, alternately sitting or pacing the carpet, Shenna waited with Kevin, and then at last, after what seemed an age, there was a doctor there, a tall, reddish-haired man with a kind expression, telling her that after emergency treatment her mother was going to be all right.

"May I see her?" Shenna asked.

He shook his head apologetically. "She's sleeping now. And I'd suggest that you go on home and get some rest yourself. You can phone up tomorrow and see how she's getting on and then come in after lunch. Bring her clothes with you. She should be well enough to go home by then."

Shenna nodded while tears stung her eyes. After a little silence the doctor asked, "Will she be all right at home?"

Shenna frowned. "All right? Of course . . ." Then she realized the implication of his question. "Yes, don't worry," she said, "she won't do anything like this again."

Her rest disturbed by recurring, nightmarish dreams, Shenna slept little the remainder of that night, and when she woke in the morning she began the wait for the hours to pass until it would be time to bring Doris back to the cottage.

Just before eleven she telephoned the hospital to ask after her mother's progress and was told that, as expected, she was very much better and would be able to leave in the afternoon. Just after one-thirty Shenna left the flat and went out to the car. As she unlocked it she turned to see Kevin coming toward her from the house. Stopping beside her, he asked how her mother was and she replied that she was making good progress. "I'm going to pick her up now," she added.

"That's good. Is there anything I can do to help?"

"No, thanks, Kevin. All I want to do right now is get her out of the hospital."

"And afterward? What will you do then?"

She stared at him for a long moment, then shrugged. "I wish I knew."

Going first to the cottage she packed a small suitcase with some of Doris's clothes and then got back in the car and drove to the hospital, where she talked to a young, attractive, dark-haired nursing sister who sat behind a desk in a small office. "You've come to take your mother home, have you?" she said. "Good. She'll make much better progress once she's back with her family. Right now she's pretty unhappy—but that's to be expected, of course. One positive thing, though—she seems genuinely to regret what she did."

Shenna nodded. "Would she—I mean—was she very sick when she was brought in last night? I know she was unconscious, but—"

"You mean would she have recovered?"

"Yes."

The nurse was silent for a second, then she said, "Without treatment, I doubt it. She'd taken enough barbiturates to be sure of the result—whether or not that was what she fully intended."

"I see."

After a few more words she directed Shenna along a corridor, and Shenna thanked her and moved away. Moments later she came to a stop outside the closed door of a private room and, after hesitating for a second, she opened the door and went in. The room was light and surprisingly pleasant and cheerful. Doris was in bed, lying propped against a bank of pillows. Her eyes were closed. Standing just inside the doorway, Shenna gazed at her, seeing dark circles beneath her eyes and lines about her mouth that she had not seen before. She saw too that the flesh on Doris's arms looked heavy and slack, while beneath the hospital nightdress her small breasts sagged against the starched cotton. Feeling a tightening in her throat, Shenna swallowed hard and stepped to the bedside.

"Mom . . ."

Doris opened her eyes at the whispered word, and Shenna smiled uncertainly, feeling the pricking of tears beneath her eyelids.

"Hi," Shenna said, and then, "I've come to take you home." She held up the small suitcase she had brought and set it down next to the bedside locker.

There was no interest in Doris's expression. "Home?" she said.

"To the cottage."

Doris nodded and Shenna stepped closer. "Don't you want to get away from here?"

Doris shrugged and murmured, "Yes," and turned her face to the window. As she did so, Shenna saw tears swimming in her eyes, tears that overflowed and ran down her cheeks. Doris began to sob. "I'm sorry," she said. "Oh, Shenna, I'm so sorry."

"Don't. Mom, don't—*please!*" Shenna moved to her, put her arms around her, and found herself weeping too.

On the way back to the cottage Shenna stopped off at a supermarket and, leaving Doris in the car, went inside and bought steak, salad makings, and other things for dinner. In the cottage she put away the food and then made some tea and carried it into the lounge, where Doris sat in a chair beside the newly lit fire. As they drank the tea, Shenna said, "Later on I'll fix us a nice supper and we'll have a quiet, relaxed evening, just the two of us. We'll watch some television, or talk—whatever you want, okay?"

Doris nodded, then said, "What time will you be going back to your apartment?"

"Oh, I won't bother going back tonight."

"But you've got your classes in the morning. You mustn't be late."

Shenna shrugged. "I won't be going in tomorrow. I'll telephone in the morning."

"Don't stay here on my account. I'll be all right. Believe me. I won't try anything else like that. I know now how stupid it was." Doris looked down at her cup. "At the time, though, I—I just wanted to die."

"Don't talk about it now."

"Before you came to pick me up I was visited by a psychiatrist at the hospital. I guess he wanted to be sure I wasn't going to do the same thing again as soon as I got out of the place. I told him I wouldn't. I guess he believed me."

There was silence in the room for a few moments, then Shenna said, "It was because of me, wasn't it? The things I said. Oh, Mom, I'm so sorry. I didn't mean to hurt you like that. But I was hurt myself and—upset and disappointed and—" She gave a shrug. "I'm just so sorry."

"It doesn't matter now. It's over." Doris sighed. "I wonder now why I lied to you. At the time it all seemed so clear, my reasons, but now—now it's all a little hazy. Like something in a dream, all clear until you examine it in the daylight." Her tone became brisker. "Anyway, it's over."

Shenna nodded. "And what will you do now?"

"Do? Me?"

"Yes. What do you want to do?"

"Does it matter?"

"Mom, of course it matters."

Doris shook her head. "No, it doesn't matter. You go and live your life. You have things to do. Don't think about me. Don't concern yourself." She gave a little smile. "And don't think I'm trying to play the martyr—I'm not. And neither am I trying to make you feel bad. I'm just trying to be real-istic."

Shenna moved to speak, but Doris went on, "I don't want you to concern yourself with me. I realized something while I was lying in that room in the hospital. I realized that I was on my own, and that I'd better start coming to terms with it." She shook her head. "I guess that's where my problems lay—in not being able to accept the situation." She paused briefly, then went on with a false note of lightness in her tone, "But not anymore. I've got to accept it now. And the sooner I start living with the idea, the better off I'll be." She waved a hand in Shenna's direction. "Go on back to school. Do what you've got to do."

"Mom . . ."

"I mean it. You go on back to your studies and I'll go on back to California. I think it's the best thing, for me to go back. It's true what you said—there's nothing for me here with you. That much is clear."

Shenna stared at her for a moment, then said, "Look, we'll talk about this whole thing later on—when you're feeling better. In the meantime I'll stay on here with you for the rest of the week."

A little later, as she washed up the tea cups, Shenna thought of her mother in the hospital, seeing again the hurt and despair in her eyes, her look of vulnerability—and she recalled how she had stood gazing at her with pity and re-morse.

With pity and remorse, yes, but not with love—and she suddenly realized that she had never loved her mother. The sudden awareness made her feel like weeping.

Shenna telephoned the school the next morning and asked Harry to connect her with her tutor, James Trandell, and a little later, when Trandell came on the line, she told him that her mother was sick and that she wouldn't be able to get in to school for the next few days. Afterward she left the house and drove to the flat in Elm Court Road, where she packed her easel, painting materials, and a number of canvases into the car. Back at the cottage in Hallowridge, she carried the items into the spare room. As she set up the easel she said to Doris with a smile, "I figure I should be able to work as well here as at the flat. I guess one north light's as good as another."

For the rest of that day and for much of the next, Tuesday, she tried to concentrate on her painting. It wasn't easy, though. Apart from the strained atmosphere in the house, she became increasingly aware of her mother's unhappiness. On the surface Doris seemed to be coping well, going about her chores with an air of calm and efficiency. At the same time she maintained her insistence that Shenna should go back to her studies and that she herself should return to California. And for a while Shenna believed that Doris had come to terms with it all, but then she would come upon her unexpectedly and find her with her guard down, and seeing the haunted, desperate look in her dull eyes, she was shocked at the depths of her mother's misery.

On Wednesday morning Shenna telephoned James Trandell and asked whether she could see him that afternoon. He replied, "Of course," and suggested that she get there around three-thirty.

Leaving the cottage after lunch, she drove to the college. As she entered and started across the foyer, Harry smiled and called out, "Ah, there you are. I've got a message for you. A phone call for you this morning."

"Oh?"

"A Mr. Alfred Carson. He left his number and wants you to ring him. Said he's been trying to call you at your home, but can't get any answer." He tore a page from a notepad and passed it to her. "You're all right, are you?" he added.

"Yes, I'm fine, thanks."

She went upstairs to where Trandell was instructing a life-drawing class. When she opened the door and looked inside he caught her eye and came out into the corridor, closing the door behind him. "I'll be with you in just a moment or two," he said. "In the meantime come and wait in the principal's office. He's not in this afternoon and neither is his secretary. We can talk there." He led the way to a door a few yards along, opened it, and ushered Shenna inside. "Make yourself comfortable," he told her. "I'll be right back."

As he turned away, Shenna said, "Do you think I could make a telephone call while I wait? I'll pay for it."

He smiled as he moved to the desk. "I think the school can run to a free phone call." Picking up the phone, he asked for an outside line and then handed the receiver to her. As the door closed behind him, she dialed, and a few moments later heard Alfred's answering voice on the other end of the line. At her greeting he said cheerfully, "Well, hello! I was wondering how you were and how the paintings are going. I've been trying to call you at your flat over the past couple of days, but there's never been any answer. I was beginning to think you'd got tired of us and had gone back to California."

After telling him that she was now living temporarily in Hallowridge with her mother she went on to say that her paintings for the exhibition were going well and that her final selection would be made in plenty of time for the catalog to go to press at the beginning of January. Good, he said; time was going by so fast. They discussed, then, the matter of her paintings being framed, and he told her that if she brought the canvases to him he would get in a framer who would do excellent work for her at a good rate. After thanking him, she added that if he wished to contact her in the immediate future he should do so at her mother's address in Hallowridge. "Fine," he said, "let me get a pencil."

After Shenna had given him the Hallowridge address and telephone number, she said with false brightness in her voice, "By the way, I saw Ian's picture in the paper a few days back. With his girlfriend—Mary."

"Yes," Alfred said, "I saw that. I suppose it's all on again with those two. I wish to God they'd make up their minds and stick to it." It was quite obvious from his reaction, Shenna thought, that he had no idea of her own relationship with Ian. She was glad.

After she had said good-bye to him and hung up she felt more depressed than ever. A moment later the door opened and the tall, lean figure of Trandell entered. "Would you like some tea or coffee?" he asked as he perched on the edge of the desk. "I can ring down for some. I think I shall have something."

She didn't want anything, but she said, "Thank you. Coffee, black—no sugar."

He nodded, lifted the intercom receiver, dialed, and asked for two coffees to be brought up. That done, he lit a cigarette and said, "So, tell me what it is. It's to do with your mother, is it?"

"Well—yes."

"How is she now?"

"Better than she was."

"What was the matter with her?"

After a little silence Shenna said, "She's been overwrought and going through a bad time lately. And I'm afraid that on Saturday it all just got—got too much for her. She took an overdose of pills." She gave a little shake of her head. "I found her in time, thank God. She was taken to the hospital and treated and they discharged her the following day."

Trandell said nothing, just looked at her in silent sympathy. Shenna continued, "Obviously it isn't something I'd like to have generally known, but I have to tell you because I don't want you to think that the decisions I've come to have been made lightly. I want you to know that there's a good reason for what I've decided to do."

"And what is it that you've decided to do?"

"She—my mother—she insists on going back to California and so I've decided to go with her. Not for good, you understand—but just for a few weeks."

"I see. You plan to leave soon?"

"Very soon. There are just a few things to sort out before I go."

"I understand you've got an exhibition of your work coming up in the new year."

"Yes, it opens at the Simpson Gallery in Kensington at the end of January. My paintings have to be selected by January fourth."

"And you're going ahead with that, are you?—the exhibition?"

"Oh, yes. I'd hoped to use the next month to do several more paintings for it, but it won't be possible now. Instead I'll have to make my selection from those I've already got. They're not all up to the standard I hoped they'd be, but . . ." She shrugged. "Anyway, I'll get the paintings handed in at the beginning of next week, then take care of a few other things—like my mother's cottage in Hallowridge—and then we'll go back to California."

"I see. When do you plan to return here?"

"In January—in time for the start of the new term. In the meantime I can spend some time with my mother, which is what she needs. We'll have several weeks together at home, just the two of us. We'll have Christmas and—well, I'm sure by the time I come back here she'll be all right again. Then I can get back to my studies. The way I see it, I'll only miss these last couple of weeks of term."

He hesitated for a second, then said, "Do you have anyone here?"

"Anyone here?" She didn't understand him.

He smiled. "I mean, is there some—special person you're

coming back to—apart from your coming back to the course?"

"Oh—I see." She turned away. "No. No—there's no one." The question had taken her completely by surprise, and for the first time she found herself facing up to what she saw as the truth. It was over between herself and Ian; she knew that now. There was no point in deluding herself about it any longer. It was over. Over. Over.

Trandell looked at her in silence for a moment, then he asked, carefully changing the subject, "Will you go back to your acting while you're in California, or have you given all that up?"

"Not for good, no. But there won't be time while I'm there."

He smiled. "I know nothing at all about such things, which I suppose must be pretty obvious." He paused. "Where are you living in London? You live quite close, don't you?"

"I've got a flat just down the road, but till we go back to California I'll be living with my mother." She took a small piece of notepaper from her purse and handed it to him. "This is my mother's address and phone number. You'll be able to reach me there if you need me."

He glanced at the paper and placed it on the desk. "Are you going to keep your flat on?" he asked.

"Yes. Though my lease runs out in February. I'll have to renew it then or move somewhere else."

He hesitated for a moment, then said, "What if your mother isn't fit again by the time you want to come back to England?"

"Oh, she will be, I'm sure."

He nodded. "Well, I hope so. It would be a shame if you let your studies go—gave up the course."

"I don't intend to do that."

"Good." He smiled. "And how are *you* coping with it all? It must be quite a strain on you."

"I'm okay."

And then all at once her lower lip was quivering and she was bending forward with tears streaming down her face. Trandell, all concern, stepped to her side and awkwardly put an arm around her shoulder. "Don't, Shenna. Don't cry. What is there to cry about?" He stood there helplessly while she continued to weep. After a while she said brokenly, "I'm sorry. I'm just being stupid, I know. But I can't help it."

"Don't apologize. You're going through a difficult time."

She shook her head. "I was doing so well, too. I know I was."

He nodded. "You were, indeed you were. But don't worry about it. You said yourself you won't miss much of the course. And the way you apply yourself, you'll soon make up any lost time."

"Yes . . . yes . . ." She nodded and wiped at her eyes with a tissue. Trandell gave her shoulder a gentle, ineffectual pat. "I'll tell the principal what you've told me; put him in the picture. I've got to phone him in a few minutes, anyway. I'll tell him then. There won't be any problem—and I'm sure he'll agree with me that no one else needs to know *everything* that you've told me."

"Thank you." Her tears had stopped now. "At the moment the newspapers don't know about my mother—and I'd hate for them to get hold of it. Although it's nothing in the way of news, they'd manage to make something of it—particularly after all this other—other business."

At the reference to Jane's death, Trandell gave a solemn nod. Then, in the little silence that followed, he looked toward the door and said, "That coffee's a long time getting here."

Shenna got to her feet. "I won't wait for it, if you don't

mind—and besides, you'll be wanting to get back to your class. . . ."

"Okay." He gave her a grave smile. "Is there anything I can do?"

"No, nothing, thank you."

"Let me know if there is."

"I will."

"So now you're going to get busy with sorting out your paintings for the exhibition, I suppose?"

"Yes."

"You were very lucky, weren't you? To be offered an exhibition of your work so early in your career."

"Yes, I was." She studied his expression for a moment, then added, "I'm not going to ask you whether you think it's merited or not."

"I already told you, I think you have talent. Though it does need tuition."

"Yes, I'm aware of that. But I know that my work has improved a lot since the beginning of the term. I can see it myself."

"Oh, it has. There's no doubt."

Still looking into his face, she shrugged. "Listen, I'm quite sure that the fact that my name is already well known in another field has some bearing on my being offered this show." She shrugged again. "But I say to myself, well, if they want to make use of that—then that's all right with me." She smiled. "I decided early on that I wouldn't spend a lot of time looking into the whys and wherefores of being offered such an opportunity. I'd just be glad it was offered. And I intend to make the best possible use of it. To make it work for me."

"Good for you. We have to take our chances where we can get them."

"That's the way I feel." Shenna started to open the door,

then stopped and turned back. "Thank you," she said, "for being so kind and understanding."

"I haven't done anything." He smiled as he took the hand she held out to him. "But listen," he added, "when you go away, just don't forget to come back."

"As soon as I can."

Trandell stood in the open doorway of the office and watched as Shenna walked away along the corridor, then he moved back to the desk and stubbed out the remains of his cigarette in the ashtray. Remembering the call he had to make to the principal, he lifted the receiver, asked for an outside line, and dialed. A few moments later Hirst's voice came on the line. For a couple of minutes they discussed a forthcoming staff meeting, and then Trandell told him of his conversation with Shenna.

"When did she say she'll be back?" Hirst asked.

"As soon as she can. In January, in time for the new term. That's what she *said*."

"Don't you think that's what she intends?"

"Oh, yes, I *do* think that's her intention. But I don't think it will happen."

"Why not?"

"I just think that once she gets over there she'll fall back into her old way of life and that will be it. Oh, I know she seems very keen on her studies, but—well, she has a lot of attractions over there, too. She'll have her film work and so many things. That apart, though, she's going back for the sake of her mother, and if her mother *is* somewhat—unstable—then who can guarantee that Shenna will be free to leave at that time? Her mother seems very dependent on her. I mean, the very fact that she came over here to be with her—that's significant. No, quite honestly, I think once Shenna leaves here that's the last we'll see of her."

A few moments later, when he put down the receiver, he turned from the desk to see the young man from the school cafeteria standing just within the open doorway holding a tray with two cups of coffee on it. Trandell shook his head. "What took you so long?" He took one of the coffees and placed some coins on the tray. "Forget the other one," he said. "It's not needed now."

When Alan had gone away again Trandell carried the cup over to the desk and sat down. As he drank the coffee, he thought again of the conversation he had had with Shenna. Yes, he was quite sure that once she had gone she would never come back. Her life and her career were in films—not struggling to make it as a painter in the face of such strong and superior opposition. And he was certain she knew it too. No matter how much she might insist that she would be back in the new year, she knew as well as he did that it wouldn't happen. Her tears had told him that as plainly as any words could have.

16

After her meeting with Trandell Shenna went out to the shops to get some coffee and then walked toward her car, which was parked near the school. As she drew near it she suddenly remembered that Wesley would be calling at the flat for her at seven-fifteen. She looked at her watch. Almost four forty-five. Right now he would still be at work. She didn't have his office telephone number, though. There was nothing to do but go to the flat later on and wait for him.

Returning to the school, she called her mother to tell her she wouldn't be back yet, and then joined Hannah and Margaret, who she met on their way to the cafeteria. As they went she told them—without going into detail—that her mother was sick and she herself was staying in Hallowridge to look after her.

In the cafeteria the girls got cups of coffee and sat at a table with other students who were talking of a bus trip to Oxford that had been planned for the coming Friday. It was scheduled to take in a visit to the Ashmolean Museum and later, at the city's main theater, the evening performance of a new production of *The Cherry Orchard*, which was on its way to London's West End. Shenna had put her name down for the outing several weeks earlier, and had since forgotten all about it.

"I haven't paid for it yet, either," Shenna said, at which Margaret commented dryly that there was something on the notice board to that effect. "But will you be able to go with your mother being ill?" Hannah asked. After a moment's hesitation Shenna answered yes. After all, she told herself, the trip was only for a day.

When the break was over Shenna went to the art history lecture—which passed a little of the time before she was due to meet Wesley. At six-thirty she stopped at the notice board in the hall. The notice relating to the trip read:

VISIT TO ASHMOLEAN MUSEUM AND
NEW THEATRE, OXFORD,
on Friday, December the 10th.
The bus will leave from the college building at 10 A.M.
sharp, so DON'T BE LATE!
The following students please contact me at once.
They know the reason why and TIME IS RUNNING
SHORT.

There followed a list of seven or eight names, with Shenna's name halfway down, next to Caspar's. The notice was signed at the bottom by the organizing instructor, David Jarvis.

As she turned away she saw that Caspar had come to stand beside her at the board. He was wearing an overcoat with a muffler around his neck. "Well," she said to him, "I guess we'd better pay up before they cut us out."

He nodded. "It looks that way."

"I suppose you're off home now to get back to your painting?"

He shrugged. "I'm afraid I don't get that much done these dark evenings. And you?"

"No. I'm just killing time for a while until I have to go and see a friend." She paused. "Look, if you're not in a terrific rush to get back home, why not come up to the bar and have a quick drink?"

He shook his head and said, "Thanks anyway, but I can't right now. Maybe some other time, okay?"

She shrugged. "Okay."

They turned then and headed for the main doors. As they reached the street he asked how her work was progressing for the exhibition. "It's going all right," she told him. "And what about your own exhibition? You were planning to exhibit your own work in the spring."

He shook his head. "Oh, I'm afraid that all fell through. The gallery went bust—just my luck."

As they stood on the pavement, there drifted down to them the sound of voices singing.

"O, Holy night, the stars are brightly shining . . ."

The sound was sweet on the cold air and Shenna lifted her gaze to the upper windows of the college building. "The more conservative element of the Christmas show," she observed, and Caspar nodded and asked why she wasn't taking part in some of the sketches. She shook her head. "I thought about it, but then decided I didn't have the time—not for a commitment like that." Now, with all that had happened, she was glad that she had kept free of it. She sighed. "Time's so precious, isn't it? And it goes by so fast. It's hard to realize it'll soon be Christmas."

Caspar nodded. They began to walk slowly along the street, and as they went she asked him what he would be doing at Christmas. He replied that he planned to go and stay with his father in Wales. "And you?" he asked.

"I'll be in California."

"California?"

After a moment she told him about her mother and her suicide attempt. She hadn't meant to, but somehow it all came pouring out. After that she went on to tell him of her decision to return with her mother to California.

"Well, don't stay away too long," he said.

"No, I won't."

As they reached her car, she suddenly realized the significance of his walking. "I've just realized," she said, "you're *walking*."

"So?"

"No, I mean, where's your bike?"

"Oh, that. I'm afraid it got involved in a bit of an accident. The thing's a write-off."

"So what will you do?"

"What I'm doing right now—walk."

"Very smart. I mean, will you get another?"

"No, I can't afford it."

She looked at her watch. "Hey, listen, I've got time before I'm due at my flat. Let me drop you home."

"No, thanks, that's okay."

"It's no trouble, really."

"No, thanks, I'm okay, really. I'll walk."

She shrugged. "Whatever." She took her car keys from her bag, unlocked the car door, and opened it.

"I appreciate it, honestly," Caspar said, "but I don't mind walking. And it's a dry night."

She looked at him keenly as he spoke. Ever since seeing him earlier beside the notice board she had been vaguely aware that there was something different about him, but she couldn't tell what. Now, though, she saw what it was. They were standing beneath a street lamp, and as he lifted his head to the harsh light, she suddenly realized that he was thinner.

"My God, Caspar," she said, "you're wasting away. Are you on a diet or something?"

For a moment he just looked at her, then he laughed and, brushing her words aside, said, "I'll see you soon." He held the door open while she got inside. When the door was closed she wound the window down. "I'll see you on Friday," she said.

He frowned. "Friday?"

"The trip to Oxford."

"Oh, yes." He nodded. "Yes, I'll see you then."

"I want to go on the trip," Shenna said, "because—well,

for one thing, I think it'll be my last chance to see the whole crowd before I go away."

"Ah, yes." He gave a slow nod, looked at her for a long moment, then stepped closer to the car, reached in, and squeezed her hand. "So long, Shenna." Then he was straightening, turning, and moving away. In just a few moments he was out of sight.

Five minutes later Shenna was in Elm Court Road and opening the door to her flat. Another five minutes later and Wesley was ringing the doorbell. When she had ushered him in he looked around and said at once, "Where's your easel?"

"Over at Hallowridge, at my mother's. Since I saw you she's been pretty sick and I've been working there at the cottage. I don't like to leave her alone anymore—not yet, anyway." She paused, and added apologetically, "Wesley, I'm afraid I can't go out to dinner this evening. Forgive me. I'm so sorry to let you down again."

Disappointment showed on his face and she shook her head. "I feel awful about it. I would have called you earlier today, but I didn't have your office number."

He took a small notebook from his pocket, wrote in it with his felt-tip pen, tore out the page, and handed it to her. "Here—in case it should happen again." As Shenna took it, he added with a rueful smile, "When d'you think we'll have that dinner? Ever?"

She sighed. "Well, I'm afraid it doesn't look likely just yet. My mother's returning to California in a few days and I've decided to go with her—and stay till she's back on her feet again."

"How long's that likely to take?"

"Not long. A few weeks."

"But what about your studies?"

"Oh, I've had to give up on that for the rest of this term—

but it won't be for long, and I don't intend to miss much of the next one."

"What about your exhibition?"

"I'll get my paintings all sorted out for that before I go. I've worked hard for it and it would be insane not to see it through when it's so close to completion. I hope to come back for the opening." She shook her head. "It's a shame about missing my classes, but—well, I've got no choice. I'm going on a trip to Oxford for the day on Friday, but after that I won't be having much contact with the school for some time."

"Then there's no point in asking if you'll be at the portrait class tomorrow evening?"

"Oh, no, I can't make that. You'll be going, will you?"

"I'd planned to." He paused. "So I doubt that I'll see you again before you go. . . ."

"Well, it'll be more difficult, for sure, while I'm living in Hallowridge."

"What's it like?"

"What d'you mean?"

"Are you having any life of your own?"

"Of course I am, but—I feel so responsible for my mother."

"Why?"

She shook her head. "Oh, I can't go into it right now, but I do."

"Why are you going back to California?"

She shrugged awkwardly and a defensive note crept into her voice as she answered, "My mother wants to. She has to."

"But why do you have to go with her?"

"I just—do. I feel I must."

"When we first met you told me you wanted to lead your own life and make your own decisions. You said you'd determined to get away from your mother and have a life of your own."

"Yes, I did say that, but—"

"And now you're giving it all up. You're going back home because it's what she wants."

"Wesley, you don't understand." She paused. "And anyway, I'd prefer not to discuss it. The decision is made."

There was a silence between them. After a moment he sighed. "No," he said, "I'm sure I don't understand. And what business is it of mine, anyway?" He stood there awkwardly for another moment, then said with a small, forced laugh, "And on that note, I think I'd better go."

He turned toward the door and Shenna stood watching as he went into the hall. At the outer door, he turned back to her and said, "I wish you weren't going. I wish there was some way to stop you."

"I'll be back, Wesley," she said.

He gave a little shake of his head. "I'd like to believe that."

When he had gone she closed the door and looked around her. Her paintings were stacked against one wall. She must get them to Alfred Carson soon for the framing. Her eyes moved on, lighting on the photograph of her father that stood on the bedside table. Beside it stood the photograph of the Hinton Peeble village church and the one she had taken of Ian sitting on the bench. The postcards from Ian were there also. After a moment she scooped up the photographs and postcards and put them in the drawer. Turning, she looked around her one more time and left the flat. As she set off for Hallowridge a few moments afterward she felt that every single thing had the ache of finality about it.

Later, at the cottage in Hallowridge, the telephone rang. "It's probably for you," Doris said, and Shenna nodded and picked up the receiver.

"Shenna?" It was Kevin's voice.

"Yes. Hello, Kevin."

"Am I disturbing you?" he asked. "Is this a bad time to call?"

"No, not at all."

"Good." He paused. "How are you?"

"I'm fine, thanks."

"And your mother?"

"Much better."

"That's good. I've been hoping I'd see you. I wanted to give you a ring before now, but I didn't want to bother you. I'm calling now to ask you how your time is fixed."

"My time?"

"Yes—I mean—is it rather restricted?"

"Restricted? How do you mean?"

"Well, I managed to get a couple of tickets for the English National Opera. *Rigoletto*. It's supposed to be brilliant. I was wondering if you could come with me."

"Oh, Kevin, I'd love to. When is it?"

"This Friday. I'm sorry it's short notice."

"Oh, damn." She clicked her tongue. "I can't make it then, I'm sorry. The school's arranged a day trip to Oxford—to visit the Ashmolean and then go on to the theater in the evening. What a shame."

"Ah, well . . ." He sounded disappointed. "We'll have to do it some other day."

"Yes. Yes, wait till I get back from California."

"You're going away?"

"As soon as I've sorted out my pictures for the exhibition." She went on to tell him then of her intention to accompany her mother back to California, to spend Christmas with her, and then come back to London, in January.

There was a little silence on the line, then he said, "I'll miss you."

"Ah, well, it won't be for long."

"That's what you say now. But you wait—you'll get back

there and that will be it. Burt Reynolds will be after you to star with him in some epic and you'll forget all about this place."

"Oh, no, Kevin." She smiled. "I've *got* to come back. We didn't finish your portrait, did we?"

He paced the room, his confused thoughts tumbling over and over in his brain, the pulse in his temple throbbing. Two or three times in his pacing he came to a halt and just stood there while the full realization of what was happening came to him and shocked him all over again. And then he would start his pacing once more, his feet keeping time with the words that drummed in his mind: *She's going away . . . she's going away.*

After a time he sat down and pulled his diary to him. Then he took up his pen. Beneath the date, December 1st, he wrote:

> *She's going away. I can hardly believe it. And will she return in January as she says she will? I'd like to believe it, but I can't. I just know that once she's gone she'll never set foot near this place again. That will be the end. But it can't be allowed to happen. It can't. When she came here it was the answer to a prayer. Surely it can't end just like that—not after everything I've done for her.*
>
> *It's ironic, really, when I think of how I once thought I might lose her. Sometimes I imagined the threat might come in the shape of her acting career—that she would be called back to some fantastic job. I never dreamed that the threat would be her own mother. If it weren't for her she would be staying on.*

On Friday morning Doris followed Shenna out to the car and watched as she got in, fastened her seat belt, and rolled down the window.

"Now don't wait up for me," Shenna told her. "I'll be very late." She started the engine and looked up into Doris's face as she hovered, bending close to the car. "Now are you sure you're going to be okay?"

"Yes, of course. You go on now or you're going to be late."

"Right." Moments later, as Shenna drove away, she looked in the rearview mirror and saw Doris standing there by the gate, her hand raised in a wave.

Shenna drove first to the flat to see if there was any mail (there was none) and then up Lee Road, parking the car in a side street near the school. The morning was cold and frosty and as she walked toward the school she pulled her muffler more closely about her throat. On the pavement the heels of her boots rang crisp and clear.

As she turned the last corner she saw that the bus had already arrived. It was still empty as yet, though, and she went past it and into the school where she found Hannah, Margaret, Colin, Brian, and several of the other students in the cafeteria. When she ordered coffee at the counter Alan smiled as he handed her her change, asking, "You off on the outing?" and she answered that she was. "Have a good time then," he said, and she thanked him and carried her cup to the table where her friends were sitting.

Brian wasn't going on the trip and when the time came to get on the bus Shenna said good-bye to him and trooped out along with the others. On board the bus she sat at the back with Hannah, Margaret, and Colin while she looked out the window for any sign of Caspar, but by the time they were due to start the bus was full and there was no sign of him.

"Where's Caspar?" she asked David Jarvis, who sat just across the aisle.

"Caspar?" he said. "Oh, he decided not to come. His seat went to someone else."

Shenna frowned. "When I saw him on Wednesday he didn't say anything about not going. Why did he change his mind?"

"I've no idea. One of the other students bought his place, that's all I know."

Shenna nodded and turned back to the window while the bus started up and moved out into the traffic. She was disappointed that Caspar hadn't come. And then she remembered his last words as they had talked together under the street lamp. "So long, Shenna," he had said, reaching in through the window and briefly clasping her hand. Now she realized he'd had no intention of coming on the trip. His words had been his good-bye.

Later, while walking through the Oxford streets, Margaret said to her in a low voice, "Between you and me, I think Caspar's having financial difficulties."

"Did he tell you that?"

"You must be joking."

"How do you know, then?"

"He's been going after some evening and weekend jobs— and I put two and two together. And there are other signs. For one thing, he hardly ever comes to the cafeteria, and he never comes to the pub anymore."

With Margaret's words, Shenna recalled how Caspar had turned down her invitation to have a drink in the bar. So *that* had been the reason—it was because he couldn't reciprocate.

It was just after five when he set out, by which time it was already dark. He wore a nondescript dark gray overcoat with a wool scarf and a dark gray hat. Getting a train from Blackheath, he made a connection with another bound for Sevenoaks, where he got off and set out to walk to Hallowridge. The walk turned out to be all of three miles, but he didn't care; the weather was dry and he had plenty of time; Shenna wouldn't be back home for hours.

When he eventually reached the narrow country road he moved silently to the cottage gate, stood there looking around for a moment or two, and then, sure that he wasn't being observed, pushed it open with a gloved hand. On soft-soled shoes he started up the path. As he walked he could see a sliver of light showing through a chink in the downstairs curtains of a room on the right, and another light in one of the rooms upstairs. Without a sound he followed the path around the house to the rear, stopped at the back door, and put his ear to it to listen. He could detect the faint sounds of music interspersed with a man's voice; it must be coming from a radio or television set.

On the right of the door was a room with no curtains drawn at the window and peering into the gloom he could see that it was the kitchen. He tried the window but found it locked. Then, very carefully, he tried the door handle—and felt it turn in his grasp. Hardly daring to breathe, he completed the turn of the handle and slowly, slowly eased open the door.

With the door silently closed behind him, he looked around. He was in the hall, which was dimly lit by a faint light that spilled out from a partly open door on the right. The music came from the same source. Then, as he stood there, he suddenly saw the shaft of light grow wider and he dodged swiftly to his left into the recess beneath the stairs.

Shrinking back into the darkened alcove, he pressed himself into the corner behind some hanging coats. The next moment he saw the woman go past him and a second later heard the sound of a latch falling into place. She was locking the back door. The sudden awareness of her action brought to him a strange feeling of elation. She was locking the door—to protect herself—and he was already inside.

The woman moved back past the recess, and a few moments later he heard the music grow louder and closer. She must be carrying a portable radio. And then her feet sounded over his head as she climbed the stairs to the floor above. Putting one hand into his pocket, he grasped a coiled piece of thin nylon cord, took it out, and wrapped one end around his gloved right hand.

He was just above to move out from the recess when he

suddenly realized that the coat hanging next to his cheek was Shenna's; he recognized its color, besides which it bore a faint trace of a perfume she sometimes wore. Briefly closing his eyes, he buried his face in the coat's folds. He remained like that for a few seconds and then, turning, he stepped silently out into the hall.

As he climbed the steep stairs the sounds from the radio grew stronger and he heard also the sound of water running. It sounded as if she was preparing a bath. Emerging onto the landing at the top of the stairs, he found that the sounds came from the bathroom on the left. Stepping closer, he saw the woman bending over the bathtub, her back toward him. She was wearing a long, blue dressing gown. He became aware suddenly of the pounding of his heart, yet at the same time he felt submerged in an icy calm. He had no regrets over what he was about to do. He had no choice.

After standing there for a few seconds he raised the cord in his hands and prepared to step forward and loop it about the woman's neck—now, while she bent over the tub. But then, suddenly, the sound of the running water ceased and she shifted her position. He froze, watching as she bent over a tall wicker linen basket and gathered up into her arms a bundle of clothing. Then she was straightening again and turning toward the door.

In the second before she would have seen him he stepped quickly back into the bedroom opposite the stairs. He didn't want to have to use the cord face to face with her, but to come up behind her and take her by surprise; it would be easier that way and he would be less likely to be affected in any struggle she would put up. Standing just within the open doorway of the shadowed bedroom, he watched as she moved past him to the stairs. And then, just as he thought he was missing his opportunity, he saw some of the articles of clothing slip from her arms and fall onto the carpet. Stopping, she bent to retrieve them—and in that moment he stepped out onto the landing behind her.

In spite of the music from the radio she must have heard the sound of his approach for suddenly, abruptly, stooped as she was, she swung her hear around. Next moment she was jerking upright, turning her body to him, in her eyes a strange look of fear and puzzlement. Then suddenly her eyes were widening in terror and her mouth opening in a piercing scream. As he brought up the cord she stretched out one hand, reaching out to ward him off while the other clutched the bundle of clothes to her breast. In the next, brief, desperate moment, instead of throwing the loop of the cord about her neck, he was overcome by panic and, pushing violently against the bundle of clothes in her grasp, hurled her down the stairs.

She went from him in a tumbling, rolling blur of blue dressing gown and articles of clothing, crashing down and coming to a thudding halt on the tiled floor of the hall below.

At the top of the stairs he stood quite still for a few moments, looking down at her as she lay sprawled near the front door. She didn't move. After a second he made his way down to her side.

Her face was covered by a cream-colored blouse. It was one of Shenna's; he had seen her wearing it. He bent, lifted the garment, and saw the woman's face. Her contorted expression was frozen in a grimace of horror and pain, her eyes wide open and staring sightlessly up past his left shoulder. Getting on his knees, he put his ear to her chest. There was not the flicker of a heartbeat. He dropped the blouse back onto the dead face and straightened. His work was done—and so much more easily than he had ever anticipated.

He stood there for some moments while his sense of pleasure grew, then, stepping aside, he turned to face himself in a nearby mirror. Taking off his hat he saw that his forehead was beaded with sweat. He wiped it with the back of his gloved right hand and briefly touched a finger to the pulsing nerve in his temple. As he moved away he smiled. Everything was going his way.

Faintly from above came the music from the radio. He turned from the sound, opened the front door with his gloved hand, and let himself out into the night. As quietly as possible he pulled the door shut behind him till he heard the lock click into place. Then, silently and swiftly, he set off down the garden path.

As he walked back to the station he became aware of the smile that still played on his lips. He had cause to smile. Shenna no longer had any reason to return to California. He had made it possible for her to stay—to be near him—and that was all that mattered.

17

The inquest was a brief affair. There seemed to be no doubt that Doris Preston had died as the result of an accident, of a fall down the stairs.

Although there appeared to be nothing at all remarkable in her death, she was still the mother of Shenna Preston, and the newspapers reported the happening—albeit briefly—and Shenna was photographed going to the inquest at the Hallowridge village hall. Interest in the incident quickly died, though, and Shenna was soon left in peace again.

A week after Doris's death her body was cremated. Cissie, her sister, had flown over for the funeral, and she and Shenna stood side by side in the small chapel, pale-faced and tight-lipped. Afterward Cissie would be taking Doris's ashes back to America with her—not to Los Angeles, but to the East Coast. There, in upstate New York, in the Orange County hills, on the farmland on which she had been raised, her ashes would be scattered.

After the funeral service Cissie and Shenna went out into the small cemetery where, among the evergreens, the oaks and the birches were stark and bare. Walking together in the damp, cold December air, Cissie asked Shenna whether she still intended to return to California as she had planned. Shenna replied that there was no longer any reason for her to give up her studies, and that for the time being she would stay on and see how things worked out.

When Cissie returned to New York two days later Shenna felt as if a chapter in her life had ended.

Doris's funeral had taken place the same day as the school term ended, and over the days that followed Shenna threw herself into a round of activity that kept her busy for many hours of the day. And she was glad of the demands upon her, which stopped her brooding too much. One of the first things she did was to move her things from the cottage back to her flat in Blackheath. Afterward she set about sorting out her mother's belongings, giving Doris's clothes to a local charity to be disposed of in one of their village sales. That done, she set about closing up the cottage and returning the key to its owner.

Two days later she left London for Bradford to spend Christmas with Margaret, her parents, and two older brothers. It turned out to be a surprisingly happy and lighthearted time. Gradually, with the passing days, Shenna found herself relaxing more and more as the horror and sorrow of Doris's death receded, and when, after eleven days, she returned alone to London, she felt more at ease than she would have thought possible. Now before her was the final preparation of her paintings for the exhibition, and in that week leading up to the beginning of the spring term she felt she could accomplish a lot.

When she got back to the flat she went through the few items of mail that had arrived in her absence. Among them was a letter from Amy who, after saying how sorry she was to hear about Doris's death, went on: *Call me. If you need an old friend at any time, call me.* Shenna smiled with affection as she read the words.

Afterward she began to get her painting materials ready for the morning. As she did so the thought of Caspar came to her mind, and after a few moments she picked up the telephone and dialed the number of his rooming house. She had seen nothing of him since before the outing to Oxford and with her own preoccupations she had hardly given him a thought.

The phone was eventually answered by one of Caspar's neighbors. The woman told Shenna that she hadn't seen Caspar about the house for a few days, but knew he was in because she had heard his radio playing. She went off to fetch him then, only to return a little while later saying he didn't answer her knock—though she was sure he was in his room. "I have a feeling he's not very well," she added.

Shenna thanked her and hung up, then, after sitting there for several more minutes she got up, put on her coat, and went out and drove away. Arriving at Caspar's address, she got no answer when she rang his bell, and after several attempts she rang one of the others. The door was opened after a little while by the woman who had earlier answered the telephone. Now, after a few words of conversation, she stood aside while Shenna entered and went up the stairs.

Shenna knocked several times on Caspar's door and softly called out his name before she heard the distant sound of his irritable voice as he called out, "Yes? Who is it?"

"It's me—Shenna." She waited, hearing nothing but silence again, then she added, "Are you going to open the door?"

Another silence, then his voice came from closer at hand: "I can't. I'm sorry."

"What do you mean, you can't? Oh, come on, Caspar, I'm concerned about you. Open the door and let me in."

"No, really, Shenna, thanks for your concern, but it's not necessary. Listen—I'll see you in a day or two. I'll give you a call."

"No, Caspar, you won't give me a call. I want to see you and I'm not going away until I do. I don't have to come in, but I want to see you for a second."

A further little silence passed and then at last she heard sounds at the door and he was there.

"Caspar . . ."

The sight of him almost took her breath away. His face looked more pale and gaunt than ever. He stood there unshaven, his hair uncombed, wearing an old dressing gown over pajamas and sweater, his stockinged feet thrust into a pair of old sandals. "Dear God," she breathed, "what on earth's happened to you?"

He forced a smile through cracked lips and said, his voice croaking slightly, "Happened? Nothing's happened. I've got a bit of chill or something, that's all."

She stared at him without speaking for a second, then pushed past him into the room. While he closed the door she looked around the room and shivered. "My God, this place is like an icebox. Haven't you got any heat in here?"

He shrugged, frowning. "I don't need it. I was in bed. I keep warm enough."

"Yeah, I'll bet. How long have you been feeling like this?—your 'chill,' as you call it?"

"Oh, a few days."

"Have you been eating?"

"Of course."

"Of course, he says. You could have fooled me. Didn't your family feed you over Christmas?"

"I didn't go home."

"I thought that was what you planned to do."

"Well, yes, it was—earlier on. But in the end I didn't."

"You stayed here over Christmas and New Year's?"

"Yes."

"Were you on your own all the time?"

"So?"

"Oh, Caspar, I wish I'd known."

"Why? What would you have done about it?"

"I don't know, but I could have done *something*. Why didn't you tell me you'd changed your plans?"

"Why should I have? You haven't been exactly free of all worries yourself, have you?"

Ignoring his words she said, "Why haven't you got any heat?"

"Listen, Shenna, I'm fine. Please don't worry about me."

"Fine?" She stepped closer to him. "You look awful."

"I told you—I think I've got a chill or something—nothing more."

"Apart from an advanced case of malnutrition."

He moved back to sit on the edge of the bed. "I'm not hungry. I'll get something when I'm hungry."

"Sure." She waved a hand at him. "Caspar, for God's sake get back in bed before you freeze." She moved to the cold gas fire. "What does this thing use?"

"Ten- and fifty-pence pieces. But I've run out of change right now. I was going out to get some later on."

"It's all right—I think I've got some." She opened her purse, brought out some coins, then moved to the meter in the corner and fed the slot. After that she found some matches, turned on the gas, and lit the fire.

"Now"— she turned away and moved to the small, partitioned-off kitchen area— "I'm going to get you something to eat."

"Really, Shenna"—the irritation was back in his voice—"I don't need you to do all this. Please. I told you, I'm not hungry."

"Yes, I heard you." Moving to the small cupboard by the gas stove she found there was hardly anything in it; she saw only things like gravy mix, ketchup, a packet of salt, a nearly empty packet of corn flakes, pickles. The small refrigerator told a similar story. As she looked into its almost empty interior she heard Caspar's voice come to her over the thin partition. "There's not much there, I know, but I've got to go out shopping soon. I shall stock up then."

Closing the refrigerator door she moved back into the room, where she saw that he had got back into bed. She looked at her watch. Just turned five o'clock. She moved to the bed, sat on the edge, and looked down into his pale face. Then while he frowned she laid the back of her hand on his brow. He felt too warm. "Do you have a thermometer?" she asked.

"Are you kidding?"

She shrugged. "I guess it was a silly question. Okay, I'm going to go out and get two or three things from the shops—and then I'll come back and make us some dinner. All right?"

Reluctantly he nodded, avoiding her eyes. She got up from the bed. "Where are your keys?" she asked.

"On the mantelpiece."

She took the keys and moved toward the door. "I'll be back in a little while."

She was back in the room just over half an hour later, carrying two plastic carrier bags of food and other items. Caspar frowned as she put the bags on the table and began to unpack them.

"I have to tell you," he said coldly, "I can't pay you for those things—today. I'm afraid you'll have to wait a while."

"Did I say anything about your having to pay me?"

"Whether or not you said anything is beside the point. I'm not about to take handouts."

She turned angrily. "For God's sake, Caspar! Can't you let up on your goddamn pride for five minutes? I want to help you—so *please* let me."

As he stared at her in surprise she took a thermometer from some tissue paper, cleaned it, shook it, and said, "Open your mouth."

"Oh for Christ's sake," he muttered.

She sighed. "My patience is running out, Caspar, so open your goddamn mouth before I force it open and stuff this thing down your throat."

"You chose the wrong career," he said dryly. "With that bedside manner you should have been a nurse. Obviously Florence Nightingale was one of your heroines."

"Yeah, and you won't get around me with smooth talk either, so just open your mouth."

A flicker of a smile touched his expression as he looked into her eyes, and then he opened his mouth and allowed her to put the end of the thermometer under his tongue. That done, she moved away and continued unpacking the bags. A little later, when she took the thermometer from his mouth, she studied it and gave a nod. "Yes, you have a temperature. Probably flu or something." She filled a tumbler at the tap and then brought it to him with two aspirins on her palm. Take these; they'll bring your temperature down and make you feel a little better."

When he had swallowed the tablets she set about heating a can of minestrone soup. When it was ready, she sat at his bedside while they ate. She was ready to cook some eggs then, but after the soup he wanted nothing more. When she had taken the plates to the kitchen she came back and sat down again on the chair facing him. "There's more soup for you later on," she said. "You just need to heat it. I'll make some tea in a while if you'd like some—but first I think you and I should have a little talk."

"Stop being so damned pushy." His smile was stronger now. "A little talk about what?"

"About you—and your situation."

"What do you mean?"

She sighed. "Oh, listen, Caspar, let's level with each other, okay? Let's not play games. I know you're broke. I just didn't realize *how* broke, that's all."

Silence for a few moments, then he said, "How do you know so much?"

She shrugged. "Things have a way of getting out. And let's face it—there are some things that're difficult to hide. I mean, I know why you didn't go on the trip to Oxford—and there's also the fact that you haven't been eating right. There are other things, too."

"It's a pity folk can't mind their own business."

"I agree—but why don't you tell me about it anyway? I'd like to help if I can."

"Thanks all the same, Shenna, but I don't see how you can do anything."

He said nothing more. She waited a few moments, then said, "Why didn't you go home to Wales? Weren't your family expecting you?"

"No."

"Oh . . ." She paused. "Won't they help you?"

"My only family is my father—and he's not talking to me."

"Why? What happened? You have a fight with him or something?"

He shook his head. "Call it just—disapproval of me."

"For something you've done?"

He paused before answering. "No. It's for something I *am*." He waved a dismissing hand. "That's enough. I don't want to go into it anymore."

"Okay."

"Anyway, my father's more or less disowned me—which has thrown quite a hefty spanner into the works, as far as my studies are concerned."

"How come?"

"I got a grant from my local council to pay for my school fees and help toward materials—and it was agreed that the rest of my expenses would be met by my father. And he was agreeable to it."

"Can he afford it?"

"Oh, yes—without ever missing it. But then, while I was visiting him in the autumn, we got into a little discussion and—well, I told him a couple of things about myself that he didn't want to know. In the past we didn't exactly get on like a house on fire, but at least we were friendly with one another. But then when I told him I—" He paused. "Well, it was as if a shutter came down. It was my own fault, of course. I should have kept my mouth shut. Anyway, that was it. He stopped all payments into my bank account."

"Maybe he'll come around in time."

"Yes, I think perhaps he will—and I just hope by then it's not too late." He shook his head. "He's a—a good man, really. Generous—quite kind. He's not been the same, though, since my mother died a couple of years back. They were very close. And I think that's one of the reasons he's so bitter and angry—because I was all he had left and I've turned out to be something of a disappointment. Right now he just can't forgive me."

"Have you tried to talk to him?"

"A couple of times, but it was no good. I won't try again."

"So what are you going to do?"

"I don't know. I've got to finish the Foundation Course and then enroll for the degree course starting in September. Hopefully I can get a larger grant. I shall be okay then."

"And until that time?"

"Well, for one thing, I've got to get a job. It doesn't matter what—in a restaurant or a pub—anything."

"When will you do it?"

"Evenings after school—and at weekends."

"My God, you'll be a wreck—even more than you are now."

He shrugged. "It can't be helped. I can't see any other way out. Anyway, I can't find anything, no matter how hard I've tried."

"But what about your *own* painting—the work you do outside of school, I mean? When will you have time for that? You won't, will you?"

"Not for a while, no, but—ah, well, I'll survive."

She stared at him for a second or two, then touched his arm. "Sure you will." She got to her feet. "I'll make that tea."

* * *

Next morning, Monday, when she called on Caspar again, she found the room warm and more comfortable. He had eaten the soup she had left for him, his temperature was lower, and he looked a lot brighter.

For lunch she prepared more soup and some lightly scrambled eggs. He ate most of it. Later, after the dishes were washed and dried, she moved back to the bed and saw that he was sleeping. She stood there for a few moments, then turned away and began to study his paintings.

The next day after calling Alfred Carson, she set off in the car for his gallery, reaching it just after eleven and pulling up in front of it on a double yellow line. A couple of minutes later Alfred was there, helping her to carry inside the half dozen canvases she had brought. When the last one had been safely deposited in the room behind the gallery she drove the car around the block until she found a parking space, then walked back to the gallery, where she met Alfred just emerging from the room at the rear. Coming to a stop in the open doorway, he looked at her with a puzzled frown on his brow.

"Would somebody mind telling me what's going on?" he said.

She nodded. "I thought you might ask me that."

He turned, and Shenna followed him into the room. There she saw that he had unwrapped the canvases. They stood on the floor, leaning against a wall. When he had closed the door behind her he said, "These aren't your paintings."

"I wish they were."

He waited for her to continue. After a moment she said, "Alfred, what can I tell you? You wanted some good pictures for your new exhibition—and here they are."

He stared at her for a moment, then picked up one of the

canvases. Reading the signature in the lower right corner, he said, "What's that? Oliver? Caspar Oliver?"

"Yes."

"Someone you know, obviously. A friend?"

"Yes. Though that's beside the point. The point is that he's got so much talent, and if anyone deserves to have his work seen *he* does. Don't you agree?"

He didn't answer but put the canvas back on the floor and took up another one. There was silence in the room for several minutes then while he gazed at the paintings one by one.

"So," Shenna said at last, "what do you think?"

"Are you sure you want to do this?" he asked, turning to her.

"Very sure."

"You're certain of it? I mean, it's not just some strange kind of reaction to—to what happened to your mother?"

"No, believe me, it's not." She waved a hand at the paintings. "I've only got to look at these and I know I'm doing the right thing. *Caspar's* the one who deserves the exposure, not me. He *needs* it, too."

"Needs it?"

"The exposure *and* the money. They will sell, won't they? His paintings?"

"I shouldn't think there's much doubt of that."

She nodded and, without going into detail or reasons why, spoke a little of Caspar's financial difficulties. When she had finished Carson said, "A well-mounted exhibition of his work should set him up and get him off to a good start on the right course. And he deserves it—you're right there." He frowned. "But do you realize that I've started work on your show? Putting out publicity for it. . . ."

"I thought you might have, but does that really matter?"

Ignoring the question, he said, "What does he think about all this—you bringing his paintings here in place of your own?"

"He doesn't know. Yet."

"How did you get them?"

"He was sleeping, and I took the opportunity to take them and put them in the car." She smiled. "And when I say he was sleeping, don't go and get the wrong idea."

He shrugged. "What business is it of mine? Anyway, how do you think he'll react when he finds out what you've done?"

"I think he'll get mad. But I don't care." She paused. "He's got talent, hasn't he?"

Carson gave a nod. "Yes, he has. A very special talent, I'd say."

"And—and you'll show his work, won't you? In place of mine?"

"If that's what you want."

"No, Alfred, you have to want it, too." She gazed at him steadily. "Do you?"

He nodded once and then again. "Yes, I do."

Caspar stared at her in amazement when she told him what she had done. He was out of bed now, and looking so much better.

"I don't understand," he said. "Have you gone out of your mind?"

"No. Just the opposite—I think in this instance I've found it."

"But the exhibition—it's *yours*. It's what you wanted so much. And you've done so much work toward it."

"I know, but it's different now. Now I want *you* to have it."

"But—but *why?*"

"Because it's right."

"That's nonsense."

"No, it's not. It makes a lot of sense this way. All I have to do is look at your paintings and then look at my own—and I know then that what I'm doing is the right thing. You're the one who should be having the exhibition, not me. And I want you to have it."

"But I can't accept it. I just can't."

"Yes, you can." She paused. "You'd be a fool to turn the opportunity down, and you know that."

There was a long silence. "You're sure about this, are you?" he said at last.

"Absolutely."

He shook his head. "I don't know what to say."

"You don't have to say anything. There's not much time and there's a lot to get done." She paused. "So your answer is yes."

He gave a slow nod. "As you said—I'd be a fool to turn down such an opportunity."

"Right."

"But—but what about the framing of my canvases? It'll cost a fortune."

"Don't worry about that. Alfred Carson will fix all that up." She wrote Carson's name, address, and telephone number on a piece of notepaper and placed it on the table. As Caspar picked it up, she said, "Give him a call. He's expecting you. He'll get your framing done and deduct the cost from your sales."

"He's sure of my making some sales, then?"

"You think he's in this business for fun?" As she finished speaking she opened her purse, took out some bank notes, and placed them on the table.

Caspar frowned. "What's that for?"

"You're going to need a few things for yourself as well. Go shopping and get some food—whatever you need. You can pay me back when you pay Alfred back. There's no hurry."

Caspar slowly smiled. "I can hardly believe it. I feel I'm going to wake up soon and find it's all a dream."

"No, you won't."

He shook his head. "You're a strange girl."

"In what way?"

"I don't know. You do something like this and—and I'm just not prepared for it. I can't say anything—except thank you."

"It's enough. Believe me, Caspar, it's made me very happy." She looked at her watch. The time was almost two-fifteen. "And now I have to leave. You're going to be pretty busy for a while, I imagine."

A few minutes later she went out into the chill January afternoon. Her car was parked in the next street, and she set off toward it, heels ringing on the pavement. Then, as she got to the corner, she came to a stop and stood quite still, breathing in the cold air, aware, all at once, of a great feeling of relief.

Over the next few days she gave Caspar what help he needed in the way of driving him to the gallery and various other places. The rest of her unaccustomed leisure time she spent in relaxed pursuits, either quietly reading on her own, visiting exhibitions, or spending time with friends. Margaret was staying in Yorkshire till the weekend, but Hannah was in town, and they visited one another and saw a movie together. She saw a little of Kevin, too, and of Wesley, with whom she went out one evening for a quiet dinner at a small, inexpensive restaurant overlooking the Thames. And so the few remaining days of the Christmas holiday went by. Next Monday, the tenth, the spring term would begin.

Her growing sense of ease came to an abrupt end on that Sunday afternoon.

After sleeping late she had got up and made herself some coffee, and while she drank it she resumed her reading of the paperback of *Bridges Are for Burning*, which she had brought from the cottage at Hallowridge. She found it to be well written and enjoyable, and she could well see what Jack Tanner had meant about wanting to cast her in the role of the girl. Later, opening the drawer to put the book away, she saw again the little collection of photographs and postcards she had so hurriedly put there, out of sight. After a moment's hesitation she picked them up.

Apart from the postcards Ian had sent, there was the photograph of her handsome, smiling father, the photograph of the little church at Hinton Peeble, and also the one of Ian himself, sitting on the bench before the pond.

And all at once the reality of it hit her. It was as if recent events had somehow submerged her sense of awareness, and now, as other preoccupations receded, she was faced with it all again. Her mother—her father—Ian . . .

After sitting there unmoving for a moment she got up, put on her coat and muffler, tied a scarf around her head, left the house, and made her way slowly up Lee Road toward Blackheath. There she went through the village and onto the hard earth of the heath itself. She walked slowly while the melancholy thoughts came crowding in. After a while she sat down on a bench—the same bench, she realized, where she had been sitting when she had gone off without her bag that time. Before her the heath looked cold and bleak, while above her the sky had about it the flat, yellowish look of promised snow. She felt lost, as if her newfound sense of freedom had become one of total bereavement. Her mother was dead and Ian would not be returning—and her father, though twenty years dead, was newly lost to her as well. And here she was, without any sense of purpose, sitting in the middle of a bleak stretch of grass in an alien country. *What am I doing here?* The words turned over in her mind like sounds from a cracked record as she sat there, oblivious to everything but her feeling of desolation. After a while snow began to fall, muffling the noises of the traffic that cut across the heath and shutting her in, cocooning her in her misery and accentuating her feeling of aloneness.

She turned, looking about her at the snow-blurred landscape, and then suddenly she saw near the church a figure, indistinct in the thick, flurrying snow. Someone was watching her. Suddenly afraid, she got to her feet, and as she did so the figure left the shadow of the church wall and began to come toward her. Hesitating for only a moment, she began to move quickly away. And then she heard from behind her a voice calling her name, a voice she recognized. With relief she stopped, turned around, and waited as the figure came closer.

"Kevin . . ."

He came to a stop before her and said apologetically, "I'm sorry if I frightened you."

She nodded. "You did, just for a moment. I didn't know it was you." She paused. "What were you doing there?"

"I was in the village, just coming out of the station when you went by. I waved to you but you didn't see me. Then I came after you onto the heath and saw you sitting on the bench. I wanted to go straight up to you, but I didn't like to. You looked rather—I don't know. Are you all right?" She nodded dully. He frowned. "Are you sure? There's something wrong, isn't there? Tell me."

She gazed at him for a moment, then burst into sobs. He stepped closer and wrapped her in his arms. "Don't—oh, please, Shenna, don't. I can't bear to see you cry."

She went on weeping. "I'm sorry," she said between her sobs. "I know it's dumb of me, but I can't help it. It's as if everything I had has gone—and I don't know what to do anymore."

"What are you talking about?"

"It's true." She spoke briefly then of her mother, of her long-dead father, and then of Ian. "I've lost everyone in just a matter of a few weeks."

He held her close to him. The snow was thinning, stopping. "You're going through a bad time right now," he said, "but you wait—once you get started back at school with your friends it'll be better. Once you get back to your painting it'll be all right again."

She turned her head and looked off into the distance. "No . . ." She paused. "That's something else I've lost—my painting—if I ever had it."

"What?"

"It was a charade—my coming here to study. I know that now."

"Don't say that."

"It's true. Who was I kidding? Oh, yes, I have a certain ability, but that's all. It's nothing that's going to turn the place upside down. I realize it now."

"No." He touched his fingertips to her chin. "Listen, I do believe that when you get back to school and get involved with the course again you'll feel differently."

She shook her head. "I'm not going back to school. Not now."

"Shenna—"

"No." She shook her head again. "I don't belong here, Kevin—whatever ideas I might have entertained. No. Now that I'm *truly* on my own I've got to make an effort to grow up—and I might as well start by facing the truth—about everything. All that romantic nonsense about my father's homeland and all that guff. This isn't my home. My home's in America—and that's where I'm going." She gave a rueful smile. "That's what most creatures do instinctively when they're hurt, isn't it? Head for home—for their den? That's what I'm going to do." She nodded. "*Before* I was going for my mother's sake. Not now. Now I'm going for mine."

She smiled up into his sad face, then shivered and linked her arm through his. "I'm cold," she said. "Come on—let's go back inside and warm up."

Later, that evening, she telephoned Amy in California. "I've decided to come back," she told her. "I'm coming home."

There was a little silence. Then Amy said, "Something's happened, hasn't it? What is it?"

Shenna hesitated before she answered. "Oh, it's a long story. I'll tell you later, when I see you."

"Okay, anytime you want. But whatever's happened, I'm glad you're coming back. I've missed you. When d'you plan to return?"

"I'm not sure yet, but soon—in the next few days."

"That soon. Will you go home to Westwood right away?"

"I don't know. My mother closed it all up and put some of the things in storage. Still, I think I'll manage there okay."

"Why not come and stay with me for a while?"

"I don't know."

"Just till you get back on your feet."

"Thanks. We'll see."

"What are you doing about your art studies?"

"Oh, I'll tell you about all that when I see you. Anyway, I have to think about that. I have to think about a lot of things."

"Well, if you think you might want to do some acting, there's quite a bit happening in TV right now. And quite a few new movies starting up. If you decide to get back into all that."

"I don't know what I want."

"No, but it's there if you want it. Bound to be for someone like you."

"Someone like me?"

"Yes, with all the talent you've got. Someone as good as you—it's a crime to see you floundering."

Shenna smiled. "Thanks. Maybe it won't be for long."

18

The following day at school Shenna told Trandell of her decision to return to California, saying that she wanted to go away for a while to do some serious thinking. She told him she would be leaving in the next two or three days, as soon as she had decided what to do with her car and had made other necessary arrangements. "So soon?" he said, and then, "But what about your exhibition?" In reply she told him that the exhibition was no longer hers, that Caspar was taking it in her place.

He looked at her closely and she nodded. "I can see you approve," she said.

"Caspar's very talented," he said. "He could use a good break like this."

"That's what I figured." She smiled suddenly. "So—now that we've sorted Caspar out, all I've got to do now is the same for myself."

When she left him she went to the foyer and put a notice on the board advertising her car for sale. The price she asked for it was low, but even so she had no real hopes of making any swift sale among her impecunious fellow students. Still, there was a chance, and if it didn't work she would take it to a used-car lot and sell it there.

Harry came by as she finished pinning the note to the board, and he looked at it and said, "Damn—I've just bought myself a little Mini—only last week. If I'd known you were selling your car I'd have waited and bought it from you."

"Shame," Shenna said, "but I didn't know last week that I'd be selling it."

After leaving the school she returned to Elm Court Road,

where she called the agents for the flat and told them of her plans to return to the United States earlier than she had anticipated. She would leave the keys with her neighbor, she told them. She was sure Kevin wouldn't mind; she'd fix it up with him later. After that she phoned to inquire after flights to Los Angeles and booked a seat on a British Airways flight leaving Heathrow late Wednesday morning. Now that she had made her decision to go, there was no point in waiting around.

When she had finished the call she went back to the school, where she joined Hannah, Margaret, Caspar, and Brian for lunch. Caspar, looking fit now, and brighter than she had seen him for a long time, had already told the others about the exhibition, and on her arrival she found it the main topic of conversation. Then, however, the talk turned to her decision to leave, the news of which had soon gotten about. "But is it necessary for you to go so *soon?*" Margaret asked. "Why don't you just relax for two or three weeks, give yourself time to adjust to everything. You might feel differently in a few days."

Shenna shook her head. "No," she said, "I've got to go back. But who knows?—maybe someday I'll return."

After lunch she went back to the flat and arranged for her paintings to be packed up and sent to Westwood. It was ironic, she thought as she replaced the receiver after calling the shipping company; most of the paintings had only just arrived from California.

Margaret telephoned when classes were finished and said that she and Hannah had been discussing the possibility of some little get-together before Shenna left and suggested that the following evening might be a good time if Shenna was agreeable. Shenna, who would much rather have left quietly, without anything in the way of a send-off, couldn't do anything but agree. Margaret said then that she and Hannah would go ahead with the necessary arrangements, adding that the party would probably be held at Hannah's flat and that they would call later to confirm it all.

Wesley had arranged to drop by that evening, and when he arrived Shenna told him of her change of plans. He shook his head impatiently and said almost sharply, "You want to make up your mind what you're going to do."

"I *have* made up my mind, Wesley."

"Until you change it again, you mean."

"No more. Not this time."

"You're not giving it a chance," he said, and now his tone was morose. "You're just reacting to—to the things that have happened."

"I don't think so."

He sighed. "It's certain now that I'll never see you again."

"Listen," she said, "you'll come over to California one day or I'll come back to England—either to work or to take a vacation—and we'll see one another." Then, before he could say anything else, she added, "By the way, some of my friends from school are giving me a little farewell party tomorrow. I'd love you to come. Can you?"

He hesitated for a moment, then said, "Oh, you don't want me there with all your arty friends."

"I *do* want you—and they're not arty. They're very nice. You'll like them. I'll know later this evening or tomorrow morning about the time and so on and I'll call you. I'll let you know."

He left a little while later, looking somewhat dejected, and not long afterward Hannah phoned to say that the party would be held at her home and would start at around seven-thirty. It would be a buffet—and if there was anyone Shenna wanted to invite, then she should go ahead. When Shenna had hung up she went across the hall and knocked on Kevin's door. She wanted him to come to the party too. There was no answer, though; she'd have to try again later.

*   *   *

She lay in bed with her eyes open in the darkness and realized that something had awakened her from her sleep. Some noise from the street—or perhaps some sound from the flat above, where Miss Martin had got up in the night? She listened. No, no sound from above, and no sound from the usually quiet street either. After a while she closed her eyes and turned her head on the pillow. And then she heard another sound, and realized that someone was outside in the hall.

Turning her head, she peered at the bedside clock and saw the luminous hands pointing to one forty-two. And then all at once she heard a sound right at her own front door, at the mail slot—a brief, faint rustling sound. Immediately she sat upright, listening.

She switched on the bedside lamp and got slowly out of bed, crept to the door, and stood listening. She could hear nothing. Then, glancing down, she saw a rectangle of white lying on the doormat. Stooping, she picked up a small envelope.

Sitting on the edge of the bed she looked at the envelope. There was nothing written on its face. She tore it open and found inside a single sheet of paper. She unfolded it and stared at the words printed there in block capitals:

DON'T GO. PLEASE DON'T GO. IF YOU LEAVE NOW
YOUR MOTHER'S DEATH WAS ALL FOR NOTHING.

The words struck a chill within her. *If you leave now your mother's death was all for nothing*. The note was from him— John Cosgray. The words went over and over in her head and she became aware suddenly of the thudding of her heart. He had come into the hall and put the note through her mail slot and then crept away again. Or *had* he crept away? Perhaps he was still there, out in the hall. . . .

Getting up from the bed, she moved silently to the door, came to a stop with her hand upon the catch, and stood listening. No sound. Nothing. Then, slowly and quietly, she drew back the catch and opened the door a foot. Holding her breath, she looked out into the hall, where the automatic timer had long since switched off the light and the only illumination came from the little that now spilled from her own flat. The hall was empty. As she closed the door again she found that her hands were damp with perspiration. She moved back to the bed and took up the note once more.

If you leave now your mother's death was all for nothing.

What did he mean? Her mother's death had been an accident. There was no doubt of that, and no one had ever thought otherwise. And who was he, this John Cosgray? She thought back to the other things he had done, and realized that they had all been demonstrations of affection, things done in an effort to make her stay in London comfortable and pleasant. And now he had come creeping round to her flat in the small hours of the morning leaving her a note begging her to stay.

She went back to the note. There was no escaping it: the words implied that her mother's death had not been an accident but had been for a purpose. For the purpose of keeping her, Shenna, there in England? *If you leave now your mother's death was all for nothing.*

And if her mother's death had not been the result of an accident, then what was the alternative—murder?

Clenching and unclenching her hands, she began to pace the room. She didn't know what to do. Should she report it? She knew what the result would be, though, if she went to the police. Apart from having to stay on in London, there would also be all the publicity. And what would it achieve? However her mother had died, nothing was going to bring her back. Besides, if there was some madman on her tracks, she'd feel safer a few thousand miles away.

She knew then what she would do. She would leave just as she had planned and she would let nothing stop her. There was only one day to go, and then she would be on the plane and all this horror would be behind her. *Everything* would be behind her and she could relax again.

She lay down on the bed after a while and closed her eyes, but it was a long, long time before sleep came.

She was awake again just after seven and after lying in blissful forgetfulness for a moment or two she got up, bathed and dressed, and ate some toast and drank some coffee. Then, soon after nine o'clock, she dialed the number of Wesley's office to tell him about the party at Hannah's that evening. She'd never felt less like going to any kind of party, but she had committed herself to it now; and anyway, she told herself, she would probably feel better surrounded by friends. The woman who answered the telephone told her that Wesley hadn't yet arrived. After leaving word for him to phone her, Shenna hung up. About half an hour later Wesley phoned back.

"I got your message," he said.

"Did you oversleep?" she said with an attempt at brightness. "Shame on you." He didn't respond in any like way, though, and she contented herself with giving him the address of the party and the time of its commencement. He started to say in a slightly aggrieved tone, "I don't know whether I can make it—" when Shenna cut in, saying almost curtly, "Well, that's up to you, Wesley. If you want to come you'll be very welcome, but do what you want."

There was a little silence, then he said, "You're angry with me. Don't be."

"I'm sorry, but—well, I've got a lot on my mind right now, what with my leaving tomorrow and—"

He cut in, "You're still going, then."

"Of course I am."

"Oh, I just hoped that—well, that you might have changed your mind."

"It's too late for that now."

"It's not too late. Of course it's not."

"Well, whatever. I can't stop to talk about it right now. I've got to get my things packed up for shipping home and then I've got to do something about selling my car. I couldn't find a buyer at school."

"I see." He paused. "Shall I call for you tonight—for the party?"

"Okay, fine, yes."

"What time?"

"About seven or seven-fifteen or so?"

"Okay, I'll be there."

The shippers who had contracted to pick up her paintings were due at eleven-thirty, and she decided she would wait till they had gone and then take her car out and sell it. In the meantime she could get on with sorting out a few other things that could go by sea and also pack her bags for the plane.

She got to work quickly and efficiently and by eleven-thirty all the packing was finished. Only her painting materials—her easel, paints, brushes, and spare canvases—remained. She would leave it all; perhaps one of the other students could make use of it. With nothing else to do for the moment, she made herself a cup of coffee and sat waiting for the representatives of the shipping company.

By twelve-thirty there was still no sign of them, but a little later a man from the company telephoned to apologize and say that the collectors had had difficulties with the van, but that they would send someone to her after lunch—by three-thirty at the latest. There was nothing she could do until then but be patient.

She tried to eat a sandwich, but left it barely touched on her plate. She seemed to be in a state of limbo—just waiting for the hours to pass till the morning, when she would get a taxi out to the airport. She would never feel at ease now until she was back in California.

The collectors from the shipping company arrived at the flat just after three-fifty and left again some ten minutes later. Shenna heaved a sigh of relief at their departure; she had very little time left now in which to find a buyer for her car—and she wanted to consult two or three if possible and get the best price she could. One dealer she intended to visit was the one who had sold her the car. On impulse, searching for another, she phoned Harry at the school and asked him the name of the dealer from whom he had bought his Mini. "You just caught me," he said, "I was just on my way out." She wrote down the address he gave her and she put it in her bag, then left the house and drove away.

A little while later Harry, driving his Mini, turned the corner into Elm Court Road. The sun was going down, but in the fading light he saw the figure of a man walk up to the front door of number nineteen. He thought he recognized him from the back, and for a moment he slowed the car in order to get a better look. As he did so the man disappeared into the hall.

It began to snow as Shenna headed for Woolwich, and in the deepening gloom the visibility swiftly diminished. Her journey was made more difficult by the fact that she didn't know the area very well. She could do nothing, though, but go on.

There was no answer to his ringing of Shenna's doorbell, and after trying two or three times more, he took a key from his pocket—the copy he had had made after finding her bag on the heath that night. Inserting it in the lock, he turned it, gently pushed open the door, and went in.

When he had closed the door behind him he hurried to the

window and drew the curtains on the falling darkness, then switched on the light and looked around him. In one corner stood her easel, and beside it two or three blank canvases and a couple of boxes that contained paints and brushes. He saw other painting paraphernalia: a roll of canvas, wooden stretchers, and a hammer. Nearby on the floor stood two suitcases. He walked over and lifted one of them. It was full, the key still in the lock. Placing the case on the bed he opened it and found it contained clothes, toilet articles, a couple of paperbacks, a notebook, and various papers.

He let fall the lid of the case and sat on the bed as the full awareness of the fact struck him. She *was* going away. There was no doubt of it. And once she had gone she would never come back. She would be out of his life for ever.

"*No. . . !*"

He cried the word aloud and then sat silent and afraid as the sound seemed to echo in the silence of the room. Then, getting up, he began to go through the suitcase's contents again.

When he had looked thoroughly through the first one he opened the second and went through that. He was searching for her passport. If he had that he could perhaps keep her here a little longer. It was not to be found, though, and in his frustration he scooped up a bundle of the clothes and hurled it across the room.

"*You can't go! You can't!*"

Sobbing out the words, he began to snatch and tear at the contents of the cases until they lay scattered all around the room. Then, in his growing fury and frustration, he turned to the boxes of painting materials and began to hurl aside the bottles of oil and turpentine, the palette knives, the brushes and the paints. After that he took up the hammer and attacked the mirror that hung on the wall. In just a few minutes he was surrounded by broken glass, smashed toilet articles, wrecked tubes of paint, and torn paper and clothing.

As he stood breathless amid the debris, the telephone began to ring. For a moment he froze and then he turned toward it and, after a little hesitation, picked up the receiver. Putting it to his ear, he said nothing at first, but just listened, then after a moment he heard a man's voice: "Hello?"

He answered then, softly, his heart thudding, "Hello."

"Hello." The man's voice on the other end sounded slightly puzzled. "Is Shenna there?"

"No, I'm afraid not. I'm a friend of hers. Can I give her a message?"

"Well, yes—please—tell her that Ian called."

"Ian?"

"Yes, tell her, please, that I shall be in London in the morning. I'm calling from San Francisco right now. Do you know whether she's received my letter? She should have got it by now."

"I've no idea."

"What time do you expect her back?"

"I—I couldn't say."

"You don't know?"

"Sorry."

"Who am I speaking to?"

"I told you—a friend."

"Haven't you got a name?"

"Not to you." *Click.* He replaced the receiver in the cradle and the call was at an end.

Ian. Who was Ian? The question nagged at his mind and with an effort he dismissed it and stood looking around him again at the chaos he had created. And then he started violently as there came the sound of a footstep outside in the hall. He stood rigid, listening. Next second there was a ring at the doorbell. He waited. The bell rang again, and again. Then there came a voice.

"Shenna. . . ? Are you there?"

Keep quiet and he'll go away.

"Shenna. . . ?" A pause, then the voice again: "Shenna, there's a letter here for you. It was delivered to my flat by mistake. . . ." After a little silence a letter came through the mail slot and fell onto the mat.

He crept to the door, bent and picked the letter up. Air mail from America. Then, putting his eye to the peephole he looked into the hall. There was a man there. He had light brown hair; he wore a brown overcoat and looked to be about his own age. He was just standing there, as if waiting and listening. Well, he could go on waiting and listening. After a while he saw him move away out of sight and then there came the sound of the outside door opening and closing.

Turning quietly aside, he moved to the bed, pulled back the cover, and lay down, burying his face in the pillow. He could smell the sweet scent of her. For some moments he lay there, reveling in the smell, and then, realizing that he was still holding the letter, he sat up and looked at it. The sender's name on the envelope was Ian Bradley. It must be the man who had just phoned; this must be the letter he had spoken of. He tore the envelope open.

At the top of the page inside was an address in San Francisco. Beneath it was written:

My dear Shenna,

I shall be in London very soon and I'm getting this note off to you as quickly as I can in the hope that it'll get to you before I do and perhaps prepare you to some extent for my arrival.

I don't know whether you'll want to see me. I hope so. I want to see you—very much, at the very least to be able to explain certain things to you—things which, I'm sure, must at present be the source of some confusion—if not unhappiness.

Shenna, do please forgive me for not writing before, as I promised. All I can say is that I very foolishly got myself involved in a certain situation—a situation that was in many ways a remnant of my past and that tended to blind me to the realities of many things. Well, all I can say now is that that involvement is over; it's in the past, and it

*will stay in the past. Now, for the first time in a long time, I can see
clearly.*

*You, in your own recent unhappiness, must have thought me the
most callous of people. I just heard from Alfred a few days ago,
however, of the loss of your mother. Believe me, I'm so sorry. I can
imagine how alone you must have felt—and at a time when I could
have given you comfort and support. Forgive me.*

*I won't stop to write more, but will just say that I hope to see you
again very soon. Until then, try not to think of me unkindly.*

Yours,
Ian

He read the letter through again. Who was he, this Ian?
One of her old American friends? Yes, probably. Surely it
couldn't be anything serious—could it? He wouldn't think
about that now. He put the letter in his pocket and got up
from the bed. It was time he left. Moving to the door he
peered through the peephole again. The hall was empty. He
turned and took a last look around the room. He was sorry
about the damage to her clothes—still, he would get her
some new things later on. Turning back to the door, he
opened it and moved to step out into the hall—and in the
same moment the outer door opened and the young man in
the brown overcoat appeared.

They stood there facing one another, the brown-coated
man looking curiously at the man who stood in the open
doorway to the flat. "Is Shenna in there?" he asked, frowning.

"No, not right now."

"Who are you?"

"A friend of Shenna's." And then, with bravado, "And
who are you?"

The other paused, then said, "My name's Kevin Brightwell. I live opposite." He stepped forward and looked into
the room—and as he did so, his eyes widened in amazement.
"Good God," he breathed. His pale eyes swept the destruc-

tion for a moment, then came back to light on the man before him. "What's been happening? Have you done this?"

There was no answer, and while the other backed up, Kevin came on into the room and slowly turned, looking around him, shaking his head in disbelief. He turned then to face the other man—and in the same moment the raised arm came down.

The hammer caught him on the side of the skull with a loud, dull crack, and he gave a cry and staggered. Again the hammer fell, carefully aimed, striking hard, smashing onto the backs of his fingers as they came up in a feeble attempt to protect his head. With a loud moan he fell to his knees. The hammer came down again and then again and blood sprayed, splattering the wall. Opening his mouth in a wordless cry, Kevin briefly turned his eyes upward to those of his attacker. Then with a final, gasping moan, he fell forward onto his face.

Breath rasping, the man stood there for long, long seconds without moving and then knelt beside the figure and turned him onto his back. He listened for the sound of breathing, but he could hear nothing and he placed a hand on the man's chest. When he detected no movement there he lifted the lid of the right eye—and saw the eye staring back sightlessly into his own. There was no question that he was dead. Quickly then, he went into action. Dipping into Kevin's overcoat pockets, he came up with a set of keys and, hurrying across the hall, he knocked on the door opposite. There was no answer and, satisfied that there was no one inside, he found the key that fitted the lock and opened the door. Then, turning, he switched off the hall light—he needed all the cover he could get—and came back into Shenna's flat, took a grip on the dead man's ankles, and pulled him out through the door.

In a few moments he had dragged him across the hall and into the darkness of the flat opposite, where he released him, letting his feet fall heavily onto the floor. Then, straightening, he dropped the bunch of keys onto the corpse, backed out into the hall, and closed the door.

Back in Shenna's flat he found a sheet of paper and took out his pen and hurriedly wrote a note to her. Then, folding it over, he printed her name in large block capitals on the face. That done, he placed it on the mantelpiece above the gas fire and then turned around to look about him at the room. He should clean up the bloodstains, he said to himself—but there wasn't time; she would be back any minute. Then he saw near the door the hammer with its bloody head and he picked it up and wrapped it in some newspaper; he would dispose of it later on. As he crossed to the door he caught sight of his reflection in the remnants of the mirror and he stopped before it and looked at himself. There was sweat on his brow and he wiped it away with the back of his hand. His dark, sparse hair was damp too. All his exertions. He briefly touched a finger to the pulsing nerve in his temple.

Turning from the mirror, he opened the door and looked cautiously out into the hall. There was no one about. He was just about to switch off the light when he suddenly saw that there were bloodstains on the hall carpet. They had got there when he had dragged the body into the opposite flat; he hadn't noticed them before. It would take too long to clean them up now, though, he decided, and rushing back into Shenna's flat he picked up a chair and carried it into the hall. Seconds later he had unscrewed the bulb and put it in his pocket. When he had replaced the chair in the flat he switched off the light behind him and closed the door.

Emerging into the cold air a moment later he looked about him. There was no sign of Shenna. Then, as quickly as he could, he set off along the street and around the corner to where the Mini was parked.

Inside he sat quite still for long moments, breathing

deeply, aware of the swift beating of his heart. Then at last he secured his seat belt and prepared to drive away. Just before he did so he moved his position slightly to look at his reflection in the driving mirror. He felt a little calmer now.

As he gazed into his reflected eyes, he smiled. Yes, it was true what she had said—the smile suited him; he should smile more often. He smiled at himself again.

"Good old Harry," he whispered.

19

She had got rid of the car—at last. After trying three dealers she had eventually returned to the second one and made the deal. It had been almost five o'clock by that time, and the snow was falling more thickly. Twenty minutes later, after vainly trying to get a taxi and only succeeding in feeding her impatience and frustration, she had eventually got directions from a friendly passerby and caught a bus.

Now, as she got off the bus and hurried to Elm Court Road, it was after six. There was very little time before Wesley was due to arrive, and she also wanted to see Kevin.

Reaching number nineteen, she wearily pushed open the main door and flicked on the switch. When no light came on she shook her head in annoyance and moved through the hall in the dark and unlocked the door to her flat.

A moment later she was inside and staring aghast at the destruction all around her. Then, as her disbelieving eyes moved back and forth over the room, she saw on the mantelpiece a folded sheet of paper with her name printed on it. Stepping through the debris, she picked up the note and read the words written there.

My darling,
   Don't go tomorrow, please. You're here and this is where you belong—with me. Just wait and everything will turn out all right. Don't go now that there is so much promise. You mustn't. Anyway, I won't let you. I love you.

John

She stood trembling. He was insane. Everything in the past had indicated it, but this left no possible doubt. The knowledge brought the terror flooding in. One could reason with a rational, sane person, but with someone like this reality had no meaning. After a while she slowly began to pick up some of the clothes and other items that had been strewn about the room. Whoever had been here had done a thorough job; there was little that hadn't been ruined.

Suddenly the question came to her mind as to how he had gotten into the flat, and she stepped quickly to the door, opened it, and looked at the lock. There was nothing about it to show that it had been forced in any way. She went then to the windows, one after the other, and found them securely locked, just as she had left them. Then whoever it was had got in with a key. But how? And then she realized. The bag that she had left on the park bench—her door key had been inside. Before returning the bag he could have had a copy made the key. Of course. How easy it would have been.

She became aware that the telephone was ringing, but as she reached out for it she suddenly stopped, thinking of those other calls from the caller who had remained silent. She waited, afraid. The ringing went on, though, and at last she picked up the receiver.

"Hello. . . ?"

"Shenna? Is that you?" The call was coming from a public phone booth.

"Yes, who's this?"

"It's Harry Johnson."

"Harry." Relief swept over her, relief that sounded in her voice. He was swift to pick it up.

"Are you all right?" he asked. "You sound—I don't know—different. Are you okay?"

"Yes."

"Are you sure?" He paused. "I just called to see how you got on with your car. Did you sell it?"

"What? Oh, yes—yes, I did."

"Good. You get a decent price for it?"

"I—I think so. I guess so."

"That's fine. I drove by your flat a while back—just to see whether you were in and had had any luck. I didn't ring the bell, though. I saw one of your friends at your front door, so I didn't stop."

"Who?" she said quickly. "Who did you see?"

"I don't know his name. I think it was one of the night-school students. I couldn't be sure, though. It was dark and that street of yours isn't exactly well lit, is it?" He paused. "You sound a bit worried."

Wesley was here, she said to herself. *Wesley was here. Wesley* . . .

"Shenna, are you all right?"

Then, hearing the note of warm sympathy in Harry's voice, the last of her reserve was swept away and she burst into tears.

"Shenna!" he said. "My God, what's the matter?"

She stood there sobbing for a moment or two. Trying to force herself to become calmer, she said breathlessly, "Oh, Harry, I'm sorry for making such a fuss. But I'm afraid you just caught me at a bad time."

"What's up? Can you tell me?"

"Harry, I'm—I'm afraid. . . ."

"I don't understand. Listen, I know you might think I'm butting in—and I don't want to do that—but I'm coming round to see you, okay? Then if there's anything I can do, well—fine. If not, then I'll buzz off again."

"Oh, please—I—"

He cut off her words: "Let me come by and see you, all right? I'll be there in a minute or two."

When she had replaced the receiver Shenna looked at her watch. It was almost a quarter to seven. Wesley would be here at any moment, and she didn't want to see him.

And she knew something else as well. She wouldn't wait till tomorrow before she left. She would go today.

With the decision, she began to move quickly, feverishly, gathering together what essential items she could salvage and putting them in the smaller of the two suitcases. There wasn't much; most of her belongings lay spoiled beyond repair. As she worked she came across the torn photographs of Ian and the church at Hinton Peeble. She found also the framed photograph of her father. The glass was smashed. She stood there looking at his face for a moment and then, shaking the remaining glass fragments free from the frame she put the photograph in the case. A few minutes later she was ready, and the case was closed and locked. That done, she hurried from the flat and stepped across the hall to Kevin's door and rang his bell. There was no answer, and after waiting impatiently for a few seconds she moved back into her own flat and began to scribble a note to him.

She had just finished when there came a ring at the doorbell. She stood frozen. Then, quietly, she moved to the door and peered out through the peephole. It was Harry.

"Are you all right?" he said when she opened the door.

She nodded. "Yes, I'm okay. Come on in." She stepped aside and he entered. He was wearing an overcoat with a dark muffler around his neck. As she closed the door behind him he came to a sudden stop.

"My God!" he breathed. "What the hell happened here?"

She shrugged, watching his shocked expression. "As you can see, I've had a visitor."

"Have you called the police?"

"No."

"Why not?" Then, without waiting for an answer, he added, "When did you discover this?"

"Not long ago—when I got back from selling my car."

He shook his head. "No wonder you sounded upset. Do you know yet what they took?"

"I don't think they took anything. I can't think of anything that's missing."

"Are you sure? Maybe you haven't checked properly."

"I'm fairly sure." She paused. "I don't think they came here to—to steal. In fact, I'm certain of it."

"What do you mean? If they didn't break in to rob you, then what did they come for?"

"I—I don't know."

He started toward the telephone. "I think we should call the police—and without wasting any time, either."

"No, no—!" She stepped quickly toward him. "No, I don't want the police involved in this."

"Why not? They ought to know."

"No, please."

"Well, what are you going to do?"

"Nothing. I'm just going to leave. Luckily I had my passport with me, so he didn't get that."

"He?"

"Whoever it was."

As she looked at him, he took off his overcoat and jacket and dropped them across the back of a chair. She stared at him. "What are you doing?"

Rolling up his sleeves, he began to gather up some of the broken glass. "I'll clear up a bit of this mess. It won't take long."

"No, Harry, no—there isn't time."

He frowned. "You can't stay here with it like this, can you?"

"I'm not staying here. I told you—I'm leaving—now."

"Are you in *that* much of a hurry?"

"Yes. I'm going to the airport tonight.

"Are there flights tonight?"

"No, but I'll stay at a hotel at the airport and get my flight in the morning. And if I can't get into a hotel—well, it doesn't matter. I'll sit up all night in the airport lounge if I have to. I don't care—just so long as I get away from here."

*　　*　　*

Everything was happening so quickly, too quickly, he said to himself as he turned away and dropped the fragments of broken glass into the rubbish bin. She was going away from him and soon there would be no time left. And that was what he had based all his plans on—time.

He could feel the nerve throbbing at his temple. He could have wept as he thought about all the plans going awry. Nothing was ready. He had prepared a room for the two of them, but that was all. He just wasn't ready.

The most important thing, though, was Shenna's feeling for him. At the beginning his vague plans had been made in the belief that she would be there for many months—in which time she would have come to love him, he knew. Now those promised months had dwindled to minutes.

Shenna watched as Harry pulled down his sleeves and began to put his jacket and coat back on. Then he said, "How will you get to the airport? Have you ordered a taxi?"

"Not yet. I'll phone now."

"I'll drive you, if you like."

"Oh, Harry, I couldn't put you to so much trouble."

"It's no trouble. You were so kind to me once and I said at the time I wouldn't forget your kindness. The very least I can do for you is this little service. I wish I could do more."

"I did nothing for you. But if you get me to the airport, it'll be the greatest help you could give me."

"We'll get you there, don't worry." He finished buttoning his coat. "Okay, ready when you are."

She reached out and lightly touched his arm with her fingertips. "Bless you, Harry. And thank you. You're a good man."

She took up her bag, her small case, the note for Kevin, and the door key. How strange it was. She had entered this little apartment bringing with her so much hope, seeing the time before her with so much promise, and now here she was, leaving it like this—creeping off, hurrying to leave it far behind, dogged by fear, intent only on getting away.

Harry stood in the open doorway as she finished her survey of the room, then he backed into the darkened hall and she followed him and locked the door. That done, she stepped across the hall and pushed the key and the note through Kevin's mail slot. Then she turned back to Harry. "Okay," she said, "let's go."

The night was cold. There was no moon visible and the sky was very dark. The snow had stopped now, but it had settled on the pavement, and there was the feel of more snow in the air. As they moved from the front gate Harry took her case and moved to the right, making for his car, which was parked nearby. Shenna followed. When they got to the car he unlocked it and put the case on the back seat. As he did so there came a call from behind them.

"Shenna . . ."

It was Wesley's voice, and Shenna turned and saw him moving toward them along the street. "Ah, your friend again," said Harry as he opened the door and got in.

Shenna nodded and said quickly, "Please—can we go?"

He leaned across and opened the passenger door and seconds later she had gotten in beside him and he had started the motor and was driving away. Her last glimpse of Wesley was as she looked back and saw him standing at the curb.

When Harry had moved the car out onto the main road he said, without looking at her, "Why didn't you want to talk to your friend?" She didn't answer, and after a moment he added, "You don't think—well—that he was responsible for what happened in your flat, do you?"

"I don't know."

"Just because I happened to see him going up to your front door. I mean, why would a friend do something like that?"

She said nothing.

"I'm sorry," Harry said. "What's it got to do with me, anyway? Tell me to mind my own business, why don't you?"

They drove in silence for some distance, while Shenna gazed unseeingly from the window. In her head the puzzling thoughts and images tumbled and shifted and drifted, mostly without any seeming form of recognizable significance, but at other times settling into patterns that lasted for brief, tantalizing moments before being swept away again by other thoughts that came churning in their wake. And through it all there was something in particular that eluded her. It was something she had seen—something that should have meant something to her—something that should have met with instant recognition. But she didn't know what it was. All she knew was that it was there, refusing to go away, hovering on the rim of her awareness, just waiting for the penny to drop. As she tried to remember, it seemed for a moment to come tantalizingly closer, and she realized that it was something she had seen very recently, something that was *wrong*, something that had jarred in her brain—but then, quickly, before she'd had a chance to reach out and grasp it, it was gone.

"What are you thinking about?"

Harry's voice came breaking into her thoughts and she turned and smiled at him. "Nothing," she said, "nothing of any importance."

"You're not worrying, are you?"

"No."

"Good—because, believe me, there's nothing for you to worry about."

The snow began to fall after a while, huge flakes that came flattening themselves against the windshield, to be swept away a moment later by the wipers. Shenna sat in silence, watching the snow, and then Harry, with a melancholy little smile, said, "Of course, you know you've thrown out all my plans—leaving so unexpectedly. . . ."

"I have? How's that?"

"I had a little going-away present for you. It's nothing much—just a little something I wanted you to have. A little—well, memento, if you like. Of our evening out together that time. That evening meant so much to me. I'll never forget it and I wanted to give you a little something to remind you of it, too." He glanced at the clock on the dashboard. "Listen, would you mind if we made a stop—just for a few minutes? It's practically on our way. It won't hold you up more than a few minutes."

Without hesitation, Shenna nodded. "Sure, why not?" She didn't care now that she was away from the flat. "Where?" she asked.

"At my home—my grandparents' house in Kew."

"Kew? You mean where the famous gardens are? I thought you lived near the school—in a little flat there?"

"Yes, but my real home is in Kew. I took the flat to be near—nearer the school."

"How long have you been there—in your flat?"

"Not long. Just since last summer."

"Oh, I imagined you'd been there for several years."

"No, just a few months." He turned briefly and smiled. "This was my first term, as well. I started just before you did." He gestured ahead toward traffic lights. "We turn off there. It's not far then."

A little while later the car moved off the main road, and after several more minutes and numerous twists and turns, came to a stop outside a very tall Victorian house set back from the pavement. Harry switched off the motor, and then, as Shenna took up her bag, he reached over to the back seat to pick up her case. Shenna said, "What's the point in bringing my case in? We shan't be here long, shall we?"

He let go of the handle of the case and smiled. "No, of course not; I don't know what I'm thinking of."

The snow was falling faster than ever as she got out, and

after the warmth of the car's interior the cold struck her like a blow. She shivered and Harry looked up from locking the car and said, "Don't worry, it'll be warmer indoors."

Turning, she gazed through the curtain of falling snow at the house. It looked huge. To one side of it was a cleared site—obviously where other buildings had once stood—while on the other stood a low, ugly bungalow with dark windows. The whole area had a lost, forgotten look about it.

Walking behind Harry she made her way up the path that ran through the long, unkempt walled garden. She could see no lights on in the house. "What about your grandparents?" she said. "Will they mind me coming in like this—without any warning?"

He shook his head. "They're not here right now. But they wouldn't mind, anyway. They're always happy to see any of my friends."

As they approached the front door she looked over to the left and saw what appeared to be a large figure. It looked to be some kind of statue. With the darkness of the night and the falling snow, however, it was difficult to see properly.

She went on, and just ahead of her Harry unlocked the front door, opened it, stepped through, and then stood aside for her to enter. When she was inside he closed the door behind her and touched her sleeve. "Come on into the sitting room," he said, and began to lead the way along the hall.

He led her into a room on the left of the hall, where he lit the gas fire and urged her to take off her coat and sit down. "I'll put the kettle on for some tea," he added, "and go and get that little present for you."

She put down her bag and, after loosening the buttons of her coat, she sat on a sofa. When he had gone from the room she sat looking around her. There were two easy chairs matching the sofa on which she sat. A highly polished bureau stood against one wall, and near to it an old windup phonograph. Seeing it, she thought of the old man in the park. The room appeared almost clinically tidy; there was not so much as a cushion that looked an inch out of place. It had an unattractive, sterile look about it.

After a while she heard the sound of Harry's feet on the stairs, and then he was entering the room once more. He carried in his hand a small wooden box, which he placed on the circular coffee table before her. He had taken off his coat and jacket, she saw, and was now in his long shirt-sleeves and pullover. She felt strangely disturbed and was aware all at once that that previous elusive image had returned and was fluttering like a captive moth in her brain, fighting for recognition.

He frowned at her and shook his head. "Why don't you take your coat off? Otherwise you won't get the benefit of it when you go out."

As he spoke he put up a hand and inserted fingers under the neckband of his shirt, and in that moment, in a flash, she saw in brilliant clarity the image she had previously been unable to grasp—the image that had so strangely disturbed her. Now in her mind she saw him once again as he had been in her flat, his sleeves rolled up, as he had bent to pick up the broken glass. She watched the scene go through her mind— like watching a scene from a movie in slow motion—and then realized what it was about the picture that had registered in her subconscious.

After their visit to the ballet he had been attacked, and his arm injured so badly that it had required many stitches. So he had said. And she had believed him. And why not?—she had had no reason to doubt him. His arm had been in bandages for several days and when the bandages had been removed he had even offered to show her the scar. . . .

Yet earlier this evening she had seen him with his arms exposed—and there had not been the faintest trace of a scar.

20

I t was Harry.

He was the one. It was *he* who had been watching her these months. *He* who had tried to keep her here, who had gone into her flat and wrecked her belongings. *He* who had written her the letters, sent her the tickets for the theater and the ballet and stolen the painting. . . .

The fear that was in her grew till it felt almost suffocating. Almost as in a dream, she watched as he lifted the lid of the box, dipped in his fingers, and brought out something that he gazed at lovingly for a moment, then held out to her on his palm.

"It was my mother's," he said. "I want you to have it."

It was a Victorian brooch, large, ornate, and very ugly. She gazed at it for a long moment and shook her head. "No, Harry," she said, "I can't accept it. Really, I can't."

"Oh, but you must. Please."

She made no attempt to take the brooch but just shook her head again and lowered her eyes. And then he was moving forward, reaching out to her. She drew back slightly.

"What's the matter?" he said. The brooch was in his outstretched fingers. "I only want to pin it on you."

Weakly she began to protest again, but then her protests died and she sat rigid while he tried to pin the brooch to her coat.

Fiddling with it at her breast, he clicked his tongue. "It won't stay closed properly," he said. "Ah, well, it'll do for now, but it needs fixing. We'll have to get it done before you can wear it out." He leaned back, put his head a little on one side, and nodded his approval. "It looks nice. It suits you, it really does." He gestured to her to rise. "Look at yourself in the glass. See how it looks."

Obediently she got to her feet and stepped in front of the mirror that hung above the fireplace. In the reflection her eyes moved to the large, ugly brooch. Above it her skin was ashen. She had to get out.

"Hey," she said, forcing a smile, "I think I'd better get going now."

"Why? What's the hurry? You said yourself there are no flights till the morning. And anyway, we haven't had the tea yet."

She nodded. "Okay. But as soon as we've had the tea . . ." Her smile felt like cardboard. "I guess once I set off I just— like to get going." There was a little silence. He came to stand behind her and she saw his face in the mirror, saw him shake his head as he looked at himself over her shoulder. Frowning, he put a hand up to his balding head.

"My hair," he said, "it's such a tragedy." His eyes went to Shenna's. "D'you think looks are all that important?"

"Of course not."

He smiled. "I knew you'd say that. It's the *real* person that matters, isn't it?"

"Yes."

He frowned again. "Are you all right? You look a bit pale."

"I'll be okay." She paused. "I think I'd like to go to the bathroom."

"Yes . . ." He looked slightly embarrassed at her words, dropping his eyes and turning away. Then, as she stepped toward the door, he moved quickly in front of her and led the way into the hall. At the foot of the stairs he pointed upward. "Use the bathroom upstairs. Second door on the right. While you're there I'll go and make that tea."

She nodded and started up the stairs. Then, several steps up, she stopped and looked back and saw that he was gazing up at her. She forced a smile at him and went on. When she reached the top of the stairs she looked back again and saw that he was still standing there. Turning, she moved forward along the landing to the bathroom, where she stepped inside, closed the door behind her, and stood with her back to it. Her heart was pounding. After standing there for a few moments she grasped the door handle and very quietly opened the door and crept out again.

Slowly and stealthily she moved toward the head of the stairs. There was no sign of him now, and after a second she started down, the occasional creak of the stairs making her stop and hold her breath while she listened for the sound of his return. There was nothing, though, and at last she had reached the hall and was at the front door, reaching out for the catch.

It wouldn't move.

Her hands wet with perspiration, she fumbled at the catch, straining at it, her fingers slipping off the metal. It remained fixed, unmoving. *He had locked it.* Then, the moment after the realization came, she heard a sound from behind and turned to see him standing there.

"Please, Harry," she said, "would you open the door?"

He frowned. "What for? Why d'you want to leave?"

"Please—open the door, will you?"

"No—I'm sorry. I can't."

She forced a smile. "Harry—what are you doing, locking me in like this?"

He didn't answer.

"Harry, you can't keep me here against my will." She tried to keep a note of reason in her voice. "You know that. I want to leave—so please unlock the door and let me out.

"Why do you want to leave?"

"Harry—just unlock the door."

He shook his head. "Don't keep asking me that. I can't let you go. I want you to stay."

"Stay. . . ?"

"Stay here with me."

"Harry, I'm going back to California. I'm going home. I've got to get to the airport to get my plane."

"No, you can't go. I can't let you. Don't you understand? It's all been leading to this—to your being here. If you leave, it will all have been wasted. You can't expect me to forget all about it now—not now when it's all coming right for me. For *us*."

"Harry—*please* . . ."

Tears sprang to her eyes and he took a step forward. "Oh, don't cry," he said. "Please don't cry. Everything's going to be fine, I promise you. I'll look after you."

"Harry, I want to leave." The tears were streaming down her cheeks now; her voice was plaintive, the voice of a lost child. "I want to go home."

"You *are* home, Shenna."

"No—no, I want to go home to California."

"That's not your home now—you know that. And you've got no one there to go back to, have you? Your home is with *me*—*here*. From now on we'll be together." He reached out and gently touched a fingertip to her tear-wet cheek. "Little tears," he whispered. "Oh, don't cry. I hate to see you cry."

"Then let me *go*."

He spread his hands in a gesture of bewilderment. "I don't know how you can ask such a thing. My God, if you only knew how I hoped for this." He smiled suddenly. "When I read that you were coming to England to study it was the answer to my prayers—it really was—and I went straight-away to the school to try to find a job. I would have taken anything that was going. Anything. There were two jobs vacant—one in the cafeteria and the other as porter. It was an absolute godsend, finding that porter's job—and it was just one more sign to me that this whole thing was planned—that it was all part of some—some great design. You might not realize it fully right now, but you will in time."

"Harry, please—let me go away from here."

His smile became a frown. "You're forgetting what I've done for you. All those little things I did for you—sending you the tickets for the theater and the ballet. Everything. I so wanted to make you happy."

"To make me happy?" she said. "When I took Caspar, my friend, with me to the theater you wrecked his bicycle. You think that made me happy?"

He frowned again. "I'm sorry I had to do that. But I told you to take a girlfriend with you, and you didn't. You disobeyed me. I didn't want to see you with anyone else—any other man. You should have realized that."

She stared at him. A little nerve began to twitch beneath the skin at his temple. "But—but when we went to the ballet together you even pretended you'd been attacked on your way home afterward," she said. "Why? I didn't go with anyone *else*—I went with *you*."

He sighed and briefly raised his eyes to the ceiling. "I *know* that," he said. "But I had made it clear *again* that you should take a girlfriend with you. Not a man. But, no—you were disobedient again."

"But—but it was *you*."

"'Yes, I know that. But that wasn't the point, was it? You didn't know it was me, did you? In your eyes you weren't taking *me*—you were taking the school porter. And that was wrong. You were not to take a man with you—*any* man. So—I had to teach you. You had to learn." He paused suddenly, gazed at her for a moment, then added, "And why did you take him, anyway, the porter? Was it pity?"

"Oh, God, Harry, no . . ."

"Anyway, that's all in the past." He smiled. "You know, I loved trying to think of little ways to make you happy. I was really pleased when I was able to get that picture for you from the museum. Oh, I realized afterward it was a mistake because it upset you—but you must give me credit for having the right motives. I was trying to make you happy with it." He paused. "And there are other things, too—things you don't know about yet. I've been preparing for your arrival here—painting our room and getting the angel for you." He gestured to the outside. "Out there. It's for you. You had a postcard of an angel statue in your sketchbook, remember?" He grinned. "And not long afterward I saw one like it. I had to get it for you. I didn't care how much it cost." He gazed at her, as if watching for her reaction. She said nothing. After a moment he went on, "I just wanted to show you how much I loved you. I'd do anything for you, Shenna, you must realize that by now."

"Then let me go, Harry, please."

"No, that's the one thing I can't do. That would be insane after all I've done for your sake. The Baxter girl, for instance. When she—"

"*Jane. . . ?*"

"Jane, yes. I righted wrongs for you. I—"

"*No!*" Afraid of what he was about to say, Shenna put her hands up to her ears, but he reached out, grasped her wrists, and gently but firmly pulled her hands down again. "You must listen to me," he said. "I'm trying to tell you—to make you understand."

"No! No! I don't want to know!"

Letting go of her hands he gazed at her with an expression of hurt in his eyes. "Oh, Shenna," he said sadly, "how soon you forget. Well, *I* don't forget. I stood there that day and saw your face when you came down the stairs. I saw how pale you were—saw the tears in your eyes. I didn't know why you were upset, but I wanted to go to you and tell you not to worry. I couldn't, of course. Afterward I learned what had happened between you and the Baxter girl—and I wanted to kill her right then; I hated her so much." He nodded. "But I was patient and the opportunity came—eventually. She would never hurt you again, I was determined on that score." He paused. "And then your mother—"

"No . . . *no* . . ." Terror flooded over her and Shenna closed her eyes, while into her mind flashed the image that was printed indelibly on her memory—the picture of her mother's body as she had found her that night—lying at the foot of the stairs in the cottage, her head twisted at an abnormal angle, dead eyes staring out. She began to weep. "Please—*stop!*" she cried brokenly. "Please . . ."

He shook his head. "I know how you must feel, but you must face the truth, Shenna. Your mother—she was an enemy to *both* of us—and you must be as aware of that as I was. Everything was going all right until she came here. Then it all went wrong. She was going to destroy all our chances of happiness together and I couldn't let that happen. She was a selfish woman—selfish and clinging, who never gave any consideration to what was right for you. And when I found out that you planned on returning with her I knew something had to be done. She had to be stopped. She was spoiling everything. So—I killed her."

He paused, gazing into Shenna's tear-streaked face, then went on, "And I'll tell you something—the way her death was taken for an accident—well, it was just another sign to me. I knew then—I absolutely *knew*, without any shadow of a doubt, that fate was on my side and that I was doing the right thing. It's happened like that all along. I've had sign after sign to help me and guide me. Like the time I was watching you on the heath while that old fool was playing his records and you went off without your bag. That was fate again, giving me a sign."

Silence followed his words. Shenna, wiping away her tears, was aware of the sound of their breathing. After a moment she said sadly, "Harry, what good has all this done?"

He shook his head. "What good? What a question. Why

do you think I wrote to you all those times when you lived in America?" He paused. "Did you ever think we'd meet someday?"

"No," she whispered.

"No, of course you didn't. And when you were here at school I'll bet you never guessed that I was the one, did you?"

"No."

"No, I know you didn't." He smiled suddenly. "Of course, the terrible, dreadful, cruel injury to my arm helped there, didn't it?"

"But—but you had photographs there in the office—of children—*your* children, you said. And your wife, too. They were all dead, so you led me to think."

He smiled again. "You know, it's the easiest way to avoid difficult questions. Just hint at some tragedy in your life. People are invariably sympathetic and they never pry. Well, it's not good taste, is it? It's just not done. They just accept what you say and leave it at that. And as for the children and the woman in the photographs—I've no more idea than you as to who they are. They were just photographs I found."

"And your girlfriend—Sally?"

"She was as real as the rest of them."

Shenna was silent for a moment, then she said, "But how—how did you always know so much?"

"What d'you mean?"

"My plans. I never told you that I was going back to California with my mother. . . ."

"You forget—I operated the switchboard. I heard a lot when I needed to."

It was all becoming clear. After a moment she said quietly, "What do you want with me, Harry?"

"What do I want?"

"Tell me."

He shrugged. "I've told you. I want you. I've wanted you

ever since I saw you in that film. And I knew then that one day I would have you. And now you're here with me, at last."

"And—now that I'm here? Harry, you'll have to let me go sometime."

"No." He shook his head. "I don't have to let you go. You're with me now, and that's where you're going to stay."

"No!" Hearing her voice rising out of control she made an effort to sound more calm and controlled. "I can't stay. You must let me go."

"Oh, I'm quite prepared for the things you say right now. But you'll change in time. And you'll come to love me. I know you can't accept that now, but you will, believe me. And you'll thank me for bringing you here tonight. You might be here against your will right now—but soon you won't want to be anywhere else."

"Please—"

He held up his hand in a gesture for silence. "Believe me," he said, "you'll love me in time. You will."

It didn't matter what she said to him, it didn't matter how much she pleaded; she couldn't reach him, she couldn't get past his blind infatuation.

Slowly, she shook her head. "Never, Harry—you've got to realize it. And more than that—I'll hate you."

"No, you won't. Don't say that."

With his words he stepped toward her and gently laid a hand against her cheek. She shuddered and drew back. He came closer, lowering his head to kiss her, and she pressed back against the door in revulsion. For a moment she watched his face coming nearer to her own and then, drawing saliva into her mouth, she spat in his face.

He recoiled as if he had been struck. He stepped back and stood staring at her while he slowly raised a hand and wiped the saliva from his cheek. Shaking his head, he said in a voice full of hurt, "What did you do that for?"

"What do you think?" Seeing his look of bewilderment, she asked herself how she could make him realize the truth, make him see that she would never love him, that all his efforts had gone for nothing. She watched his face, waiting to see the realization there, but he just stood in silence for a while, then shook his head and said, "No. It's understandable. You're upset right now. It was my fault. I should have expected you to react in such a way—a girl like you."

"A girl like me?"

"Yes." He nodded. "I know what you're like. In spite of those films you were in, I know that none of it was the—the real you. I've always known it."

"Known what? What are you talking about—the real me?"

"You," he said, "*you*. Why do you think I was so attracted to you? Because of what you are. *Perfect*. To me, you were perfect. Pure . . . perfect." He paused. "And I've never thought otherwise. At the school I've watched the other girls carrying on, making fools of themselves. Not you, though. You were different. Not that I would have put up with it if you'd been—tempted. That's another reason I wrecked that student's bicycle that night—though I didn't need to worry about him, as it turned out."

She stared at him for some moments, then said coldly, deliberately, "You've got the wrong idea about me, Harry. I'm not special. I'm just like every other girl."

"Oh, no. I know that's not so."

"It is."

"No, you're not like the others. All those other girls—the way they sleep around. How can you say you're like them? You're not."

She was silent for a second, then she said, "What makes you think I don't sleep around?"

He looked at her sharply, frowning, then shook his head. "No. I know."

"You *think* you know."

"I *know*. I know *you*."

"Do you?" She gave a calculated, sardonic smile. "You know nothing. Nothing at all."

"Please." He shook his head and turned away. "You're only saying that. Why? Why do you say such a thing?"

"Because it's true."

"No." He sat down on the stairs, facing her. "You can't make me believe anything of you that I don't want to."

"No—you've got an idea of me fixed in your mind—and it's nothing like the person I am." And now, suddenly, she could see a flicker of doubt in his eyes. She couldn't let up. "I'm nothing like the idea of me that you have," she added.

Minutes of silence went by as he stared at her, as if trying to read what was in her mind. Then he said in a low voice, "Who—who is Ian?"

"Ian?"

"Yes. Ian—Bradley."

"How do you know about him?"

"I know about him. He telephoned your flat while I was there earlier this evening. And there was a letter from him too. Who is he?"

Ian had written and telephoned. . . . She hesitated, then, carefully choosing her words, she said, "He's my lover. I love him."

Briefly he closed his eyes, as if in pain. "I don't believe you," he said.

"You don't *want* to believe it. You think I'm so different from other girls. I'm not. Of course I'm not. Where do you think I was when I wasn't at school? What do you think I was doing when I wasn't studying? I'll tell you: I was in his bed. In Ian's bed. I was with him every chance I could get. And if I get the chance in the future, I'll do the same again."

He waved a hand, as if brushing her words away. "Stop it!" he shouted. "Stop talking like that. I don't want to hear!"

"You're afraid of facing up to the truth—that I'm not the

paragon of virtue you thought I was—that I'm the same as everybody else. Well, face it, because that's the way it is."

"No . . ." He stared at her for some seconds, as if he were suddenly seeing her for the first time. After a while he said, "Once when I wrote to you I said I had invested my life in you. Do you remember?"

She shook her head. "No, I don't remember. But why should I? And why should I care what you said? That was up to you, if you wanted to invest your life in some—some fantasy. And anyway, what makes you think I ever bothered to read your letters?" Her voice was heavy with scorn; she was relentless; it was the only way. "Why should I bother to read the outpourings of some stranger who never meant a damn thing to me? You know what you were to me? You were just another crank. We used to laugh about you, my mother and I."

"*Don't!*" He clapped his hands over his ears. "Don't say that."

"It's the truth."

"No, no, no, no, no." He shook his head violently from side to side, mechanically, like a puppet. "I don't want to hear!" As he spoke, she saw, suddenly, the glisten of tears in his eyes. She wouldn't let up. "You were wrong," she said. "You were wrong about me in every possible way. I'm not different from the rest. And I'll tell you something else: I hate you. Get it into your head once and for all, Harry. *I loathe you.*"

Slowly, he got up and stood staring at her, his arms hanging loose at his sides, the tears still in his eyes. He looked totally bereft. Several moments went by and then he said, "It's not possible. How could I be wrong about you? How could that be?"

She shrugged. "We all make mistakes."

"I was wrong about you—all this time?"

"Yes."

"I was wrong about you," he said again. "I was wrong."

"It doesn't matter anymore. Just let me go."

He gazed at her with a frown deepening on his brow, then turned full circle, moving as if lost, disoriented. After a moment he sank back on the stairs and put his head in his hands. Watching in silence, Shenna saw his shoulders begin to shake and then heard the sound of his sobs. She said nothing. It would be all right now, she knew. All she had to do was to be patient a little longer. Soon she would be free.

The minutes ticked by while he continued to sit there with his face buried in his hands, and Shenna stood silently waiting with her back to the locked door. And then, at last, he raised his head and looked up at her. When he spoke a moment later his voice had a strange, hoarse, tight quality about it.

"What I wrote in my letter," he said, "it's true. I did invest my life in you." He paused. "And now I see that it was all for nothing."

She kept silent.

"It was all for nothing," he said again. "And now I've got nothing left to live for." He gazed into her eyes across the space of the carpet between them. "You were my life—the whole meaning, the whole purpose of my whole existence. I made you the total reason for my being—for my living. And now you've taken that reason away. You've taken everything away from me. I've got nothing."

She couldn't help herself. "Don't say that. . . ."

"Nothing. *Nothing!* I've got less than I had before. Don't you understand?" He shook his head. "I've done so many things for you. Given you so many things. So many gifts. Gifts—for you. Even murder. I killed for you. *I killed for you*. And what have you done in exchange? Thrown it all up in my face. And I've got nothing. You've robbed me of everything. Of my life. You've taken away my life."

Throughout his torrent of words she had seen a change

coming over him. His eyes now were shining with tears of anger, glittering in a face from which the blood seemed to be draining away.

"Harry—" she said, stepping forward.

"Be quiet"—he got to his feet—"*bitch!*"

He spat the words at her, and she shrank back against the door again. Now she saw in his deathly white face a rage that distorted his features and brought a new fear rising up in her throat and set her heart pounding against her ribs.

"You've killed me," he said. "You've killed me as surely as if you'd taken a knife and pushed it into my heart."

"No, Harry, I—"

"And now you expect me to open the door and let you go, just as if nothing has happened."

For some moments he stared at her, his breathing hoarse, his eyes blazing, and then he stepped toward her.

As he reached out for her she screamed and dodged quickly to the left, arms flapping, warding him off, and the next moment she had pushed past him and was dashing along the hall toward the rear of the house.

Coming to a door at the end, she wrenched it open, flicked a switch, and found herself in the kitchen. Seeing in the far wall a door to the outside, she dashed forward and grasped the handle. The door wouldn't budge. Desperate, panic-stricken, she turned. There was another door over to the right. She dashed toward it, flung it open, and found herself in a small utility room. In the spilled light from the kitchen she saw shelves of linen, a washing machine, a clothes basket, and a pile of old clothes heaped on top of two large plastic bags stuffed with clothes.

Her hands scrambling on the wall, she located a switch and flicked on the light. Then, by the feeble overhead glow, she moved to the window and tried to push it open. It was locked. He had thought of everything. Sobbing out loud in her despair and frustration, she searched around for something with which to smash the glass. She could see nothing. Then, frantically reaching down to the pile of clothes for some garment that she could wrap around her arm for protection, she grasped a piece of fabric and pulled.

As she did so, the two large plastic bags toppled and fell at her feet, and she peered down in the dim light and realized that they held not clothes, but what appeared to be a pair of dummies. Bending closer to the grotesque, horrifically misshapen figures, she saw that they were an old man and an old woman. She stood there as if mesmerized, staring in horror at their battered, distorted features and the dark crust of dried blood in their matted hair and in the hollows of their eyes as they stared out through their transparent prisons. Then she opened her mouth and screamed.

21

When Ian reached Elm Court Road just before seven-thirty, he found Wesley standing at the door to number nineteen. Giving him a token smile, he asked him whether he was waiting for somebody.

"Yes—Shenna Preston," Wesley replied, giving a sudden shiver of cold. "I'm a friend of hers. I was to call for her at quarter past seven."

"I gather she's not in."

"No. I got here just in time to see her drive off. I called out to her, but she didn't stop. I don't know why. She saw me all right, I know. I'm hoping she'll return soon. We're supposed to be going to a party."

Ian shrugged. "Well, if she's expecting you, I've no doubt she'll be back before very long." He reached into his pocket, took out his keys, and sorted out the one to Shenna's flat. "Excuse me," he murmured. He moved to the front door and pushed it open. The light in the hall didn't go on when he flicked the switch, and in the darkness he went to Shenna's door, unlocked it, and went inside. A minute after switching on the light he was on the phone to the police.

When he had replaced the receiver he went outside to where Wesley still waited and asked him to come inside. Wesley followed him into the flat and then came to an abrupt halt and stood looking aghast at the wreckage all around.

"And it looks as if somebody's been injured," Ian said, pointing to the bloodstains. Then he added, "But you saw her, you said. . . ."

Wesley nodded. "Yes, I saw her drive away—with some fellow from the art school. I told you—I called to her, but she didn't answer."

"Did she seem—all right? Did she look as if she was—hurt in any way?"

"I couldn't tell, but I don't think so. I only saw her for a moment. She seemed to be in a great hurry."

"Who was she with? Do you know him? One of her student friends?"

"I think he's a porter from the school. I've seen him at the reception desk a couple of times in the early evenings."

"D'you know his name?"

"No."

As they stood talking, there came a ring at the doorbell and they turned to see a uniformed constable standing in the open doorway. Entering the flat he looked around, coming to a stop when he saw the bloodstains near the door. Wesley told him then of Shenna's hurried departure with the school porter. As he listened, the constable made some brief notes and then immediately put out a call for assistance.

By the time a plainclothes detective sergeant arrived a little while later, the constable had found a spare light bulb in the kitchen and replaced the one missing from the hall. That done, they found the bloodstains leading to the door opposite. Soon afterward, with Ian and Wesley standing by, the two officers had forced a way into the flat and found Kevin's body.

In no time then, it seemed, the place was swarming with police.

Shenna's scream was still echoing in the tiny room when she looked around and saw Harry standing on the threshold. As she turned to face him he stepped forward, reaching out, and she screamed again as his arms came about her, wrapping her close. She pushed at him, struggling violently, and then felt his hands move up to her neck. His fingers came around her throat, tightening their hold, his thumbs pressing in, harder, harder. She tried to cry out, but no sound came. She couldn't breathe and it seemed as if the light in the little room began to grow dim. Then, drawing on all the last re-sources of her strength, she braced herself and with all her force brought up her knee and smashed it violently into his crotch.

His head snapped backward and he gasped out, while in the same moment his hands fell away from her throat. With-out hesitation, she brought her knee upward again and, as he fell backward, doubling over in pain, she thrust him aside, pushed past him, and dashed away.

Staggering, still reeling from the pressure on her throat, she almost fell into the hall. Then, recovering her balance, she ran on. Knowing that it was useless to try to escape by the front door, she made for the stairs and started upward. Halfway up, she found the flight bisected by a small square of landing and she turned on it and continued her frantic climb. Seconds later she had reached the first floor, seeing ahead of her a wide, spacious landing stretching away with numerous doors opening off it. Briefly she wavered, wonder-ing whether to seek refuge there, but the next moment she was dashing on, plunging up the next flight of stairs to the floor above, clutching at the banister, her breath coming in great, gasping sobs. Reaching the third floor landing, she paused briefly to look down the well of the staircase and she suddenly saw Harry come into view below as he pounded up the stairs. Turning, she fled on toward the next flight.

As she reached the lower step she found on her right a switch and she snatched at it, bathing the stairway before her in a dim, cold glow. These stairs were narrower than those below. She climbed on upward, and moments later she had reached the pitch darkness of the top landing where, fran-tically, her heart thudding, she groped around until she had found a light switch. Flicking on the light, she looked about her. There were no more stairs. In blind panic she turned to the right, to the left, seeing before her only a series of closed doors. From the stairs below she could hear already the sound of footsteps coming closer. At any moment he would be there.

The seconds seemed like hours as she spun, not knowing which way to turn. In desperation she ran to one of the doors and tried the handle. Locked. Turning away from it, she wrenched at another door—it was locked as well. The third door she tried opened easily under her touch, swinging inward on silent hinges. Beyond it, in the dim light that spilled from the landing, she could make out a small room with shelves along one wall. As she gazed in she heard again the sound of Harry's approach. Without hesitating she hurried inside and swiftly and silently closed the door behind her.

Gasping for breath, she groped about for a light switch. She couldn't find one, though, and she immediately turned her attention to feeling for some fastening for the door. Seconds later her frantic fingers had located a small bolt and, sobbing with relief, she pushed it home.

Turning, she tentatively moved forward, reaching about her with outstretched hands, and a moment later felt her fingers touch the shelves, finding that they held what seemed like boxes and tins and various tools. She needed something to use as a weapon, and her fingers searched in the dark, scrabbling around until they had found a length of iron pipe about eighteen inches long. She grasped it firmly. He must be close, so close. At any moment he would be outside. Her rapid breathing sounded harsh and shallow to her ears and her hand holding the iron pipe was wet with the sweat of her terror; she knew the weapon would prove ultimately useless against his insane determination and it would be only seconds before he discovered where she was hiding; the flimsy bolt wouldn't keep him out for long.

Stepping to one side, she felt beneath her shoe the softness of a cushion or mattress, and then her knee came into sharp, painful contact with some slanting timber support, and she reached out with her free hand and found a flight of wooden steps. She couldn't guess where they might lead to—perhaps an attic, she hoped—someplace where she could secure herself away for a while and in that time think of some way to make her escape or attract attention from outside. She had no clear idea in her mind of anything beside the frantic desire to keep some distance between herself and *him*. She climbed onto the steps and started up—and in the same moment she heard from the landing the sound of footsteps as he reached the top of the stairs.

As she crept upward, she listened to the sound of his moving feet, of doors being opened and closed and then, seconds later, he was at the door right behind her and she heard the handle turning as he tried to open it. She held her breath, listening as he met the resistance of the bolt and then as he shook the door, at first gently and then with violence. She moved farther up the steps, her terror soaring. Then his voice came, low and close to the door.

"Shenna?"

She kept silent.

He spoke again. "Shenna? Answer me." There was a pause. "Don't worry, I know you're in there, *bitch*. I'll get to you in a minute."

The door rattled and then was violently shaken as he hurled himself against it. The small bolt wouldn't hold out long against such pressure. Sobbing, she moved farther up the steps. Then, reaching up, her trembling hand encountered some kind of door with a handle—no, not a door, a pair of window shutters. She pulled and the shutters opened and next moment she found herself looking out at snowflakes whirling down out of the dark night sky. Finding beneath her scrabbling hand the window catch, she fumbled at it and felt it spring beneath the pressure of her touch. Then she was pushing the window wide and a blast of icy air was striking her in the face like a blow. Looking down, she found herself looking onto the roof, on either side of her sloping upward to its apex, while immediately below was a flat section bordered at its edge by a parapet—all of it a pale carpet under its blanket of snow. Behind her, she heard the door shaken again and again, followed by the sound of splintering wood. The next moment she was scrambling through the open window into the night air.

She fell into the snow on her hands and knees, the impact numbing her knuckles as she clutched the iron pipe. Then, swiftly rising, she slammed the window shut, seeing as she did so that there was now a light on in the little room. Unless she could stop him, he would be out of the window behind her at any second. She hovered for one brief, panicked moment of thought and then, fingers groping in the snow beneath the window, she located some unevenness in the structure. Quickly she jammed one end of the iron bar into it and the other against the window frame and pressed down hard on it with her foot. Hurriedly, she turned to the right, where the parapet ran along the edge of the roof. The snow was driving in a blinding, icy blur and she had to screw up her eyes in order to see, but she could just make out beyond the far edge of the roof the distant blur of a street lamp. That was the direction she must aim for, and with determination she fell to her knees and began to crawl. As she did so she heard through the noise-deadening snow the muffled sound of blows on the window frame as Harry tried to push it open.

With the snow saturating her jeans, she crawled, sobbing, along the level strip that ran between the steep slope of the roof and the parapet. By keeping low, she hoped to remain hidden long enough to get to the front of the house and so attract the attention of some passerby. Unaware of the coldness of her hands in the snow, she crawled on, intent only on reaching her goal. And at last, after minutes that seemed like hours, she reached the far side of the roof and raised herself on her knees before the parapet. At the same moment she heard Harry's voice, muffled through the falling snow, coming from somewhere behind her.

"Shenna? Shenna?"

How soon he had gotten out onto the roof! After a moment his voice came again.

"Shenna? Come on inside in the warm." A pause, and then: "You're going to catch your death out here." And then he laughed.

Trying to shut out the sound of his voice, she looked out over the parapet. Beyond the walled front garden the snow-covered street lay dimly lit by the street lamps. Gazing through the curtain of driving snow, she peered intently, trying to see if there was anyone about. There was no sign of anyone, not even the light of a passing car. Despair sweeping over her like a wave, she got to her feet and lifted her head and screamed out into the night.

"Help me! For God's sake, somebody help me!"

As the sound of her voice faded in the air she became dully aware that the snow was dying. And then, peering down, she made out in the shadows beyond the garden wall the shape of a figure with a dog and a shifting beam of light. A woman with a flashlight. *"Help! Help me!"* Shenna cried out again and then saw the little beam of light come up, as if it were trying to pierce the space between them. The next moment she turned at a sound and saw Harry standing just a few feet away.

The sight of him almost took the breath from her body. She gasped for air, her hands reaching up to her mouth, her knees weak. He took a step toward her and she backed away.

"Oh, God . . . Oh, God . . . Oh, God . . ." She found herself muttering the words under her breath. The snow had all but stopped now, and through the last drifting flakes she watched him standing there quite still, just looking at her. Then he turned his head and gazed out over the parapet at the old woman and her dog. Turning back to Shenna, he smiled, a strange, cold little smile. "I wouldn't waste your breath yelling to old Mrs. Medlin. That crazy old woman can't do anything to help you." He shook his head. "In fact, it doesn't matter how much you scream for help. There's only you and me—and nobody can get up here—at least not in time to be of any help to you." He gestured back over his shoulder. "And don't get any thoughts about making a run for the roof window. I'd stop you before you got five yards."

"Please, Harry," she said imploringly, her voice breaking on a sob. "Please let me go. *Please*."

He shook his head. "No. And don't bother pleading with me. Earlier, downstairs, I might have listened. Not now. I'm wise to you. I know what you're like. I realize now what you've done."

"Harry, I've done nothing to hurt you."

"You've done *nothing?* You took away from me all reason for living. And there's nothing now that you can say or do to change anything. It's over." He took a step toward her and she gave a little gasp of fear and backed away.

"Listen, Harry,"—her mind was racing—"just let me go and they'll—they'll take it into account, you know they will."

"Who's *they?*"

"The—the police."

He laughed. "The *police!* Oh, don't worry, I shan't be having anything to do with the police. Oh, no." He shook his head. "When I say the charade is over I mean it's *over*. There won't be any players left out of this particular little play. This is the end for both of us."

"No—Harry, no . . ."

"*No, Harry, no,*" he mimicked bitterly. "Yes, I'm afraid so. The end for you *and* for me." He stared at her for a moment across the space of snow-covered roof between them, then lowered his head. "There's nothing for me anymore. And I've come too far with all the things I've done. There's no turning back; there's no way I can make a new start—not now." He raised his head and looked at her. There were tears on his cheeks. "Perhaps now you can understand what you've done to me. Can you?"

"Harry—I'm sorry you've been hurt. And if I can make it up to you, I will. Just give me a chance to try. Please."

As if confirming some thought, he said resignedly, "No, you don't understand. I should have realized you wouldn't." Roughly, he brushed a hand across his cheek. "It doesn't matter now, anyway. There's no more time for you to think about it. Time has run out—for both of us."

As he finished speaking, he stepped forward, arms lifting toward her. And then, almost in the same moment, there came into the sudden, deathly silence the sounds of a police siren and a car engine coming close, fast, into the street. Harry halted in his stride, turned his head, and looked down. In the street below a car with a flashing blue light swept into sight and, with a screech of brakes and in a flurry of spraying snow, came to a halt before the house.

Even before the car had come fully to a stop, the doors were opening and the figures of four police officers in dark uniforms were getting out. Moments later the old woman was directing their gaze to the couple on the rooftop. Shenna, snatching her glance briefly from Harry, raised a hand, frantically waved, and shouted in desperation, "Help me, please! He's going to kill me! *Help me!*"

Harry, standing just a few feet away, paid no heed to her cries; he didn't even seem to hear her. He stood as if mesmerized, gazing down in fascination at the scene of erupting noise and activity, watching as one by one the men looked up and saw him and Shenna standing there against the sky. A powerful beam swept up and caught him in its light, and he put up a hand to shield his eyes from the brightness. And then another beam wavered upward and sought out the figure of Shenna and stayed, trembling, on her, bathing her in its glow. She saw two of the men enter through the gate and run up the path toward the house, to be hidden from sight by the obstructing parapet. Harry gave a humorless laugh.

"They're wasting their time. It'll take them ages to get through that front door."

There came a man's voice from the street below, "Shenna? *Hold on.* Just hold on. We'll have someone with you in another minute."

Laughing, Harry leaned down over the parapet. "A minute?" he shouted. "A minute will be too late." He turned to Shenna. "Don't you wish you were in America right now, where all the cops carry guns? They could have picked me off by now with no trouble."

"Johnson?" The voice called from below. Harry said nothing and the voice came again. "Harry Johnson—can you hear me?"

"Yes," Harry shouted down, "I can hear you."

"Listen—leave the girl alone. Don't touch her. We can get this all sorted out. Just don't do anything foolish."

Harry's answering laugh rang out in the cold air. "Don't do anything foolish? No, I won't—not anymore. What I'm doing now is going to be the smartest thing I've done in my life."

When he had finished speaking he turned and looked at Shenna, and she knew instantly that the moment had come. There would be no more talk. With cold terror clutching at her heart, she raised her hands to ward him off, and in the same moment he lunged forward. With a scream, she dodged to the side, trying to make a break toward the rear section of the roof, but he was too quick for her. In seconds he was right behind her, had caught her by the coat, and was dragging her, screaming and struggling, back toward the roof's edge. *"No!"* she screamed. *"Don't! Don't! Please!"*

Deaf to her cries, he pulled her nearer to the parapet and there, coming to a halt, held her in front of him, his body pressing into her back, arms tight around her waist, holding her fast. She struggled and kicked in his grasp, but he held on. And then, over the sound of her desperate cries, he yelled out to the watchers below, his voice ringing out like that of some music-hall master of ceremonies: "And here she

is—Miss Shenna Preston—famous star of stage and screen."
He paused briefly, as if enjoying his performance. "You've
seen her in some wonderful finales, right? Well, here's a fi-
nale to top them all." Then, lowering his face above Shenna's, he added, "It'll be over very soon now."

With his last words he brought one arm up across her
throat and with the other circling her waist, dragged her
frantically struggling body to the very edge of the roof.
Choking for breath, she reached up to claw at the arm that
held her in its vicelike grip—and as she did so she felt the
Victorian brooch scrape against her wrist. Desperately her
fingers encircled it, closing around its ornate face. Then,
snatching its long pin free from her coat, she blindly stabbed
back and upward with all the force she could find.

Harry screamed and stepped back, releasing her from his
grasp. Shenna, thrown completely off balance, reeled and
fell forward across the parapet. The beam of light holding
her in its glare, she clutched with frantic fingers, scrabbling
at the stone balustrade in a desperate effort to hold on and
prevent herself from falling over onto the pathway below.

For long, long seconds she seemed to hang there on the
very brink of the drop, but then at last, forcing every last
vestige of strength into her hands, she pulled herself up to
safety. In the next moment, as she dropped to her knees in
the snow, she became aware of a strange, animal-like cry.
Turning her head, she saw him.

The sound from his gaping mouth was one unending
scream as he moved across the roof in the glare of the searching lights. His hands were held up to his face, covering his
eyes, while blood ran down his cheeks and fell into the snow.
Gazing at him in horror, Shenna watched as, looking like
some grotesque marionette, he spun drunkenly first to the
left and then to the right. She watched as, hands plucking at
his eye, he blindly cannoned into the stone post of the parapet's corner. She saw him reach out to find his bearings,
hands groping, fumbling in the air. Then, as he turned back

in her direction, she saw his face. The Victorian brooch was embedded in his right eye, glinting brightly in the light of the beams like some macabre decoration. And even as she gazed at him he stumbled, and she watched as his knees caught the edge of the parapet and he toppled forward. To her horrified gaze he seemed to hover there on the edge for endless moments, like someone caught by a slow-motion camera, tilting slowly, slowly out into space. Then, with a shriek that echoed in the air, he was gone.

After a while there were policemen on the roof beside her, helping her up and leading her back to the window. Down the stairs they moved, in a little procession, toward the hall where other policemen milled about. As she reached it, stepping from the stairs, a young woman constable came to her holding her beaded bag. "Is this yours?" she asked and Shenna took it, murmuring her thanks.

Moments later she was being led out through the front door and down the porch steps. As she emerged onto the snow-covered pathway, her eyes were drawn over to her right, where two uniformed men stood beside the stone statue in the arbor.

"Don't look," the young policewoman said, but it was too late. Shenna had seen what was there, taking in the scene in one glance.

In the now brightly lit snow-covered arbor stood the statue Harry had talked of, the angel he had bought for her. Earlier, arriving at the house in the falling snow, she had barely noticed it. Now, lit up by the lights, it looked like some bizarre tableau. There was the angel. And there, too, was Harry.

He lay in the concrete angel's arms, his body impaled on the bronze sword.

22

Shenna spent the night in a private room at a local hospital. "Keeping her in for observation," the police doctor called it. Then, just after ten the next morning, as soon as he could be admitted, Ian was there, followed by a plainclothes officer from the CID and the young woman police-constable who had come to the house the night before. A little later, while Ian retreated to sit in the waiting room, the officers spent two hours taking a lengthy statement from Shenna, after which, with a request to her to keep them informed of her whereabouts, they left.

After their departure Ian took her out of the building, successfully evading the throng of reporters who had learned of her involvement in the sensational happenings and were waiting at the hospital's main entrance. She couldn't dodge them forever, though; it would only be a matter of time before they caught up with her and she was forced to run the gauntlet of their questions. She was resigned to it, but until it happened she could take a brief respite, safe in the knowledge that it was all over and she could get on with her life again.

The rest of the day she spent in the quiet comfort of Ian's Knightsbridge flat, where he proved loving and attentive. She was glad of his strong, supporting presence.

In the evening, after dinner, they sat together before a crackling wood fire, and he put his arms around her and held her to him. After sitting for some time in silence, he said, "Can you forgive me?"

"Forgive you?"

"For what I did. . . ."

She turned and smiled gravely into his eyes. "And what did you do, Ian?"

"You know—not writing, not calling—all that."

"Because of her, wasn't it? Mary. Mary Carroll."

He hesitated before he spoke again. "How much do you know about her?"

"A lot more than you realize." After a moment she told him of seeing him and Mary together, and also of having seen his airline ticket with the date of his arrival in London that previous time. Afterward he looked away, his face set with shame. "I don't know what to say," he said, "except that I'm glad you know."

"Are you?"

"Yes." He began, then, to talk to her about his relationship with Mary, but Shenna put a finger to his lips. "Forget it," she said. "It's no longer important."

"Well, then, just allow me to say that it was a big mistake, and that it's over. Completely." He paused. "And one other thing—that *through* it—*because* of it, I realized just how much you mean to me. Can you understand that?"

"Yes, I think so."

"And can you believe me when I say that I love you?"

"Yes."

At her response, his hands came up on either side of her face, which she turned toward him. "Yes," he said, looking into her eyes, "you must believe me. I love you, Shenna. I love you."

After a while she told him of how she had given up her studies at the art school and of her plans to return to California. He nodded. "Yes, your friend Wesley already told me. So, if everything had gone according to schedule, you'd be on the plane right now."

"Yes."

"And I would have missed you. I almost did."

"Almost."

"You'd have gone off—leaving no word."

She shrugged. "Ian, what would have been the point? I hadn't heard from you. I never expected to hear from you again. I thought it was over."

"I'm sorry."

She pressed his arm. "Still, that's all in the past now, isn't it?"

"Yes, *yes*."

He went on to say that in a few months he would be leaving London to move to San Francisco. "And I've been thinking," he said, "perhaps we could go together. I thought we might get a place there—some nice house in the city or out in Marin County—or wherever you fancy. You could paint—or do what you want. You told me how disenchanted you've become with the movie business, so—why not take a couple of years off? Look around for a while—relax and decide what you want to do. And if you decide you want to make a movie—well, Los Angeles isn't that far."

"You mean for us to live together?"

He nodded. "I know it's coming a bit sudden, but—well, you've got to make some decisions anyway about what you're going to do, haven't you? And there isn't that much time, is there? Oh, listen, I know we could be happy. And besides, I think you need looking after. You need someone around to make sure you don't get into any more trouble."

"You sound a bit like my mother."

He laughed and then, serious again, said, "Well, what do you think?"

She smiled and put up a hand, brushing fingers through his thick, dark hair. "Ian, I don't know what to say. Everything's happening so fast, and I don't know that I'm in a fit enough state to take it all in. I can hardly believe I'm not still up there on that roof."

He took her hand and pressed it to his mouth. "You poor kid. I'm sorry; I didn't mean to rush you."

She was silent for a moment, then she said, "I'd have to go home first. The house in Westwood is empty. I'd have to get that sorted out."

He nodded. "Of course. I've thought about that. I thought perhaps, if you like, we could fly out there in the next few days—or whenever you want—and arrange everything. Let the place—or sell it, or whatever. We'll do whatever needs to be done."

She smiled. "I'm not surprised you're so successful at your job. You think of everything, don't you?"

"I try to. Anyway, I just want to take away some of your responsibilities for a while. Give you a break. You've been through a hard time." He paused. "And then I thought—once that's all sorted out—your house—we could come back here and just take it easy for a while—or maybe we could stop off to spend a week on the Continent—if you'd like that—Florence, Rome, or Paris."

"It sounds fantastic."

"Right. Then we could get back for your opening."

"My opening?"

"Your exhibition."

"Oh, that. It's not mine anymore."

"What d'you mean?"

"I gave it away. To a friend of mine at school."

He stared at her. "Are you serious?"

"Yes, of course. His name's Caspar Oliver. He's a student—and he has far more talent than I'll ever have."

"And that's the reason you gave it to him? Because he's talented?"

"Not only that. He needed it. He was having a rough time. He was really down on his luck."

"And so you just—gave your exhibition to him. Just like that."

"Just like that."

He smiled and frowned at the same time. "You sure he's just a friend, this Caspar?"

"Yes," she smiled. "Don't worry—he's just a friend."

"Aha, so you say." He shook his head incredulously. "Oh, come on, Shenna! You'd do something like that for another student? Somebody you haven't known more than a few months?"

"Yes. Why not?"

"Are you quite sure he's nothing more to you than that—a friend?"

"That's all. Why is it so hard to accept?"

He didn't answer. "But what are you to *him?*" he asked.

"The same."

"*Shenna* . . ."

She laughed, a touch of impatience in the sound. "Ian, get it into your head—I don't think of Caspar in that way and he doesn't think of *me* in that way. For God's sake, he's not interested in *any* girl, let alone *me.*"

"You mean he's queer?" He gazed at her for a moment then sighed. "Well, of course, it's your business, my love, but I don't understand you, I really don't. After all that slog, all those months of work, you go and give away your exhibition—the most marvelous shop window you could ask for. You moaned to me about the lack of opportunities but when you do get one, you give it away. Here it was—handed to you on a plate—and you give it away to some little fag who comes to you with a hard-luck story. It's beyond me."

Shenna stared at him for a second, then turned away.

"I'm sorry," Ian said, putting his arm around her. "I suppose I was just looking forward to the whole thing. I guess I'm just a little disappointed. But anyway, it's your affair." He turned her around to face him. "Forgive me, please. I think I must be in the wrong business to be able to fully understand. In the advertising world one soon gets rid of all notions of altruism." He paused. "You forgive me?"

"Forget it. It doesn't matter."

He smiled at her. "Teething troubles," he murmured. "And I guess we'll have a few more. But we'll get over them, you'll see."

Later they lay in bed side by side. Ian yawned. He still hadn't caught up with his sleep from the flight over. "And I was up for hours last night," he said, "wondering and worrying about you. God, you had me scared." He drew her to him, tenderly wrapping her in his arms. "I'm so sleepy." He yawned again and nuzzled into the warmth of her neck. "Still—I can always find the energy for you."

After they had made love they lay in one another's arms. Ian fell asleep almost at once, but it was some time before Shenna eventually slept. When she did she dreamed that she was back on the roof again. But this time there was no snow. Instead it was warm. Harry was holding her, his arms wrapped around her. She struggled to free herself, and even while he held her she could see him, another Harry, lying across the arms of the angel, the bronze sword thrust upward through his stomach. She screamed out, pushing the wrapping arms away and struggling out of their hold. Then she was opening her eyes while Ian took her in his arms again and soothed her.

"It's all right, it's all right." He ran his hand gently, rhythmically over her shoulder. "You had a bad dream, that's all. You're safe now."

She sat up and turned on the bedside light and leaned back against the pillows while her heartbeat and her breathing slowed. It was good just to be awake and to be aware of her safety. Against her side Ian lay curled, his arm across her thighs, his eyes closed. Bending her head to him, she murmured, "I think I'll make myself a drink," and then realized that he was asleep again.

Gently moving his encircling arm aside, she slid out of bed. He didn't stir. She wrapped his robe around her and went out to the kitchen, where she made herself a cup of weak tea. Bringing it back into the bedroom, she stood gazing at him for a few moments in the dim, soft glow of the lamp, then went over to the window, drew back the curtain a fraction, and looked out onto the street. In the dull yellow shine of the streetlight she could see snow falling. There was no one about. Letting the curtain fall back into place, she turned back into the room and saw that the time was one thirty-two.

She moved to a chair near the bed and sat there looking down at him as he slept. Then her glance moved on to the chair nearby, on which lay all her things. After she had sat there for some time she got up, picked up her clothes, shoes and bag, and crept across the room. In the doorway she turned and looked back at him and then went out, silently closing the door behind her. In the kitchen she dressed, poured some more tea, and sat slowly drinking it at the table. When the cup was empty she put it down, got up, and went to the telephone on the wall. Beside it was a list bearing various numbers, including two or three for taxis. She dialed, and when an answer came she asked in a low voice for a taxi to come around immediately. "Only don't ring the bell," she said. "I'll be watching for you."

She went into the hall and got her coat, bringing it back to the kitchen. She would go to a hotel for tonight and in the morning she would call the CID officer and tell him that she was going home to California, but that she would return to London whenever she was needed.

She put on her coat and then stood there thinking that she should write Ian a note. After a moment or two, though, she decided against it. There was really nothing to say.

She took her gloves from her bag. And as she did so she saw there the paperback of *Bridges Are for Burning*. When she got back home she would call Jack Tanner and see if the role was still open. And if not, well, it didn't matter; there would be something else coming along very soon. For one thing, she could help with the promotion of *Chain Letter*. But whatever—she knew now where her future lay; she no longer had any doubt.

Another thought crossed her mind. The house in Westwood was all shut up. So, she asked herself, what should she do about somewhere to live until the house was back in order? Perhaps she should call Amy and go and stay with her. After all, Amy had invited her. "Why not come and stay with me for a while?" Amy had said. "Just till you get back on your feet." Now Shenna momentarily pursed her lips in decision. Thanks, Amy, dear friend, but I'll go to a hotel till I get the house sorted out. I've found my feet at last.

Moving back to the door she switched off the light and let herself out into the hall. There was only the front door and then she would be free. And really free this time. Another minute and the front door was silently closing behind her. She stood on the step, watching as the snow fell on the quiet street and the lights of the taxi came into view.